**To
The
Castle**

To The Castle

by Dorothea Malm

 Appleton-Century-Crofts, Inc., New York

To
The
Castle

One

TODAY, IN THE COURTYARD of the Savoy, as I was setting
out on the last of the errands that had brought me to London, I
saw my dear father again, still in exile from that splendid Château
de Ferronçalles that he once ruled with so subtle a tyranny. But I
was prepared against the possibility of a chance encounter—he lives
chiefly in England now. So was he. We did not speak.

It was a gloomy, rainy day, and taxis were hard to come by; there
were quite a few people clustered about waiting impatiently for
them. The man in charge was doing his best to be fair, but he could
not haul people back by force if they nipped into a newly vacated
taxi out of turn, and a stout Briton none too sure of himself
who stood midway between my father and me soon began to feel
slighted. "You're getting a bit peeved," a friend remarked to him,
and he said, "I certainly am getting peeved, I'm going to make a
row! Look at that!" Another taxi had come up, a woman with a fur
piece and a dog over one arm was getting out, and already getting
in on the other side was a triumphant man who had only just come
through the glass doors from the hall. My father smiled slightly to
himself.

He was looking very well, his handsome face a little worn by
time, a little subdued by life, but his bearing quite unchanged, and
that was odd, because he had suffered a great deal. He had lost
his position of power in the world; he had thrown away the devotion of one who would have been loyal to him through everything;
and worst of all for one who worshipped the name he bore and
valued his descent as few men find it practical to do nowadays,

[7]

he had broken his word and so destroyed what had always seemed his indestructible self-esteem.

And here he stood in the busy midday gloom of the Savoy court-yard on a rainy day, with wet taxis turning their tight circles past him, and here stood I, a dozen feet away, and not speaking. It seemed to me that our past stood open to the world at that moment—the relentless cupidity that had begun it all, the profound inner heartlessness of him, the ugly struggles between us, and the final bursting of his golden bubble with a death that was really a happy escape and an attempt at death that was pure tragedy. In the next moment, by one of those swift reversals of perception that show us the two sides of truth, I saw how safe we had always been from the world's guesses, for family quarrels are common enough, and that was the name the world had been bound to give to our quiet four days of horror. There had been no public parading of our troubles, only a quiet quarrel, a wedding almost as obscure, and after that a quiet life again, undistinguished except by those events that do not stir the curiosity of strangers because they happen to everyone—good things, tiresome things, inevitable things.

And now he was being put into a taxi by an apologizing doorman, and the angry Briton was making his silly row at last, and I turned and went inside again, caught fast in a dream of the Château de Ferronçalles during one winter month long ago, when I went seeking the Duke my father and was not welcomed.

He seems to have forgotten; I am glad that I have not, though there is such grief in it. The sight of him brought it all back more living and real than the murmurous hall that I walked through or the cage of the lift that carried me up, but smaller things than that have done it—the smell of old wood-smoke in a cold room, the sudden silence of footsteps going from gravel to grass, the cold rough touch of wet stone, a bedroom fire at night rousing itself from embers to flare silently for a minute or two. Once it was only the sound of a train hurrying along the distances of a quiet countryside; once it was the deep note of an almost inaudible bell fading on the wind; and once it was three lines of a poem written a hundred years ago by someone who guessed at the truth of love and guessed right. "Cold in the earth," it began, "and the deep snow piled above thee, Far, far removed . . ." and something about a grave, and then, "Have I forgot, my only love, to love thee?"

[8]

which was no question but a proud cry of triumph over time. It was my cry too, for I have not forgotten, and I never shall. Though I should never see that lovely castle again, its slate roofs and weathered pale stone walls, its long terrace overhanging the little river that washes its strong foundations, its panelled rooms and carved stone chimney-pieces, the colonnaded quadrangle of the great courtyard, all sunlight and shadow and silence, I shall never forget it, or the events that happened within it, or the people who lived there.

Now I hear again the enormous murmur of London, the large aimless untiring music of traffic that never reaches a climax of any kind. That winter month is far away and very long ago. But when I listen to the present sounds they are like a ticking clock telling the wrong time.

There is no hunger harder to bear than a hunger for what is gone. It is painful when the past seems obdurately remote, and equally painful when everything lost comes close against all one's senses and seems more real than what is there. It makes one a captive invisibly held, estranged from the real world, dumb and helpless, a sleeper desperately trying to wake from a nightmare of now.

There is no waking; there is no recovering what is gone; there is only remembering. But all I can bear to put down is what I could not bear to live again—which is, in some disguise for decency's sake, all this:

My first recollections of myself in a city called Wichita in the State of Kansas are of someone unwanted and out of place. I lived in the country of my birth, which is France, till I was old enough to take notice of it, but I was removed from it before I was old enough to remember what I had noticed; and my mother was always careful to impress on me that I could hardly belong to a country where I could not even remember having been. "I am French, yes," she would say to neighbours who inquired, "but this one—I don't know. Who could say?"

"Well, she's American now, anyway," they would remark kindly, adopting me as easily as they in turn had once been adopted.

"American?" my mother would say then with a snort, much amused. "Look at her!" I was and am very dark, swarthy, what is

[9]

called in America foreign-looking. "No, she belongs to no-man's land, that one. . . ."

In the same way she always made it plain that I was fatherless. Indeed, I knew that she was my mother, that I was not merely a foundling forced upon her by the obscure customs of a distant land, only because I heard my stepfather speak of her as my mother. One day I traced in dictionaries in the school library the meaning of an epithet that she often spat at me in moments of anger—*sale bâtarde*. The *sale* I had understood, the meaning of *bâtarde* was new to me. I had taken it to mean brat, or something of the sort. Even then, of course, I did not for a moment believe it. I thought it only something to be said in moments of anger, like brat. Later, when I learned that it was true, I could not forgive my mother for having used the truth as so casual an insult. It was something that should not have counted with me at all, so wholly not my fault it was. If anything, I deserved apologies for it. I deserved being given an opportunity to forgive. But my mother reproached me with it from the beginning. She was not, however, a pleasant woman in any way.

She was coarse and vulgar; and I did not use the word "spat" in any figurative sense. She was a woman troubled with a superfluity of saliva; a sucking sound, which meant that she was trying to get the situation under control, preceded every outburst. And she was not one to be embarrassed when she sprayed somebody as she vehemently talked to him. She was also swarthily dark and incurably unkempt. Her black hair straggled; her clothes were always twisted in an unattractive way; she was greedy and noisy at table. I even saw her once or twice absently pick her nose in public. In a way it was all good for me. A bad example can be as educating as a good one. I was trained by the shock that her ways made our neighbours feel. And she was an energetic housekeeper, and she was far from unhandsome. She had vivacious eyes and straight, superb features; it was a face with character.

Until I was thirteen we lived in Wichita, Kansas, in a narrow two-story grey frame house on Grove Street. The flat Kansas accent still clings to me; I still say *cain't* when I am stirred up. My first stepfather was a carpenter who had fought in the war—the first of the world wars. My mother had met him in Paris, passing herself off, I suppose, as a widow, and he married her and took us home with him to Wichita, where he coughed his life away doing easy jobs of indoor carpentry, repairs and remodelling, in a slipshod, in-efficient fashion. He was kind to me and told me to call him Papa, which I did, but without pleasure, because hearing me do so made her laugh sardonically at us both. When I was thirteen, he died, and we buried him decently, sold the house, and moved to New York, where my mother was soon employed by a number of small households as a daily or weekly cleaning-woman, a job she per-formed very well. She worked hard, she did not steal, and she did not tell lies. By the time I was beginning to get over my shy and secret nostalgia for dear, flat, sunny Wichita, she had met and mar-ried a British sailor, a small, eager, thoughtful man, kind-hearted and romantic, and we moved to Liverpool. I was then at an age when one begins to think of one's independent future, and I dared to ask her, one day, about my real father—her sailor had told me that I could call him Dad if I liked, but I could not feel that he was going to belong to me even in so small a degree as the car-penter had done; I was getting too old for that.

"What father?" she said, laughing, her eyes glowing. "You are a bastard, you know. Bastards don't have fathers. Don't count on any-thing from him. He begot you, and that finished it for him. He isn't wasting any thoughts on you. He doesn't care if you're alive or dead."

That idea seemed to gratify her. What could I do? I drew down my shell and cowered behind it and said no more.

We crossed the Atlantic third-class, my mother and I, sharing a hot little inside cabin in the bow of the ship; and it was like living for a week in a small elevator constantly in erratic motion. My mother was seasick all the way, and I had to take care of her be-cause the stewardess refused to go near her—my mother was al-ways disgusting in illness. And so, for the first time, I got some in-formation from her.

One day, when I was looking out a fresh nightgown for her—she did not want it, but I could no longer endure the old one—I found a picture-postcard in her suitcase, a glossy deckle-edged pho-tograph with a soiled blank back. At right angles across the middle of the back was the name of the photographer, a French name with a Paris address, but there was no message written on it, and it had never gone through the mails. An upper corner, where presumably the picture had been identified, had been broken off. The back, as

I say, was soiled, but it was not yellowed. The postcard did not seem very old. I wonder now if she played the thief for once in her life and stole it from one of the apartments in New York where she had worked. Or perhaps she boldly asked for it. The glossy picture was of a castle, a real castle, pale, beautiful, majestic, reflected in the tranquil water of a river.

She was between vomitings at the moment, weak and panting; her head ached badly; she had almost no resistance. But she would not tell me names or places.

"*He* lived there," she said with a curious indefinable colouring of emotion. It was not bitterness; it was not tenderness. Perhaps it was only an awareness that once in her life she had mated for love. But I, the child of love, was a dirty bastard prying where I had no business to pry. "Put it back where you found it!"

"My father?" I said, entranced. The ship rolled slowly, hung motionless at a slant, and rolled a little farther; the open suitcase slid from wall to wall, a short distance; the woodwork creaked as the ship rolled back and righted itself; and the floor lifted and sank, lifted and sank, smoothly, sickeningly, as the pitching began again. "Where is it? Who is he?" She stared at me with, as I see it now, a smug, peasant insolence. This was ground that was her own, and she stood guard on it. "What a liar you are!"

She was insulted. "No! He's a duke. . . . Truly . . ." she said, and then she sank watchfully into herself again, peering out at me malevolently from the fortress of her secret. But I did not get an impression of permanence from her withdrawal. It seemed that what she had said seemed to her to require the saying of something more, which is the only way I can put into words the subtle sensation I had then.

I was, of course, utterly uplifted by what I had heard. It was far more gladdening, more comforting, more warming than a dream of future glory, this glimpse of actual glory in the past. I had often dreamed of justifying—no, more than that, of making splendid my cheap existence by winning fame, fortune, and admiration from the world; this was—just then—better.

My excitement did not shut me away from events of the moment. On the contrary, it made me more keenly sensitive to them. I waited, and before long she said, "You have the eyes of that family," and once again the emotional quality of her words was difficult to judge. She was looking not into but at my eyes, and she did not seem to be so much coveting them as gloating over them, as if they, or at least their peculiar conformation, were her own property. There was jealousy in her voice, but it seemed the jealousy of possession. She was like some fond mother watching her baby in another woman's arms. Then she said with unequivocal bitterness and a conscious sense of theatre, "Your eyes are your birthright," and began retching again.

That was the end of the second of our three talks on the subject of my father. When next I went weaving down the passage to the lavatory, I took with me the mirror from my mother's handbag. It was quite a large mirror, about two inches by four inches, backed with cardboard covered in brown rayon faille. I locked myself in one of the compartments and studied my face very carefully and respectfully—because it had just become the face of a duke's daughter. Why it should be better to be the illegitimate daughter of a duke than to be the illegitimate daughter of a plumber or a grocer or a sailor, I do not know, but I was uplifted by the thought of it, as I should have been crushed by the thought of the other. The idea of being a bastard scarcely troubled me any more because my mysterious father was a duke who lived in a castle. I did not resent his seduction of my mother or his failure to look after me; resentment came later. Just now I studied my face with enormous interest and respect.

I was a few weeks past my fifteenth birthday, but my face had already pretty much found its final shape, and I was within an inch or two of my final height, which is better than five feet nine inches in my stockinged feet. I saw that I had my mother's nose, long and straight, and my mother's strong and stubborn jaw. But my eyes were quite unlike hers. They were long and narrow in shape and in colour a pure dark blue, but the most unusual thing about them was a kind of crease or fold under them, which gave the lower lids more prominence than is ordinary. It was a kind of incised line, not a shadow. It made the eyes look always slightly narrowed. But their blueness might also be considered odd in so swarthy a face, black-lashed, black-browed, and framed in a thick tangle of black hair.

For weeks afterwards I was more conscious of my eyes than of any other part of me; I seemed to myself to be wearing them. But that feeling dwindled and disappeared and the glory of my birth dimmed in the long Liverpool years. In Liverpool I felt American, as I had never really felt American in the United States, because I so despised Liverpool. I hated the fog and smoke and mud, and the yellow Mersey, and the rusty freighters and tankers anchored in it, and the dull streets and the dull people, docile in misery, patient in poverty, and I began to feel that it was indeed God's country on the other side of the Atlantic because He certainly sent all His finest weather there, as the saying goes. Liverpool seemed the place most neglected in all the world by everything joyous and hopeful.

My mother's second marriage suited her no better than the first. She was passionate, and the carpenter had been sickly, and the sailor was often away. As far as I know, she was never unfaithful to either of them, but I do remember that her temper was always short in Liverpool, and mine was too. We took in lodgers, but they did not stay long—because the times were hard, and they lost their jobs or got into debt and had to go, or because my mother by chance mixed the foxes and the geese one way or another and they chose to go, indignant that my mother could think it possible for a retired housekeeper still a maiden to sleep in a bedroom whose closed door faced the closed door of a bedroom where slept a solicitor's clerk, or for a solicitor's clerk to share an attic with a greengrocer, or for a greengrocer to sit at the same table with a plumber, though the plumber's hands were quite clean, but what can one expect of foreigners! And one foggy dripping winter night, when everything I touched was clammy with damp and a choking smell of coal-smoke and soot permeated the heavy air, in a sudden storm of despair I cried out, "Oh, damn that Duke in his castle who lets me live in a hovel in this ugly town for all my days!"

"He doesn't care *that* for you," my mother said cruelly, snapping her fingers.

We sat in the dank, shabby, orderly kitchen with the gas oven lit and its door open for warmth—a mean expedient, I thought—and the old cold odours of fifty years of other people's cooking polluted the air sordidly. "*Or* for you!" I said with bitter triumph.

"Or for me," she agreed, for once peacefully at my side in contemplation of our mutual past. "Ah, well, he was only a boy. He was only sixteen. . . . What could he do?"

This shocked me. I knew that my mother had been twenty when

[14]

I was born, and I had thought of my father as a man much older than she, a suave, wicked, experienced duke for whom I would be a natural consequence lightly shuffled off at the time, but very possibly an object of interest later. Now I became an inept accident, something to be ashamed of, to dread the sight of. There is something queerly distasteful about having for a father a boy of sixteen. Sixteen when I was born, then fifteen when I was conceived—horrible! Or sixteen when I was conceived, therefore seventeen when I was born—could I hope for that?

My mother felt my shock without clearly understanding it and turned against me once more, roused by it from her dream of the past. "Yes, sixteen!" she said spittingly, grinning at me. "Just sixteen!" She was as dark and vehement and spiteful as a gypsy. Her teeth were strong and white. There was hatred in her eyes.

"Who was he?" I said fiercely, but without hope. "Where does he live?"

"Ah, you'd like to know that, wouldn't you, little bastard, and go begging for your rights? . . ." Her eyes were hot depths of darkness.

And so perhaps it was only jealousy after all, the jealousy of possession, that made her dislike me so much when my father came in question. Boy though he had been, he was nevertheless the great thing in her life, her point of contact with the grand upper world of money and ancestry and power—and I had a better claim on him than she had, I who had never seen him, who had suffered no pain for him, I whom he had never seen. But she had other natural reasons to hate me. She certainly had not gone with him into the bushes, or wherever it had been, in order to have a child. I had been a most unwelcome by-blow from the beginning, and a nuisance later on. Perhaps it was greatly to her credit that she had not abandoned me on the doorstep of some Paris orphanage, that she had, indeed, let me be born.

We were spared the trouble of burying my second stepfather. He was drowned from the deck of a tanker in the Bay of Biscay. We then went to London, and not long afterwards, soon after my seventeenth birthday, my mother married for the third and last time. He was middle-aged, Swiss, and a waiter in a Soho restaurant, a stout man with cheeks so red and mottled that they looked diseased. Then I left her, robbing her of that picture-postcard as I went. I had taken a business course, at the suggestion of and financed by her kind-hearted sailor, and I got a job as a file-clerk in the office of a button factory, then as receptionist-typist with a firm of young architects. I went from them to a publishing house in Bedford Street; and while I was working there, my mother died, at forty-one, in childbirth, and I was alone in the world.

But here the paths divide. I can see very clearly my mother's daughter at twenty-one, a tall, thin girl with unusual blue eyes in a swarthy face, black bobbed hair, a soft, flat Kansas accent, good French, undependable manners. But when I think of that girl, who called herself Isabel Regan, she does not seem to be myself. I remember her as if I had been an onlooker in her life, an interested observer. I can recall her thoughts and feelings, but I can hardly believe that they were ever mine. I feel the closeness of blood-ties with her, but I also feel the distance that exists between any two people, however nearly related they are. Isabel at twenty-one puzzles and irritates and embarrasses me; it is Isabel at twenty-two who was my inseparable, unanalysable self. The break, the change, was as quick and complete as that, because it was not so much a change as an awakening—the awakening that comes when through a child's illusion of being a passenger on someone else's ship breaks the realization that one is all by oneself in a little boat of one's own—but that the boat can be rowed and steered somewhat in the direction, at least, of the destination one chooses. There is all the difference in the world between those two states of mind. And so it is not strange that I cannot find myself, the self that I have known since then, in that girl who lived in so heavy a spell of passive expectancy and watchful waiting. She is someone else, someone I once knew very well and remember very clearly, but someone I cannot now speak for in my own person.

And so, *she* was private secretary to one of the directors of Blakeney and Potts, a difficult man—his secretaries never lasted long—and *she* shared an office with one of the two readers, Daphne Small, who was some years older, who had been at Oxford, who went home at week-ends to Holme Manor in Hampshire, where her family had lived practically since time began, and who was very pretty in a blunt, fair-haired, pink-and-white, orthodox British fashion. And her manners were irreproachable. How Isabel did envy her . . . and pity her!

I remember very well that mixture of depressed envy and proud pity which for a while magnified Daphne Small into an obsessing symbol, and I can remember the mixture of romantic hope and realistic discouragement that nourished it. When week after week went by and nothing happened, when Isabel saw how she was becoming established in spite of herself with a good job and a place to live and habits of independence and an increasing background of commercially valuable experience, all of which were turning her willy-nilly into a self-sufficient working-girl, she envied Daphne Small, who had all that and so much more besides. She saw that a father is only what he gives—a roof overhead, food on the table, clothes to wear, protection, kindness, guidance, and a name. If he gives those things, he is a father. If he gives nothing, he is nothing, and it counts for nothing that he happens to be a duke. He might just as well, for all the difference it makes, be a beggar, a butcher, a carpenter, a sailor—anything.

Thus she reasoned, trying in dejection to convince herself that the grapes were sour, but behind the cold logic there loomed a wraith that belonged to a different order of reason. Her father *was* a duke—a fact that meant nothing but still would not be dismissed. It was no more than a habit of thought in her head, five intangible, weightless words linked together to make an idea, yet it influenced her unreasonably. Any other five words would have had the same effect if she had accepted them as true—which made it so particularly unreasonable. If her mother had let her think the carpenter was her father, that would have made him her father—but she was very glad her mother had not done so, for then she would not have been richly haunted by the existence of that unknown other man; then she would not have been able to feel, whenever her life seemed specially drab, that the real materials of her life were yet to come, then she would not have been able to pity Daphne, whose possibilities were all known.

Consequently, she never dared show anyone the postcard picture. She could not risk learning that it was merely a picture of some desolate national treasure inhabited only by history.

She shared a flat not far from the office with two other girls, one a typist with Blakeney and Potts, the other a clergyman's daughter who was trying to go on the stage. Miriam had a sleek and sleepy beauty, pale-skinned and red-haired, that would have provided her with a lively social life except that she was serious. She went out only on business, to show herself at the right places; otherwise she stayed at home and read aloud from Shakespeare in a prim, precise, emotional voice. The emotion in it was always the same—sweet pathos asking unanswerable questions of life. The typist was another sort altogether—a plain girl, a thoroughly nice girl, a peacemaker, an apologist. The clergyman's daughter once said she thought Isabel looked like someone with a romantic past, and Isabel loved her for it. The typist, however, levelled everyone. She was the sort of person who fancies that kings and commoners are very much alike at heart, and she looked at all ranks with the same mild, matter-of-fact compassion that took all the colour out of the world.

It was a small flat for three people, bedroom, sitting-room, and kitchen-bath, with a cover for the bath when it was not in use—small rooms all of them, facing north and east; and the three girls were not specially congenial types. Still, they rubbed along, taking sides with one or another against the third over particular irritations, but making no permanent exclusive alliances of offence and defence. Betty and Isabel quarrelled with Miriam over the negligent theatrical ways that she was earnestly cultivating—a trick of being always nonchalantly half-dressed unless she was on the point of leaving the flat, a habit of balancing her cup and saucer precariously to free her hands for gestures, the use of makeshift ashtrays when conventional ones were all over the place. But Betty and Miriam took sides against Isabel about opening windows wide at night to let the smuts blow in and settle on everything, so that one could not even simply get dressed in the morning without getting one's hands dirty. And Miriam and Isabel took sides against Betty on the question of veal and pork instead of mutton and beef for dinner. They had one rather funny debate on food once—it lasted a whole evening—with Betty attacking the myth, as she called it, that British cookery was not the equal, in its way, of any in the world. It ended, I think, when she brought the King and Queen into it somehow.

And so, for a while, it was up in the morning, a quick wash, coffee and toast eaten standing, then clip-clop on high heels down the stairs, and outside into the fresh morning or the raw dawn, depending on the season, to hurry through Covent Garden to Bedford Street, picking one's way between vans and great dray-horses and carts, with the clatter and bustle of grey, busy London as a second alarm to complete the awakening. Then past the low, old, time-sagged windows of Blakeney and Potts, up the two long flights of narrow, carpeted stairs to the sunny office—wide-windowed, its walls distempered a jonquil yellow—that she shared with Daphne, and "Good morning, Miss Small!" and the day began.

Henry Dolphin, whose secretary she was, had his office down a flight and at the front of the building. It got no sun, but it was large and furnished to his taste—grey walls, thick grey-green carpet, a small set of open shelves, displaying an austere selection of books —Henry James, Stendhal, Dorothy Richardson, and so forth—and a black oak table and thinly cushioned black oak chairs.

Henry was then thirty-two or three, the great-grandson of the niece of the original Blakeney, tall and spider-thin, fair-haired, with a mask of a face and grey, impassive, intelligent eyes. He was a bachelor and lived alone. His only close relative was a sister who was a rather distinguished professor of economics at one of the provincial universities. He had many French friends; half his correspondence was in French; and Isabel took that to be his chief reason for putting up for a time with their not infrequent disagreements. He was an unreasonable man. He wasted her time gossiping about authors and agents and then complained that she never got things done when she should. He grumbled tediously about decisions the other directors made that he disapproved of, not blaming her for them but permitting her to observe at close range and in explicit illustration the sour humour they evoked in him. He would sometimes announce in the morning, "I am definitely not feeling my usual genial self today," and that would have to serve as apology for a whole day of snappings and snarlings.

In other respects he was rather sweet. He did not seem to mind if she forgot to call him *sir*, and sometimes he climbed the long flight of stairs himself to give her some task to do rather than summoning her down to him, and he could be very amusing about authoresses, whom he detested, especially those unpretentious ones who liked, as he said, to make light of their mediocre accomplishments. That sort were simply irritating to him; they ground down his soul on the wheel of their gay modesty, he said, while the pompous ones he could laugh at and almost enjoy in an angry way. He was a difficult man.

And there were days when Isabel could almost have wished he would fall and break his neck or get run over by a bus—he was notably impetuous on stairways and in traffic—so arbitrary and contradictory he could be, so cruelly distracting at busy moments, so blithely offhand in his overriding of other people's routines.

Their little difficulties never came to anything very serious, however, until one January morning when he misread the entries in his appointment book and took it upon himself to put through some telephone calls that scrambled his whole day. Isabel unavoidably felt some reluctance about taking over the straightening out, and she let her reluctance show.

After the short, sharp discussion that ensued, she ran up the long flight of stairs, burst in on Daphne, and said, "Well, do warn my successors of that loose rod fourth step down, or Henry's secretaries will be dying like flies."

"Oh, my dear, not the sack?" said Daphne incredulously.

"The sack," said Isabel, emptying the drawers of the desk of her private belongings.

"Oh, my dear, don't do that; he'll be relenting any moment now."

"I don't think so. And if he does, I shan't." She was very angry. He had been unjust.

"Oh, my dear, don't stick in your toes. These aren't the times to be out of work."

"Something will turn up," she said, and at the foot of the stairs, or perhaps merely from the door of his office—he had a carrying voice—Henry shouted, "Miss Regan!"

Daphne laughed. "Well, there you are!" she said gaily, but Isabel went on stowing her things into a string bag that she had meant to use for some laying in of stores that evening. "Now, look here, my dear," said Daphne, sobering, "you simply must not be obstinate. It's so silly. It's so unwise. You'll feel all proud and triumphant today, but tomorrow you'll be kicking yourself. It isn't easy to find a job now. I've a cousin who's simply haunting the publishing houses, trying to find any sort of opening—trying for months and months. He'd take your job in a flash—"

"Well, give him a ring," Isabel said, but then Betty came in at the door, mild and reasonable, seeing all, guessing all.

"Isabel," she said, "Mr. Dolphin wants to see you in his office at once."

"Oh, all right," Isabel said weakly, and Daphne looked relieved.

Henry was standing by his pale windows, silhouetted against daylight, but the winter daylight was dim, and his face could be seen plainly—not that much could be read on it. "Well," he said when Isabel came in and stood by the table, "I see I'm not to expect any sort of apology from you." His voice was cold.

She said nothing, and for a very good reason. She had weakened enough to regret the scene they had had ten minutes before. The thought of unemployment really did scare her; but she felt that his regret was not decided enough for an apology to do much good now. He was troubled by the scene, which had been undignified, and he was dreading the inconvenience of breaking in a new secretary to his dear whims. But his dread was not so high a wall that he could not see beyond it to the *status quo ante* that would follow a reconciliation—and the look of it did not really tempt him. She did not suit him, actually; he wanted a willing slave. He found their conflicts interesting and rather a pleasant test for himself, but if he had had a willing slave in his office he would have been glad to look for his entertainments elsewhere. If she had said, "I'm sorry, Mr. Dolphin, very sorry," he might very well have made up his wavering mind and said, "But it's no good our trying to go on together, is it?" And she would have lost what upper hand she had.

He walked a wide circle round her to close the door that she had left open. "I've never known what to make of you, and that's the truth," he said, coming back to sit down at the table, his hands clasped behind his head as he stared up at her. "Don't just stand there sullenly silent," he said bitingly. "If you won't apologize to me, you may as well ask me to apologize to you."

"Would you?"

"Definitely not," he said, taking his hands down and sitting up straight with some satisfaction.

"Well, then."

"Well, then, as you say. I just can't analyse you," he went on with a vague sweep of his hand through the air, peering up at her with grey, sharp eyes. "You seem to have a very peculiar idea of

[21]

yourself. I should say the basic element in your character is resent-fulness. What have you got to be resentful about? You baffle me. You stalk about like Sarah Siddons herself, putting something of grandeur into every gesture. . . . Sombre, morose, and unforgiving. Who wants a tragedy queen typing his letters? I ask you, who does?"

"I type very well."

"That's very true. But you really had no business telling me to do my own dirty work, had you? . . ."

"I suppose not."

The telephone rang. He picked it up and said, "No, I won't. . . . No. And don't put any more calls through to me for the present, please. I'm engaged. I'm at war with Miss Regan." And so she knew that she had got the sack all right. He would not have said that if he had meant to keep her on. "And justice and fairness had noth-ing to do with it, had they?" he continued, replacing the telephone.

"Oh, I think they had, morally," she said, sitting down with-out leave on the chair near the table, her usual chair for taking dictation.

"Stubborn Miss Regan. I suppose it's the Irish in you."

"There's no Irish in me."

"Regan?"

"It's really Régan. And it's my stepfather's name, anyway." He waited abstractedly, cat at the mouse-hole. "That's all," she said, grinning at him.

He lifted his fair brows without looking at her and laughed a little. "All right. . . . I play that game," he went on as if chang-ing the subject, "of guessing at the lives of people one sits opposite to in trains. I've always thought myself rather good at it. But I've seen a good deal more of you, and the closest I can come is that you're a dispossessed princess waiting rather impatiently to be re-called to a throne."

"Oh?" she said, feeling stabbed.

"Merely waiting. Doing nothing whatsoever about fomenting a revolution, or whatever it is dispossessed princesses do to advance themselves."

"I believe in fate," she said because nothing more repressive oc-curred to her.

"Ah, that fits in very nicely. And said very superbly, too, quite

[22]

in the tradition. Sarah Siddons at her best. Sarah Siddons typing letters and believing in fate at some two pounds a week. . . ." He looked at her, looked away, and said, "I may as well say quite frankly that I'm doing my best to make you cry." He sounded a bit ashamed of himself.

"Go ahead and try," she said doggedly.

"When a horse throws one, one must get up on him again at once, not to lose one's nerve. But if one doesn't mean to do that, surely the horse must be punished somehow, so he won't go off thinking he can get away with it. Or she, as the case may be."

"And it will also make you feel so much better about everything."

"About being called an unjust, bullying coward trying to crawl out from under at someone else's expense. . . . Yes, exactly."

"I apologize, Mr. Dolphin."

"Well, I'll be damned," he said, really surprised. "With all your heart?"

"For saying it. Not for thinking it. It was perfectly fair to think it."

"And there we are again," he said, slapping the palms of his hands down on the table. "What I ask myself is, what's going to become of you? There aren't any thrones left in the world, Miss Regan; there aren't any King Cophetuas; there aren't any Prince Charmings. Well, yes, there are: one has only to read the newspapers—but what I mean to say is, they aren't to be counted on. You're quite good-looking enough to snare a duke, I grant you, but you can't live your life in that expectation, trusting to fate— my God!—because it's very apt not to happen, don't you see? The chances are a million to one against it."

"I don't want to snare a duke."

"Well, what do you want?"

She thought for a moment and finally shrugged her shoulders slightly. "I don't know."

"Fate. Destiny."

"More or less."

"And who am I to say you're wrong?" he said, sighing and smiling, but looking thoroughly exasperated none the less. He got up and paced the room, troubled, it seemed, by indecision at a decisive moment, and the murmur of London mingled with the silence for a minute or two. "Obviously," he said at length, "we have come to a parting of the ways, have we not?"

"That would appear to be the case," she said evenly, but her fear was very real, and it made her regret very sharp. She saw herself standing in the rain in queues at employment agencies.

"I can't keep you on when you're so insubordinate a subordinate, can I? Well, at least I got my apology, such as it was. . . . I expect I shall miss you, Miss Regan, in a happy sort of way." His face was flushed; he looked oddly guilty and oddly defiant, too, as if he had an idea in his head that he did not mean to examine too closely before he acted on it. "Have you anything in mind for yourself? No, of course you haven't; you must wait to be kicked upstairs by destiny. But is there anything in the offing for you, or have you been unforgivably insolent while standing at the end of a plank, so to speak?"

"More or less," she said again.

"Well," he said, pacing about, hands in pockets, his coat rucked up round the neck by the hunching of his shoulders, "there's my friend Yves d'Ayz, who's a cousin of the Duc de Ferronçalles . . . not a very nice chap in many respects, he'll probably try to seduce you, but I shouldn't allow that if I were you. It would come to nothing and be a waste of time, destiny or no destiny."

"Who's not a nice chap, the Duke or M. d'Ayz?" she said quietly, anxious that he should not stop talking and start thinking and perhaps change his mind.

"I don't know anything about the Duke, I've never met him. . . . I met his sister once; she's a very nice woman. . . ." He stopped in his pacing and faced her. "You aren't related to that family, are you?"

She felt an awareness of motion deep in her mind, slow and heavy, overcoming inertia, gathering momentum, something large getting under way at last, a great ship slipping its tugs in the night and starting its engines to proceed alone. She said, "Not to my knowledge. Why should I be?"

"I've always wanted to ask you that," he said, a bit ashamed of himself again. "It's none of my business, of course. No, I believe you. It's just that you have the look of that family, the height, for one thing, and something about the eyes. You could be related in some out-of-the-way fashion, you know. I mean, it's entirely possible, isn't it? . . . Well, the fact of the matter is, Miss Regan, Yves wants a secretary to help him with a book he's writing. He's suddenly decided to be an author. God! It sounds a thoroughly dull book, I must say, a turning-out of some minor dirty-linen cupboard in history, but I suppose we shall have to have a look at it if it ever comes to anything. . . . He's about one-third done, I think, and he's doing both the French and English versions himself, tandem-style. Silly. But you could be useful to him; you know how a manuscript ought to look—and it would spare me a good deal too, I must say."

"Oh, yes, he's the one you're always writing to about idioms. I remember."

"And it's been a bore. As you know. Well, there it is. As a matter of fact, I've thought of sending someone over to take a look at what he's done so far—Miss Small or someone else minor who wouldn't be too inflating for his ego, just to see if there *is* anything in it for us. He's been begging me to, and we really owe him that much. He's the one—do you remember? No, it was before your time—he's the one got us that Grand Prix du Roman book we were so hot on. . . . And he saved the day for us with Miss Marple, that time she took offence—he gave her a round of merriment in Paris and introduced her everywhere as the most subtle and unappreciated of English realists, which pleased her, you can imagine, with her silly books selling like hot cakes in the railway stations. . . ."

"He sounds rather nice."

Henry made his most expressive face, which expressed the vagueness of dubiety. "The one great drawback would be that I don't think he's ever had a secretary before; this is rather a departure for him."

"That's no drawback."

"I mean, he'd not know the proper care and treatment of secretaries—oh, I see what you mean." He laughed. "The horse that's never been ridden. No training, but at least no bad training. True. . . ." He drifted to the window and looked out on winter greyness. "No, he's not such a bad chap, I suppose. . . . A bit of a tease at times, that's all. So I shall send him you. That should pay him off, don't you think?" he said, glancing over his shoulder with a smile. "No, he's not a bad sort. An out-and-out egotist, of course, as selfish as they come, really fantastically self-absorbed; but

[25]

clever, and not really unprincipled, I think. . . . I'll tell you what," he said, turning, "if you go, we might send Miss Small over at the same time for a look at that book. Give Miss Small a little excitement. You could protect her."

"Do you mean that—protect her?"

"No, of course I don't! Good Lord! I shouldn't recommend you for the post or the post to you if there were anything at all like that— I'm not an evil old man! He'll pay fairly well, I should think; and if he doesn't, you must see that he does, that's all. Make yourself useful, in a business way— I'm serious about that, by the way, that wasn't quite a joke—and then put the screws on."

"Where does he live?"

"In Paris. He has a very charming house there. He collects things, rather knowledgeably. . . . You'd have to find lodgings for yourself— I could recommend you a good inexpensive hotel to start with. Or do you know Paris?"

"Not at all."

"Well, are you interested?"

"Very much."

"Destiny calling?"

She laughed, he laughed, too, but dubiously. "No, thank you very much, Mr. Dolphin, I'm really very grateful; it's very kind of you."

"Then would you," he said, coming back to the table, "as a special favour, reserving your right of protest, straighten out the mess I've made of my appointments this afternoon?"

"Yes, Mr. Dolphin."

He sighed and sat down and folded his hands over his concave middle. "I breathe again. You might start with Mrs. Devereaux. There the rub is I talked her into cancelling another engagement to lunch with me. You haven't much time, so get cracking. And you might telephone the agencies some time today and see about a replacement for yourself—it'll take a week or so to get things arranged with Yves, so you'll have time to break her in for me. And the appointment with my tailor is one you mustn't sacrifice, no matter what. That's important."

"Yes, Mr. Dolphin."

"So get cracking, will you!"

"*Yes*, Mr. Dolphin!"

[26]

There was an immediate and fabulous flowering of expectations, an infinite branching of bubbles each enclosing a picture of the future, some of them very contradictory. She imagined dozens of differing welcomes of herself, and dozens of family situations all of which contained an inevitable niche for her, and she could hardly keep her mind on any task. At the back of her mind, like a dark ground for the bright pictures, was the idea of a possible cruel rejection, but that did not really dismay her. She was young enough to feel that there must be pleasure in tragedy. She could even look forward to being perfectly miserable—in a castle.

All her pictures of the future had the castle for their background. She leaped confidently past the meeting with the Duke's cousin to the meeting with the Duke himself. She was sure that it would come.

Miriam envied her; Betty thought her a fool to take a job with foreigners. But Betty helped her shop for a secondhand suitcase —she could not get all her possessions into the two she already owned—and made lists of what she should buy. But they were not very practical, those lists. She could have lived comfortably on a desert isle with what was on those lists, but she was not going to a desert isle: she was going to Paris. And she had nothing like enough money to supply herself on that scale, in any case. She contented herself with a spare toothbrush, six handkerchiefs, four pairs of stockings, and a pair of black leather gloves.

In applying for a passport she made a rather sad discovery. Her mother had travelled to England as an American citizen, having become one by marrying the carpenter from Kansas, but she had become British when she married the sailor, and she had remained that when she married the Swiss waiter, who was also a naturalized Briton; and all the while, Isabel, as a minor child, had been faithfully following her mother through these changes. There was no question about it. Though she was born in France and transported out of France by no impulse of her own, Isabel had been for a while an American citizen and was now a British subject. At least it made the obtaining of a passport a simple matter.

When that was done, there was only one thing more to do, and it was something that she could do very gladly. She said good-bye to Betty's brother John. He was a diffident, gangling young man of twenty-three employed at Thos. Cook and Sons, and he had for some time been persecuting her with invitations to dinner or to see a film or to go to the ballet, which he may well not have been able to afford, and she was running out of excuses for not accepting them. He had fallen a little in love with her, but she did not know that, or knew it but would not admit it—it was her first experience of the kind, and it was unfortunate for both of them that he was too much benumbed by his own shyness to be aware of her feelings and that she was too unimpressed by him to care about his. Her treatment of Betty's brother John was one of the things that Isabel at twenty-two remembered with shame. But at the time he was merely someone clumsily thrusting the facts of life before her in a very unattractive guise; and she was very glad to see the last of him.

Finally, on a Sunday afternoon, the day before her departure, too restless to do anything else, she took a last walk through the streets of London. She suffered from the empty feeling of apprehension and excitement that all travellers must feel, however used to travel they are, because people are born to put down roots, and every journey, even from hotel to hotel, is an uprooting. Her roots had always been shallow, but she found out that they existed when she prepared to go.

It was a cold, bright day, not a typical day. Footsteps were loud on cold pavements, and the clear air seemed to put all distant views of London behind glass, making of them marvellously life-like panoramas stilled and remote. She said good-bye to Eros, for tradition's sake, strolled up Regent Street and down Bond Street, along Piccadilly to Hyde Park Corner and back through the Green Park to St. James's Street, took a last look at Nelson's lions, and then went down to linger on the Embankment, leaning on the parapet to look at the river, the great Thames taking its slow curve past history two thousand years deep on its banks.

But as she stood there she realized that she felt not like someone setting out on a journey, but like a visitor on the eve of going home. What she suffered from now was the impatience, the sudden hunger for home, the sharp nostalgia of someone who has been too long away, but will not be away much longer.

She hardly noticed London any more; her thoughts were all on the future that had dimly begun to glow on the horizon, on the southern horizon towards which she gazed.

Two

EARLY ON THE MONDAY MORNING, because there was fog, Isabel taxied to Victoria station with her three large suitcases, arriving there—after a tedious and nerve-racking progress through dark, wet, indistinct streets that once or twice involved waiting in vain for suspected cross-traffic—not much in advance of the train's departure. In the dark, enormous cavern of the station, sounds of metal striking against metal, sounds of iron wheels rolling on concrete platforms, low voices, loud voices, footsteps walking, footsteps running, whistles, clinkings, hissings, compartment doors slamming —all these sounds multiplied themselves in the cold, raw air, reverberating to fill the great enclosure with a hollow, murmuring overtone, background to the immediate sounds endlessly repeated. She felt a bit yawny with nervousness and excitement; and she walked unsteadily as she followed her porter, several times almost bumping into people. It was cold. She wore a thick dark-blue coat over a woollen coat and skirt and jumper, with a blue felt hat pulled down well over her ears and her new leather gloves on her hands, and she still felt cold and consequently depressed as well, deeply doubtful of the enterprise she was engaged in.

She did not come upon Daphne in the station, but that did not matter because their seats on the Golden Arrow had been booked at the same time and would be together. It had been decided definitely only on the Friday before that Daphne would use the ticket bought for her—Henry had wavered desperately between going himself, sending her, and sending no one—and that afternoon had been complicated by an exchange of wires with Yves in Paris. Yves's acknowledgement of the final decision was so innocently overjoyed that Henry had been tempted, he said, to change his mind again and break the man's heart after all. But he did not.

Inside the train the air was dry and warm, and Isabel felt better about everything. Daphne was there, looking pink-and-white and very pretty in her light-blue travelling tweeds.

"*There* you are, my dear!" she cried. "At last! Was it the fog? My dear, isn't this luxury?"

"But you can't want to sit facing the engine—"

"Honestly, I don't mind at all. Isn't it cold?"

"Awfully," said Isabel, hanging up her coat and sitting down opposite Daphne, who smiled. Isabel smiled.

The first almost imperceptible movement of the train gave her the thrill of memory roused. She had not been on a train for four years, and she had forgotten that heavy gliding motion of immense weight and power that seems to run on stored momentum; she had forgotten the slow clicking thud and clank over rail-joints that quickens into a speaking rhythm saying portentous things, and the sense of being on one's way, beyond the power of a change of mind. They ran out of the heavy fog as they left the suburbs behind, but the day was still grey, misty, and dripping, and the backs of row dwellings that occasionally appeared along the tracks, all alike and all mean, did not make the leaving of England something to be regretted, whatever was ahead.

Two hours later, as they left the train at Dover, the wind whipped at Isabel's heavy coat, and Daphne said, "Smell the sea!" and another passenger behind them remarked wisely, "We're going to have a rough crossing. . . ."

It was a rough crossing, up and down, up and down, all the way, like riding on the pedal of a bicycle, but they stayed on deck, where the wet, cold, salty blasts of wind were a counter-irritant, and rather enjoyed the motion, which was, as Daphne dangerously remarked, really quite pleasant in a sickening way. None the less, it was dismaying, on the windy quay at Calais, to hear the wise passenger remarking, "Not too bad, after all!"

The French Golden Arrow seemed enormous after the little English train; it brought to Isabel's mind dim recollections of big American trains; but this car was not only large but also elegant. It was French. There were French porters in smocks and berets outside on the windy platform; there were French people settling themselves in the train with little exclamations of pleasure and satisfaction, reviving into the confidence that being on one's own soil brings; and English travellers had turned sprightly and a little loud: they were in France.

The tables were laid for lunch.

"Feeling better?" said Daphne, taking up the menu. "This sounds very good." She laid the menu down before Isabel. "And I am famished."

"So am I," said Isabel.

The engine made a little startled scream; the train moved.

After lunch, over good coffee, Daphne offered Isabel her cigarette case; they shared a match; and fumbling her words a bit—this was a departure!—she suggested that they might use each other's Christian names, at least when it wasn't business. . . .

"All right," Isabel said, watching France through the wide, clear window . . . a lonely rural landscape, not wild but lonely, little villages, white-walled, red-roofed, posters saying VICHY . . . DUBONNET . . . empty highways. Behind her, a French couple were talking quietly together, subdued by the approaching end of their holiday; they were wondering if they would be met at the station; they reminded each other of little troubles at home that they were returning to; they sighed; once they laughed, but not very gaily. Nevertheless, they were returning home, to a house or flat that they knew well, where they would be welcomed, if only by familiar rooms and well-known homely odours.

"And oh, that business!" said Daphne. "I feel that any power of judgement I ever had is simply seeping away down cracks and crevasses. I'm so dreading I shall read it and think it frightful when it's really marvellous, or the other way round, which would be quite as bad. . . ."

"Oh, no, you'll know," said Isabel, looking out at lonely, frozen fields streaked with snow here and there, at leafless trees and heavy grey sky, as she sat inertly swaying with the motion of the train.

"But Mr. Dolphin's depending on me, you know—he says he means to follow whatever lead I give him, and I don't want to let him down."

"You'll be all right when the time comes," said Isabel, taking a fresh cigarette from her own case, which she left doubtfully open on the table between them.

An attendant came by to present the luncheon bill, counting the chalk marks on the cloth for extras; and dusk deepened outside, lights twinkled in the blue winter twilight, points of brightness far away, bright streaks across the darkness nearby; and now she could see her reflection in the glass of the window, a shade travelling at her elbow, obsessed by its inaccessible memories.

She did not try to think seriously of what she was travelling to. It was too large to be thought about. It was the rest of her life. It was reunion, the discovery of reality, of the true foundation, of the solid earth itself. It was the awakening out of a nightmare of not belonging to the busy world round her. It was finding out what she really was, because it was finding out her context. When she looked ahead, it was to beguile herself, almost consciously, yet half convinced of what she dreamed, with a vision of the Château de Ferronçalles and its Duke as they must be if they were to have a welcome for her.

It would be a beautiful and luxurious castle. He would be a duke to his finger-tips, above the world's narrow standards, but kind and responsible and understanding, too. He would have a charming wife, benevolent and sympathetic, with whom he was very happy. It would be a happy household, the perfect picture of a happy household, as static and lovely as the picture-postcard of the castle itself. Everyone in it would love everyone else. There would be no flaws that her arrival could widen into ugly chasms of disagreement. And then from his cousin in Paris would come strange news. A girl had turned up bearing an unmistakable likeness to the family. In all innocence, before seeing her, his cousin had hired her as secretary. But now it seemed that she, too, had been innocent in the affair, for she asked nothing, expected nothing, and so deserved everything. Then he would come in haste to Paris, and she would meet him.

But under this manageable pastel confection of the future there was a dark reality of the past that swam away from her whenever she reached for it. She had been here before—in that tragic time of Flanders and the Marne and Château-Thierry and Verdun she had lived in Paris—but she could not remember it. She had left Paris by train with her mother and stepfather in winter weather like this, bundled for warmth, he had told her, in an army blanket, but she had not slept, he had said, she had looked out bright-eyed at everything; yet she could not remember it now. There seemed a kind of membrane between her thoughts and the past; they could not break through, though the membrane was so thin that almost she felt the stir of life beneath it.

One reminding word to direct their effort was all they needed, she felt, but no reminding word came, only Paris itself, the Gare du Nord, a surly porter in beret and blue smock and leather strap; endless cold cement platforms and ramps; a cold, train-smelling gloom; fresh, cold, night air; lights.

In a taxi travelling dangerously fast they rode through dark, slanting, busy streets to the hotel that Mr. Dolphin had recommended, and Daphne took charge there. But all her happy composure had abruptly disappeared. She was distant and subdued, and it seemed that everything had begun to bore her. She demanded a sitting-room, bedroom with twin beds, and bath in a high, listless voice, her eyes focused anywhere but on the clerk to whom she spoke, as if she hoped for very little from what she gave herself the trouble of saying. Isabel wondered whether she was tired or whether she disliked the look of the hotel, which was certainly not impressive, though it was fascinating—they stood in a narrow, stone-floored corridor at the hall-porter's counter, and at the far end of the counter, on the other side, the hall-porter was sipping unobtrusively at a glass of dark liquid, which, by the expression on his hard, pleasant face, was possibly medicine, and behind him a canary in a black wire cage was singing under its breath, possibly so as not to attract the attention of a great mouse-coloured cat sleeping on the table below the cage, and at the end of the corridor, through glass doors, one could see the evening traffic of Paris moving fast in the cold night air.

But when they were alone in the sitting-room of their suite, Daphne had no criticisms to make of the hotel. She went to the window and opened it slightly for fresh air—with six degrees of frost outside! But the room was stuffy and stale-smelling. It was a red room—red velvet, red plush, red carpet, papered with red roses; on the white marble mantel of the chimney-piece was a vase of dark red *immortelles* reflected in the mirror above the mantel. The window overlooked a glassed-in court, dimly glowing; there were a few lighted windows in the opposite façade. She closed the window and jerked the curtains shut and moved to the mirror. After a moment she said, "It *is* too blue. I always did think so."

"Your suit? It's lovely!"

"Too blue," she said gloomily.

"No!"

She took off her hat and pushed at her fair curled hair, made a face, shook her head, and turned away from the mirror. "Oh, Lord," she said, and then she said, "Sorry." Isabel gave her a puzzled, inquiring smile. "Never mind. It always affects me this way, somehow; I don't know why."

"Paris?" said Isabel, remembering that Daphne's change of mood had come as the train slowed to a stop in the station. "Or just travel abroad?" she continued doubtfully, but as she said it, she felt sure that no other city could have had that effect on Daphne—not Rome or New York or Amsterdam or Madrid. Italians and Spaniards would be natives, New Yorkers and the Dutch would be provincials, any Briton could make his own rules among them; only Paris was formidable. The French were not natives in Paris, they were Parisians, and formidable.

"Well, here we are," said Daphne snubbingly, and then there was a knock on the door and a page came in with a letter for her that had been, he said, waiting for her arrival, only the clerk had forgotten it till now. She laughed dryly and seemed to feel a little better about things. "It's a wonder they remembered it at all," she said when he had gone, opening it brusquely and looking first at the signature, which was her way of doing things at the office. "Oh?" she said, and then she frowned over the letter itself, which was handwritten and difficult and quite long. "But what's all this about?" she said, laughing again. She looked up. "From our friend M. d'Ayz. Come and see."

She sat down on the red plush sofa, Isabel sat down beside her, and they read the letter together. It was an odd letter. The first long paragraph was an elaborate, an almost Chinese welcome of Miss Small—and Miss Regan—to Paris. The next was a string of rather mysteriously undefined apologies for his manuscript; but they were followed by a lavish defence of it, which concluded the first page. The next page was utterly baffling. The first half of it thanked her for granting a request that had not, so far as they could see, been made; the final paragraph spoke of railway stations and a noon train to Tours that would be met by him there with very great pleasure.

"Why on earth?" said Daphne.

"Turn back; there was a sentence I skipped; it was so unreadable—"

"Good Lord! half of it was unreadable; we shall have to go through it word by word. . . ."

They went through it word by word, and Daphne got out her little silver pencil and circled the words that they could not make out, and they held the paper off at all angles and squinted at each word in turn and tried to catch it unawares to make it take a more reasonable shape than the one it persisted in holding. They got rather hilarious, as people always do over such problems; they giggled a good deal.

Then Daphne said, "But three words won't change the meaning, and it's obviously all about his book, anyway—what does he *mean*, meet the train at Tours?"

She had got her courage back. In a moment she decided to telephone him and get the matter cleared up. There was no telephone in the suite; she had to go down again to the hall-porter's cubbyhole. But she went very gaily, like a schoolgirl on an adventure. Her background had risen up round her again, strong and unassailable, shielding her even in the middle of Paris.

Ten minutes later she came pelting back, very much excited. "My dear," she said, "will you come? It's quite beyond me; my French simply isn't up to it. He isn't there—I gathered that much—but the servant seems to know all about it. Do come."

Isabel, who had been sitting in a kind of stupor of expectancy, rose and followed her along the dim, narrow, red-carpeted corridor and down the curve of the little red-carpeted stairway to a tiny office behind the hall-porter's cubby-hole, where the telephone waited off its hook. The hall-porter had put the call through for Daphne, and he watched from his counter with quizzical interest as Isabel undertook to carry on where she had failed.

But the servant's French was her mother's French, clear, distinct, and meticulous, and she had no trouble with it even reduced as it was to the vibrations of a little black diaphragm. M. d'Ayz had gone on Saturday to the Château de Ferronçalles, and he expected them to join him there. "Yes," she muttered, feeling cornered, and she turned and told this to Daphne, who said incredulously, "But how frightfully inconsiderate!"

"I thought it must be that," said Isabel, who was equally dismayed. It would be death to all her hopes if she walked in without warning to embarrass her father before his family.

She had got the impression that Madame d'Ayz had not gone with her husband, so she asked politely to speak to her. There was no Madame d'Ayz, the servant replied, perceptibly astonished; M. d'Ayz was not married. Then could he, Isabel suggested, himself arrange to show Miss Small the manuscript here in Paris, either at this hotel or at M. d'Ayz's house? No, he was very sorry, he had not the authority to do that.

She told this to Daphne, who said, "It's most awkward and difficult. How can we thrust ourselves on a perfectly strange household? —I don't know what to say."

"Would you want to go? I mean—"

"I'd like to do the job I was sent to do, that's all," said Daphne sharply. "But I don't see—"

"Perhaps he's on terms there so he *can* invite— Then you could go, and I could stay here and see about lodgings for myself, or something—"

"I *couldn't* go *alone*—" said Daphne, and of course she was right: they both had to go or they both had to stay; they both had to make the same choice, so that they would not seem to criticize each other.

"Well, wait," said Isabel, and she spoke into the telephone again. But the Duchesse de Ferronçalles, she said, was she aware of this invitation that M. d'Ayz had taken it upon himself to give on her behalf?

There was a pause.

The Duke was a bachelor also, the servant answered uncomfortably, troubled by this close questioning, and he was quite sure that, in effect, any suggestion of M. d'Ayz's would be approved—that she need not concern herself with any question of—

Isabel could not speak for a moment. If ever she had doubted the power of destiny, how could she doubt it now? He was a bachelor, he could not be embarrassed by her unexpected arrival—at least, not in any way that required her sparing him. She would have had to respect the feelings of his innocent wife; but he had no wife—

and besides, it was not her volition that was taking her there, but his cousin's. It was working out. She felt an awed elation about the way it was working out. It promised well.

"What did he say?" asked Daphne. "You look so shocked!"

"Wait a moment." But was there, then, no lady, Isabel said into the telephone, residing at the castle? For now she remembered Henry's warnings about his friend, and they did not seem fantastic to her as she stood at the scarred desk in the little queer-smelling office of this hotel in Paris.

Oh, yes, he said; indeed yes. At present there was the Comtesse de Varaisne, who was the Duke's sister. And he sounded then rather sweet and kind, as if it had come to him that this had been the difficulty all along, and sympathized, though he could not help being a little amused too.

So she thanked him very much and apologized for taking so much of his time, and he said it was nothing, and she replaced the telephone in its cradle and smiled at the hall-porter. "Good news?" he said, laughing, as he came to let them out of his realm, and she laughed, too, as she passed him, with Daphne behind her.

They said nothing on the way back to their suite. Daphne unlocked the door, which had no doorknob on the outside, only a keyhole, with a large stationary knob in the centre panel for pulling it shut. Then she said, pushing the door shut behind them, "Now tell me everything," and Isabel repeated her exchange with the servant.

"I suppose I've got to go," Isabel concluded.

"Must you? Yes, I suppose you must. It's your job, isn't it? But . . . I was sent here to read a manuscript. How can I go back without even having seen it?"

"Well, you could go and see it."

"And find perhaps he's gone dancing off to—to Biarritz or somewhere with it tucked covetously under his arm—"

"But why should he do that?"

"I don't know why I said that! Only, the whole thing seems so irregular," Daphne complained, sitting down on the red plush sofa. "I mean, so—so casual! Oh, I may as well tell you, Isabel. Mr. Dolphin as much as said he wasn't a very dependable chap. I was to be very guarded. I'm going to have a cigarette." She got up, took her cigarette case out of her handbag, chose a cigarette, struck a match for it, picked up an ashtray from a little table that was well out of reach of any chair, and sat down again on the sofa with the ashtray in her lap. Then she leaped up and said, "*Sorry!* Did you want one?"

"No, thanks," Isabel said, chiefly to spare her feelings. She sat down again.

"The fact of the matter is, I don't think I should let you go alone. I'm a bit older, and . . . well, Mr. Dolphin told me to keep an eye on you, see you settled in, so to speak. . . ."

"He told me to keep an eye on *you*."

"He didn't!" She looked up at Isabel, and then she laughed. "Oh, that man is a wretch," she said affectionately. "One never knows where one is with him. All the same . . ."

"Perhaps he *had* to go, M. d'Ayz—perhaps he was summoned. . . ."

"Then why couldn't he have made arrangements for me to see the manuscript here?"

Isabel thought about that, grasping the cool edge of the marble mantel with both hands and staring into the red *immortelles*. "Well, couldn't he be wanting to show you off to his family—to impress them?"

"I love the way you put that. It sounded so Irish! But that's ridiculous. Impress them with *me*?"

"Well, as the representative of Blakeney and Potts come specially to see his book, even though it isn't yet finished," said Isabel, whose face was flushed, but she kept her back turned.

"But that sounds so innocent!"

"You mean you think it's some kind of plot?" said Isabel, turning her head slowly to look at Daphne and feeling as if she peered through a murkiness of shadowy motives that she had been trying to guess at. The strain of an exhausting day of travel had overtaken her, and the strangeness of knowing that outside the curtained windows was busy Paris on a winter night bewildered her.

"My dear, I could think anything; it's all so hole-and-corner and complicated and unnecessary—no, in point of fact I meant—well, unsophisticated. So sort of childish."

"Well, people do get unsophisticated and childish about books they write. You know."

"Oh, Lord! Yes. But a Frenchman, cousin to a duke, with tons of literary friends. . . ."

"But his first book."

"It's possible. But how selfish!"

"But perhaps he thinks what a treat it'd be for you—for us—to see the château. . . ."

"I know! And it would be! If only that had been the arrangement! I suppose it didn't occur to him that I couldn't decide for myself where I went and how long I stayed? . . . I mean, people who've never worked for a living—that's it, of course. He simply doesn't understand. . . ." Isabel saw that she was talking herself into going, and did not know whether to be glad or sorry. Being alone might have made the great meeting simpler and easier for everyone, but having an observer would be protection if something went wrong. "I don't want to offend him. But on the other hand . . ."

They discussed the matter for some time, and Isabel, without any conscious intention of doing so, found herself shifting her arguments to keep Daphne passive. When Daphne began to worry about taking too much upon herself after all, she suggested wiring Mr. Dolphin at his flat, asking for instructions. But when Daphne began to compose the cable she felt compelled to point out that if he strongly disapproved, he would think ill of Daphne for not seeing the unwisdom of the change of plan for herself, whereas if he thought it an obvious necessity, he would accuse her of making a mountain of a molehill and tease her about it at the office for evermore.

Isabel settled at last into a course of minimizing the step—probably only a day or two more away from the office, and Daphne had brought work along to do at odd moments, anyway, and only the extra expense of a round-trip ticket to Tours, which could not amount to much, and she would merely be doing what she had been sent to do, which was to take a look at M. d'Ayz's manuscript, never mind where—and saw then that she was behaving like an amateur painter afraid to do anything more to a picture that had accidentally gone very well. She wanted to leave well enough alone.

As it turned out, Henry would have been furious if Daphne had not gone, so that was all right, but the worry of not being sure on that point made Daphne rather irritable for a while, though she tried to hide it. They had dinner in their suite, and food made a difference.

Sipping coffee after dessert, Daphne said at last, "You're very silent, Isabel," and the brittleness had gone from her voice. "All on edge about the new job?"

"It's been a long day," Isabel said, and she at once realized that the day was now over. There was nothing that she could shelter behind now. She had already started on the last movement of time that would take her to face her only living parent. Dinner had been the last barrier between herself and the swift, dark descent into sleep and the morrow—the station, the train, the journey, the castle.

In the morning Daphne had several business errands to do for Mr. Dolphin; Isabel trailed along with her. They had a very early lunch, and at noon they settled themselves in the coupé of the Orléans train at the Gare d'Austerlitz.

It was a short journey—not much more than three hours— through rolling fields and woods, frozen and leafless now, but it was dull as are all journeys on railways, which take their long, straight diagonals through scenery so arbitrarily, so unresponsively, that they seem thereby to turn the scenery against them, so that it shuts them out. Daphne had a manuscript to read. Isabel spent her time trying not to think of the cousin whom she was shortly to meet, because she remembered his letter now as that of someone quite unprepared to be kind to a new relation. In every phrase of it there had been egotism and conceit and an airy disregard of reality. She could not believe that he was really ignorant of Daphne's lowly position in the firm. She felt that he was wilfully deceiving himself, probably on the principle that the British always understated things, or else that he was wilfully determined to force the acceptance of his own evaluation of the facts. She did not like the way he ignored the personality, the humanity, of his new secretary, referring to her always in an afterthought, as if she were something that existed only to link him importantly to Blakeney and Potts, almost as if she were on loan from them. She felt that a girl really on her way to take a job with him could have looked forward to a thin time of it. And she felt that her actual situation might be even worse, as long as she was at his mercy. What would such an egotist, prepared to receive an unknown hireling, do when he met instead a long-lost relative with claims on his family? If Henry had noticed the resemblance, he would certainly do so. How would he respond to the necessity of revising a scene that he had planned along quite different lines?

It seemed possible that he might behave very badly indeed. She could imagine him hotly refusing to have anything to do with her, abandoning her in the station, driving off with Daphne; and she saw herself hiring a car somehow with promises and pleadings and arriving at the castle to find great gates barred against her. A nightmare of involved frustrations, each more impossibly absurd than the one it grew out of, swelled up darkly before her. Destiny had sent her across an ocean and three-quarters of the way across a vast continent, and then had brought her back in slow steps, from Wichita to New York, from New York to Liverpool, from Liverpool to London, from London to Paris, and then one step farther. But now that the goal was so near, she could not quite believe that she would be allowed to reach it, after all. Something would happen to prevent her. Or perhaps in some obscure part of her, fearing what she longed for, dreading the irrevocable reality of her dreams, she only hoped that something would happen.

When the train slowed, slowed yet more, glided, and halted with the faintest of jolts in the station at Tours, she felt half sick with excitement and alarm. She got herself out of the train by assuring herself that her cousin would not be there, that it was all a mistake, that no one would be there, that they would have to telephone and send wires and perhaps turn round and go back to Paris again, and how irritated Daphne would be. . . .

But he was there, unmistakably himself, just beyond the gate. For the first time in her life she had the sensation of recognizing a relative, of feeling round her the ramifications of family. And almost at once she became aware of a great flatness of disappointment—because no sudden instinctive affection for him rose in her. Instead, she felt unexpectedly hostile and far more separate from him than from a stranger. For there he was, well-dressed and comfortable and careless, and there she was with her ill-fitting clothes and a practically empty purse, caring too much. She almost hated him.

He was tall and thin, in his late thirties, blue-eyed, more brown than dark, with a large forehead and a short, square, stubborn chin and elegant hands that were slender and rather small; and for a moment he looked purely triumphant as he saw that they had indeed come at his summons, the representatives of his English publishers-to-be. He wondered which of them was which; he looked from one face to the other—and then quickly, unbelievingly, back to the first face.

And then he stood like stone, still staring, and the expression in his eyes changed slowly from simple astonishment to ridiculous protest as he realized what she must be. It was proof enough that she carried her birthright in her countenance, and far more plainly than she had supposed. Just before it was time to speak, he managed to look away. He glanced at his watch, glanced over his shoulder at a traveller in a red hat, acted out the idle curiosity of a man at ease, glanced at Isabel, said spitefully with a pleasant smile, "Such a bean-pole!" and turned to shake hands with Daphne.

It was a cruel greeting, but there was an intimacy about it that established her in the family whether he meant it to do so or not—she knew that he could have spoken like that at first sight only to a young relative. She felt accepted—and slapped. For a moment the world rocked. Then the shock collected her; it made her see him clearly as a petulant dragon that she must get past in order to reach her father's protection.

Daphne was shocked, too, whether by the simple rudeness of his remark or by the impropriety of such a welcome from an employer to a secretary, Isabel was not certain, but she was somehow quite sure, after a moment, of what Yves was feeling. It was all there in his curiously trivial face. His first instinctive revulsion had become futile, petty anger. If he had been some thirty years younger he might have doubled up his fists and viciously kicked at her because she had come to spoil his lovely party. It was really no wonder he was childishly upset, however. Other things had very recently gone wrong for him; he had come to the station with much on his mind. This was a last straw for him.

His car was outside, drawn up carelessly at a slant to the curb. It was a grey Rolls-Royce and very beautiful; it made the other cars in the square look like derelict machinery. Isabel was put in the back seat with the luggage piled round her feet; Daphne sat in front beside Yves; and off they went very fast through a fair amount of traffic—cars and trams and pedestrians—across the station square, to the left on a boulevard, to the right on a long avenue, and over a bridge across a broad, quiet river with islands in it. Isabel looked back once to see the twin towers of the cathedral at Tours rising above the little rooftops, but she quickly and nervously faced front again, because they were going very fast indeed—seventy miles an hour, perhaps—on a good sandy road through the empty winter countryside; on the wrong side of it, of course, as it seemed. But after a while, abruptly, he took his foot off the accelerator. He had realized that his angry speed was taking him home too quickly, before he had thought what to say when he got there. They almost crawled the rest of the way. Daphne glanced at him once or twice, puzzled but grateful. He paid no attention to her. He was thinking hard and getting nowhere with his thoughts. Their speed did not triumphantly rise again.

Isabel opened her handbag wide and without taking the picture-postcard out looked at it, at the pale walls and towers serenely reflected in water, stared at it, studied it, and looked up from it at intervals to see at last in the distance the incredible reality of it.

It was just like the picture, and it was altogether different. It was a majestic huddle of shabby grey masonry under a winter sky—grey, time-pocked walls and towers, heavy rooftops. People had lived there for hundreds of years and were living there now. It was real. Her mother had known it; she had travelled the road Isabel was travelling now.

The road curved; the castle disappeared; and she did not see it again till they were passing through the single street of a tiny village under its eastern wall between hillside and river—peaked-roofed houses and a shop or two on the one hand along the river, on the other, doors and windows in the hillside itself, opening, she thought, into storage caves of some kind. A large brown dog ran behind the car, barking and snarling at its tires. At the end of the street the highroad turned sharply north, but the car continued straight on up a steep cobbled incline and turned at the top of it to the left into an old paved courtyard.

Then she was within the castle. On all sides its ancient walls rose to the cold sky; there was silence except for the chirping of a melancholy little bird. And Yves had still not thought of what to say. He sat motionless. Daphne glanced at him inquiringly. He did not

[43]

notice her glance. Perhaps it was occurring to him how much wiser it would have been to leave his new-found relative in a hotel at Tours, so that he could have made his explanations unhindered by her presence, because he lifted his hands in a little futile gesture of disgust and struck the steering-wheel. It was too late. Servants were coming out of the house: a middle-aged man in black with a pinched, sad, plump face as pale as wax, a footman in a sort of livery. On the other hand, it might not be too late—he could take her back there now and return alone. An air of uncertain purpose came into his posture; he half turned, as if to speak to her. And by instinct, without thought, she leaned forward and opened the door for herself and stepped out of the car. Having reached her goal, she was going to cling like a barnacle to it, by instinct. He got out of the car, too, then, and Daphne got out, and the footman began lifting out the suitcases. He was well-trained; he did not look up; and neither did the butler.

"Well," said Yves desperately, "shall we go inside?"

"It's all so interesting," said Daphne, much relieved, "so lovely and still," as she moved towards the carved stone porch and the great dark door that it sheltered.

But as Isabel took a step to follow, Yves moved into her path and stopped her, motioning the servants to go on without them as he spoke privately to her. He still had not recovered his presence of mind; he was still futilely rebelling. And he would not look at her. It seemed he could not bear to look at her. It seemed that she disgusted him, by-blow of a casual passion that she was.

"Why in heaven's name did it have to be done like this?" he said. "Why couldn't there have been some warning? Perhaps I could have arranged something, if I'd been warned! Yes! But now I can't do a thing!" He was fiercely angry, but it was not the anger between strangers or friends that puts a space between them for a moment. It was instead the enclosing sort of family anger that shuts the world away while two relatives settle their differences. It made her feel that she belonged where she was even while it greatly unnerved her. "You've made things impossible for me, that's all. Bringing this disgrace down on him—*inviting* you here! He'll be unmanageable. And just when it was particularly important that—"

But he was only concerned for himself, and she stopped listening to him because at that moment, through the door that the butler was holding open, a new voice came, a slow voice, dark, as some voices are, and though what it said was gay enough, there was something reluctant in the gaiety: "Good afternoon, Miss Regan or Miss Small, have you had a pleasant journey?"

Isabel had turned her head towards the sound. Now she looked feverishly at Yves, her eyes asking for confirmation of her guess at who the speaker was. But he had turned his head, too, and was still gazing at the door. "Oh, God!" he said. "Of course he would choose to be civil today . . . for a change." And then he shrugged his shoulders and resigned himself to what was coming, perhaps trusting himself to manage, perhaps weakly giving up. "Do you have a sense of humour?" he asked her with the calm of the doomed. "There is a wayward one that runs in the family— Do you have it? Because the comical thing is—" He stopped, turning his head again, distracted by what the other man was saying in amazement within the hall:

"But what's wrong? What is it?"

"No—no, nothing," Daphne was heard to say in a stammer. She seemed hardly able to speak at all. "Nothing— It's just that—" Yves made a face—and made up his mind. He went swiftly inside.

His dismay should have prepared Isabel for the reception she was going to get. But it did not. Reality was steadily eating away the edges of her hopes, but she only retreated from it to deceive herself tenaciously a little longer—and if she had not been able to do so, I suppose this affair of forcing her way into the household of strangers would have been too much for her. She followed him as if drawn by a cord round her neck into a large echoing gloominess with people in it.

He had already begun to speak, and his plangent, tenor voice was as distracting, as annoying as a buzzing fly. "Miss Small," he was saying, "wants her tea. Wants it in every sense of the word—isn't that right, Miss Small? You've met my cousin? The Duc de Ferronçalles, Miss Small, of Blakeney and Potts, the English— But you will want to go to your room, I know, and relax a bit after this tedious travelling— Arnaud, will you show Miss Small to her room, if you please—and take the luggage up at once, Joël?" But he was accomplishing his purpose; he was making a stir through the tensions and clearing the hall.

If he had not done that, they would all have been standing frozen in silence, as Isabel and her father were standing. For the comical thing was that she looked enough like him to be his daughter in anyone's eyes—in the eyes of the most casual and unobservant stranger, and therefore how much more so in the eyes of the household servants, of his sister, of his friends! He had no choice of explanations. There was only one explanation that anyone could believe. Her claim on him was indisputable.

He looked as if he were drowning in the realization of that. His face was tilted up, like that of someone neck-deep in water. He looked down his nose at her, amazed, incredulous, trying to understand what had suddenly appeared out of the blue before him. And the dimness, the high ceiling lost in shadows, the echoing stillness gave the moment a solemnity that awed her. He was a remarkably handsome man, tall and dark, heavy-browed and sombre, and quite unapproachable, quite formidably distant, not at all the kind of person at whose lapel one could catch and make protestations to. He would always choose his time to listen. She did not try to speak; she waited. But her blank stare must have seemed to him purposeful and implacable, instead of awed and expectant. Shyness is often mistaken for hostility.

At last the expression in his long, narrow blue eyes altered. He was searching—she knew this, she was certain of it—for her mother's face in his memories of the past. He found it, closed his eyes for a moment that seemed long, opened them, and said to his cousin in a growl of finally exhausted patience, "What are you trying to do? What are you up to now?"

"But I did not know!" Yves said earnestly. "Honestly I did not know, I swear to you, Mathieu, I give you my word of honour—"

"Oh, I can smell the complicity," said the Duke, still not raising his voice, but he looked taut as a bowstring. He was frightening—to her, and also, she saw, to his cousin. "What are you up to? But it won't do. You've gone too far now." There was silence. Then he said to Yves, "I think you and I will have a talk now; this anger is too good to be wasted," and Isabel thought him the more formidable that he could make this quaint declaration without the slightest subsidence of his wrath. He turned to her. He was taller than she, much older than she, and standing on his own ground, and he used these advantages to make her feel mean, futile, and defenceless. "What has he been telling you?" he said severely. "That I was

[46]

a meek soul, easily cornered, easy prey for any kind of blackmail? Well, he was wrong. . . . Come along," he said to his cousin, and Yves followed him, beginning new affirmations that were answered and interrupted with growling exclamations of disbelief.

She was alone in that large, cold, bare hall, staring round her with dazed eyes. It was slightly furnished, but not in any way that made it hospitable. The floor was of small square tiles, worn stone-coloured, but in the corners traces of glazed colour remained, bright and floral. The walls were panelled in wood that was cracked and warped and blackened with age. There was a great fireplace with no fire in it.

She was suffering, and there was, after all, no pleasure in suffering. She did not feel noble in grief, she felt flayed and loathsome, and the remedy she instinctively found for a sensation of ignominy too great to be endured was to take sides against herself and flog herself a little more, thus climbing up on her own bowed back to raise herself to the level—or almost—of her oppressors. She cruelly reminded herself of the scenes of welcome that she had imagined —august embraces, eager questions, tender reproofs for not having come back long ago—and she explored her deeper heart to uncover other expectations even more humiliating: the return of the prodigal, an aged butler putting out a trembling joyful hand, a white-haired housekeeper breaking down in happy tears, young maids gathering round, awed and interested. . . . "But you are one of us, mademoiselle—you are obviously one of us. . . . You have come home!" The dispossessed princess returning in open triumph to her throne, while poor Daphne stood neglected, wondering at it all. . . .

Then she felt utterly crushed with shame; she moved across the hall because she could not bear to stand still with the ache of it; and her footsteps sounded hollow and lonely in the silence.

She was not left there very long. Another footman came hurrying in, sent, it was plain, to get her out of sight quickly, and she had her first experience of a household that reflected the moods of its master unthinkingly. The servant was barely polite. She felt that he could not have been told to treat her so; he had merely absorbed that tone from the tone of the command given him, and it had not occurred to him to make his own judgement—or even to be neutral.

"Through here, mademoiselle," he said, pushing open one wing of a double door in the south wall.

There was a passage beyond, stone-walled, stone-floored, and at the east end of it a spacious circular staircase, a strangely graceful open-work of stone for half its circumference, the other half solid outside wall with two or three narrow windows cut in the thickness of it. The stone treads were worn into treacherous cups near the newel. He kept to the wall as he led the way up; she did so, too. When they left the staircase they were on a polished wooden floor that creaked. He went to the nearest door and held it open. She went in and heard the door grind shut on sagging hinges behind her.

She was in a small, cold room with dark panelled walls and a faded rug on the parquet floor. In one corner was a hooded stone fireplace where a fire was laid but not lit. There was also a narrow bed, a wardrobe, a small chest of drawers, a wash-stand, a deep shabby wing-chair, and very little room for walking. Her three suitcases stood in a row under the single window, which had curtains of red-flecked cotton to match the quilted coverlet on the bed. She heard a noise behind her, and Daphne said uncertainly, "What a cubby-hole they've put you in!" She turned and saw that there was another door in the room, a narrow door panelled like the walls. Daphne peered past it, nervously smiling, but her eyes avoided Isabel's eyes just as the servant's had done after one startled stare. Isabel would almost rather have been stared at. "Haven't they! Never mind. They told me you'd be in here, and I've been hoping you'd come up in time to have some tea. Do come and have some tea."

Daphne's room next door was spacious and beautiful, all gilt and rosy silk. There were four great windows in the south wall framing a misty, twilit view of the open countryside beyond the river, and when Isabel turned from the view she saw that there was a fire glowing and flickering on the hearth in the north wall. The busy, pointed orange flames were brightening as the dusk darkened, lighting the tea-table pleasantly, warming the air. It was the first open fire that she had ever stood beside, and for some mysterious reason it made her want to cry.

"Do come and sit down," said Daphne. "I'm going to have another cup," she said, looking into the teapot. "It's really very good. . . . Here you are. Cake? The cake's really very good. . . . Now if

I can only get my hands on that manuscript—and I don't mind telling you I'm a bit more hopeful than I was. . . . All this"—she waved her hand—"rather pins our friend down, doesn't it? . . . I do so wish I knew more about it. . . . When one thinks that Francis the First may have walked in this room—may even have slept here! Or Henry the Fourth. Or Sully, or the Duc de Guise. They say that should be pronounced Gweeze, not Geeze. Do you know?"

"I don't know."

"Tired?"

"Yes."

"It's been a tiresome two days. Exhausting. Have some more cake. . . ." But she looked at Isabel so little that it was plain she wanted to look a lot and study the face that was so like another face just seen, and her talk simply skated along on the surface, unregarded and uncontrolled, as she thought of something that was not the castle nor the business that had brought her there nor the good tea and good cake. When she spoke her mind at last, it was as if she had skidded into a break in the ice and plunged by accident: "I *can't* help wondering, *are* you connected with this family in some way?" Then at once she tried to scramble out again. "Sorry, sorry, sorry! When will I learn that children should be seen and not heard! There's still some tea left—"

"No more, thank you," Isabel said, standing up. The windows were tall rectangles of pallor, very far away and very large, or very close and small, it was hard to tell in that light, and though she knew which it was, she pretended she did not. "I imagine there is an out-of-the-way connection of some kind or other, so my mother told me." She folded her arms, hugging herself. "I'd forgotten about it."

"Oh," said Daphne, flushing as she bent to tease the fire. Her hair was like sun-coloured silk in the firelight. Isabel suddenly and sharply envied her that innocent fair hair. "I see."

"Where do all these doors go?"

"Into empty rooms, my dear—enormous empty rooms." She shook her fair head ruefully. "How I shall feel when the lights are out and things start creaking—!"

"I think I shall go and have a bath. . . . What sort of arrangements are there, do you know? Any? None?" said Isabel, leaving the door between their rooms open. Her cubby-hole was very dark now. She felt in her pockets for a box of matches, found one, and struck a light.

"They brought me a can of hot water. . . . Did they you?"

They had not. Isabel examined the room. There was a small door in the marble-topped wash-stand that did not promise well, and it did in fact contain a nice white porcelain chamber-pot, and neither of the two doors in the room had a bolt on it. Daphne giggled from the doorway. The match burned low; Isabel blew it out, waved it to cool it, and put it back in the box.

"No," said Daphne, "as a matter of fact the maid who brought the tea did say something on that subject. Actually she gave me very elaborate directions, down the passage and to the right or to the left—the awful thing is I've forgotten which. Shall we explore?"

Isabel did not think she should, but after three hours of train and forty minutes in a car and all that tea, she really had no choice. They set off down the dim, creaking, ancient corridor. The cold air smelled of history; the silence was the grave of sounds that had had their moment of life centuries ago. Once again, for some odd reason, she wanted to cry.

There were now one or two lighted lamps in brackets on the wall of the passage, which was T-shaped. A door at the juncture of the stem and cross-piece of the T opened into an empty room with uncurtained windows glaring grey. The next door opened on a little circular stairway like a fan unfurling downwards into darkness. Someone was coming slowly up. Isabel stepped back, and Daphne stepped back too, for different reasons.

"Hullo?" said the Duke, emerging on the creaking floor.

"I'm so sorry," said Daphne meaninglessly.

"Are you lost?" he said to her, laughing. But he seemed tired— his heart was not in his laughter.

"Yes—no—"

"What are you looking for?"

"Nothing at all, really," she said hesitantly. She must have despised her sudden freak of bashfulness, but could not help it—he a man, and French, and a duke, and she a woman differently made.

Isabel was staring at him, fascinated and frightened, but he did not seem to know that she was there. He waited for Daphne to decide that she had indeed been in search of something and to explain what it was. But Daphne could not speak, and Isabel said at last in a hurried mutter, meaning to spare them both, "We were looking for the lavatory."

He gave her a slow sidelong look of displeasure, as if she had spoken very much out of turn. But it was a mechanical look, his heart was not in that either, and he only said, "Oh! Along here," walking along the right-hand turn of the passage to a door at the end of it. He opened the door, reached inside to switch on a light, and waited there politely so that he could close it on them when they had entered. "And the bath is the first door round the corner on the left as you come back. Quantities of hot water." They were inside. He closed the door on them.

The room was larger than Isabel's bedroom and quite unfurnished except that in one corner, all lonely, stood a little water-closet, perfectly round, with a polished oak seat and a tank high overhead and a handle on a long chain moving slightly in a perpetual draught.

"I think," said Daphne with the palm of her hand over her face, looking through her fingers, "I shall just wait outside. . . ."

When Isabel came out and she went in, Isabel did not wait for her. She could not play any longer the game of happy schoolgirls having an adventure. She could not giggle and joke.

He had been taut with anger before; now he was weary and quiet in triumph. She walked back along the dim old creaking passage and heard a murmur of voices as she passed one closed door —ghost-like voices in subdued concord. Someone had come to her room while she was out of it. There was a copper can of hot water on the floor beside the wash-stand, and on the chest by the bed a pair of lighted candles in a polished copper candlestick. The red-speckled curtains at the window had been drawn, but the fire was still unlit. A decision had been made; Yves would not defend her; Daphne could do nothing for her.

She washed in the hot water, opened one of the suitcases and took out her blue frock, the only dinner dress she had ever owned, bought at a sale, never worn before, and not wholly a successful bargain—the sleeves were bunchy, the skirt had to be forever twitched at to make it hang straight. She shook it out and put it doubtfully on, and combed her hair. Then she went into Daphne's room because she could not bear the cold any longer and did not want to be found by Daphne huddled in her coat by an unlit fire.

[51]

Daphne was dressed for dinner, too. The fire on her hearth was leaping and hissing; the curtains of faded rosy damask were drawn.

Isabel did not know whether or not she was expected to appear at dinner, but she trusted that Daphne's presence and ignorance would shelter her, and she did not want to be left behind. One does not earn wages in this world for four years without learning how to endure slights and rebuffs, but one still gets hurt by them, and what had happened to her in this house had been more than commonly hurtful.

They went down together, uncertain of where to go. The staircase was lighted now by a hanging lamp; so was the L-shaped ground-floor passage, from which they went into the great hall of their first entrance into the house. The hearth was still bare and dark, but another hanging lamp lighted the room dimly, and a footman came in as they hesitated there. He was the one who had taken Isabel to her room, fair-haired, heavy-cheeked, country-bred. He came through a pair of doors in the north wall, and when he saw Daphne and Isabel he went back to open them again.

Isabel followed Daphne into a long room dark in tone and richly ornamented. Walls and ceiling were panelled in squares of dark wood intricately carved, and at either end, in the short walls, were chimney-pieces of stone sculptured with a delicacy and grace that made drawing-room ornaments of them. It was a beautiful room, and it was warm—wonderfully warm—the first warm room that she had come upon. Magnificent fires leaped richly on both hearths, and the warmth from them met in the centre of the room; it did not lose itself and dwindle away in coldness, it met its likeness and grew.

When the Duke came in, he gave Isabel only a glance, his brows raised, and turned at once to explain his sister's absence to Daphne —it seemed that the Countess had taken cold and could not leave her room. Once again Isabel felt that rudeness was the next thing to welcome. She knew that he would never have treated the most hateful stranger so. Even treating her that way seemed to make him uncomfortable, though his discomfort only increased his anger with her. As the talk went on and she sat ignored, she tried to keep up her courage with that reasoning. Daphne said that she lived at Holme Manor in Hampshire and that they were quite sure they had a ghost. He said there were no ghosts at Ferronçalles. She said she was glad to hear that, with night coming on, but wasn't it a shame, and surprising, too, in so old a château, which she pronounced as if it were "shadow" spelt with a "t." He said that they had cows and ducks and chickens and pigs and horses; did that help at all? She said that she adored pigs. They talked about pigs. He had an English accent, as his cousin had, but he had not caught the true clipped casualness of it; his speech was slow and distinct, giving full value to every complicated vowel, which made it sound like an unkind mockery of English at times.

Isabel studied him covertly but with intense interest, hardly able to believe that she really was at last seeing him with her own eyes. She thought him uncannily handsome—uncannily because he looked so like herself, and her own face, dark, stern, heavy-browed, had never pleased her much. Miriam had had all sorts of nice phrases for it—an antique face, dusky plum-coloured hair, a profile on a coin—but Miriam had thought Queen Nefertiti the most beautiful woman that ever existed, which showed what her taste was. Isabel would have liked more bloom and softness. But the austerity that displeased her in her own face charmed her in his. She admired the dark brows that almost met, the severe carving of eye-sockets and nose. When he talked, he always glanced away and twiddled his thumbs and appeared to be hardly aware of his audience; his face was softened by a shadowy inward look that made him seem withdrawn and dreamy; and he listened with the same apparent inattentiveness; but just as she was beginning to hope that Daphne was boring him, he laughed, and it was such honest laughter that she turned to stare at the fire, the great glowing cave of living flame, framed in pale stone exactly as it had been framed for hundreds of years, and felt bewildered by the unnaturalness of everything else.

She had come back to her home after twenty-one years wanting really only a welcome and a private acknowledgement, nothing else; but she seemed to have walked into a maze of trivialities and formalities of distrust and social embarrassment and customs and habits—so that here she sat, ignored, while he was able to laugh with a stranger who meant nothing to him. And she did not know what to do about it now that the open anger had gone and she was opposed only by trivialities and formalities.

Then Yves came in, to be greeted much as Isabel had been, for he, too, was in disgrace, and he, too, was a relative; but there was a difference, the contempt and dislike did not have to be so plainly expressed in his case because he would feel them if they were only hinted—and could not be, for that matter, because he was Daphne's sponsor, and she must not be made uncomfortable. Moreover, he expected it and was unabashed. Then the double door on the other side of the room opened, and the butler, Arnaud, appeared to announce dinner. They went into the dining-room, which was an altogether different sort of room, massive and severely simple. Its stone walls were whitewashed, the beams in its dark ceiling were exposed, and the floor was of stone, too. The fireplace was beside the door; Isabel did not see it as she entered, she saw instead the warm waves of firelight moving up the white walls to fall softly back, as gentle as an ebbing tide, and almost as old a motion.

Back in the drawing-room for coffee after dinner, as she sat in silence with strained eyes trying to occupy themselves in some natural way, she noticed how the room had been wired for electricity, with exposed wires stapled to the beautiful panelling, and how worn the carpet was near the doors, and how comfortable the chairs were. Some of them had loose extra cushions and large hassocks, and near them stood the kind of plain but useful lamps that throw a good light for reading. To the right of the door into the dining-room was an ebony lowboy inlaid with disks of mother-of-pearl, a remarkably ugly piece of furniture, and on it was a gilt-and-marble clock with a very sharp tick and a very sweet chime, but it struck at six minutes past the hour, and it did not strike the hour that the hands had just told. On the far side of the table there was a third door, narrow and tall. The other end of the room was well furnished with tables, chairs, and a sofa, but it looked somehow disused despite the glowing fire that lighted and warmed it, as if no one had the habit of sitting there.

While she took note of these things, Daphne and the Duke and Yves were conversing, but not very successfully now. Instead of laying the groundwork for conversation during dinner, they had exhausted it, and now there were only spasmodic remarks and longish pauses. It would have been an awkward party in any circumstances —two men and two women of disparate ages and different backgrounds paired by numbers in an intimacy that had no foundation —but with one of the four not being spoken to, and one of them increasingly disturbed by that fact, and one of them obviously getting sleepy, and the fourth fretting inwardly about his own affairs, which had unexpectedly gone so very wrong, it was all hopelessly awkward. Daphne got up at last to put an end to it, and everyone was glad.

They gathered briefly at the door, and good nights were said by everyone but Isabel, who had no voice to trust after her long silence. And then somehow she and Daphne were crossing the cold, dim hall together and the door was closed behind them with Yves and his cousin still in the drawing-room, and almost at once, beyond the closed door, Yves's muted voice rose naggingly. The quarrel was being resumed.

But there was no exchange of glances, no sharing of relief and amusement between Isabel and Daphne as they crossed the hall and walked side by side down the passage to the great circular staircase, where the hanging lamp swayed in a draught and cast confusing shadows through the brass open-work of its shade. And when they had climbed the stairs and arrived at the door of Isabel's room, Daphne said only, "Well, it's been a long day . . . good night," and went on to her own door. Undoubtedly she was feeling dissatisfied with her management of the evening, undoubtedly the sound of her own shrill, nervous voice making inane comments after dinner was echoing painfully in her ears, but that is not a sensation one likes to be alone with. But she did not want to be with Isabel now, playing the game of happy schoolgirls on an adventure.

Probably she was as much affected by Isabel's failure to confide in her as by the manner of Isabel's reception in the house; but Isabel did not see that, and she went into her small, cold, dark room and closed the door feeling rejected by the whole world, feeling utterly friendless, utterly despised. She stood motionless. It did not seem worth her while to move or make a light or go to bed or do anything at all.

Then she heard someone shout outside, and she bumped through the dark to the window and pulled back the curtain to look out. The curtain smelled rather chokingly of dust, as curtains always do. Her warm breath fogged the cold glass.

Outside, cloudy moonlight vaguely showed the true lights and darks of things—pale walls looked pale, dark roofs looked dark, and in the centre of the pale stone courtyard stood the dark, foreshortened figure of the Duke. He was shouting to a dog, and the dog came, a large dark dog with a topknot and a tasselled tail. It came with hateful servility, slower and slower, drooping lower and lower, crawling the last short distance to his feet. He stooped and touched it, and it seemed to swoon with joy. When he straightened and turned towards the house, it scrambled hastily up and trotted anxiously after him. They went out of sight under the stone roof of the porch.

She dropped the curtain, groped here and there on flat surfaces for her box of matches, found it, felt for a good match among the burnt ones, and struck it and lighted the candles, struck another and lighted the fire, struck a third and lighted a cigarette. Then she pulled the wing-chair close to the fire and sat down and put her feet up on the low stone curb of the hearth. The tinkling rustle of consumed paper was overtaken by the roar of kindling wood; bright flame moved up through the artfully arranged logs; warmth flowed towards her. Now at last she felt only angry. She had been treated very badly for no fault of her own. She had not asked to be born, but she had been born. She was alive and human, not something to be thrust disdainfully away because her presence made someone uncomfortable. She belonged here as much as anyone did. She had rights; he had obligations. He had behaved with shameful unkindness; the whole world would agree to that. He had behaved selfishly and heartlessly; there was no denying it. And there was no excusing it.

She sat for a long while staring into the brilliant fire, moving only to take more wood from the basket by the hearth and throw it recklessly on the blaze, growing almost exultant as she considered her wrongs. But beneath her exultation the darkness of disappointment gathered round her heart and clung there, as soft and bitter as smoke; and when she went to bed at last, she cried over her wrongs for the first time in her life and wanted to die.

She woke to another grey day, washed in cold water, put on the thick navy-blue suit she had worn the day before, and winding her watch, wandered to the window and saw the Duke, bareheaded, dressed in breeches and gaiters and a brown tweed riding-coat, talking to Daphne in the courtyard. He was looking up at the opposite façade, pointing out some detail of the architecture; she was looking up at him and smiling.

Isabel went downstairs, through the great hall, and outside. After passing through the bitterly cold hall she was surprised to find the day so mild, chilly but not sharp, cloudy but irresolutely so. They were still standing in the courtyard, much as before, though now both considering each other as they talked, instead of details of architecture. "Good morning!" she said, standing in the stone porch like one in possession, her hands thrust in her pockets.

They turned. "Good morning," said Daphne neutrally, and he said to her, "Excuse me," and to Isabel, approaching with long, slow steps that brought him unexpectedly soon to the porch, "Will you come with me, please?"

She followed him inside again, through the hall, into the passage, and to the right past the staircase through a series of bare rooms that she had not seen before; and as she bumbled along behind him, watching the back of his beautiful dark head and broad shoulders while empty rooms swam past in a slow blur, her only thought was, "There he is; and how charming, how charming; and how I would try to please him, if only he knew. . . ."

They came into a room that was furnished, and he turned at once to leave her there, saying, "My cousin will be here before long."

"But I've had no breakfast!"

"You've had no breakfast?" he said, looking directly at her for the first time since the first time, but doing so as if he meant to catch her out in a pointless lie. His blue eyes were cold and sharp in his dark face. "Did you not ring when you wakened?"

"There's no bell in my room," she said, which was true.

"Where have they put you, then?"

"In that—that *little* room next to Miss Small's."

Very unexpectedly he laughed. "You don't like small rooms?" he said jovially, his face alight with amusement, and for a moment his involuntary laughter made everything warm and easy. But then he remembered his suspicions and turned away, his laughter fading; and everything stiffened again. "Oh, but you must be fed; I'll have them bring you something here."

"Coffee and toast will do very well," she called after him carelessly, and he stopped, his hand on the handle of the door, then went on, straightening his shoulders with a little movement that showed quite well his reception of that remark.

She turned from the closed door to look at the room, but not triumphantly—no, sickly. She had not meant to be insolent; she only

[57]

had not wanted to crawl, as the servile dog had done, and her voice had found the wrong note.

It was a lovely room, long and narrow, graceful and serene. At one end of it was a fire, a bright fire exquisitely framed in golden marble; above the mantel was a painting of a forest picnic, lords and ladies in pastel satins in a green scene of shaven lawns and shady trees that seemed to contain the reality of deep midsummer warmth; and in addition, thin sunlight had begun to trace the shapes of eight tall southern windows on the flowered rug.

A plain, dark maid brought coffee and toast—precisely that—on a tray. She did not smile or look at Isabel; she only pointed to a corner of thick white paper sticking out from under the saucer and departed. It was a short letter, three spiky lines written in black ink with a thin sputtering pen:

> *My cousin is informed of my wishes in this matter and will convey them to you. Whatever may have to be done for you, you will not in future attempt to come here again.*

She remembered then her mother in moods of muttering resentment, when her dark eyes were hot and watchful and suspicious as they looked out at a world that was an enemy; and for the first time in her life she seemed to stand behind the façade of that mood in the glowing tangle of her mother's nerves and taut sinews and tensed muscles. She more than understood her; she was her. She saw the world as her mother had seen it at such moments, and knew both her own powerlessness and her own integrity as her mother must have known hers. And so she was collected in anger, though she was also blocked and frustrated. She was as formidable as her mother had ever been.

She ate her breakfast in haste, to get that necessity out of the way before the battle; and time passed. After a while she got up to walk restlessly back and forth in the room, from the chimney-piece to a pair of glass doors at the other end of the room and back again. The glass doors opened on a terrace bright now with sunlight, sheltered from the wind on three sides, and so long that the door at the far end seemed only inches high. The tall columns that supported its roof cast delicate shadows aslant on the weathered stone floor. She walked back towards the fire, pausing at the pretty writing-table in the centre of the room to put out her last cigarette in a silver ashtray. There were other useful trinkets there: a paper-scissors, a clear glass paper-weight as big as her fist, with a nosegay of spring flowers imprisoned in it, a calendar printed on ivory leaves, a thin gold pen; and there was a tin of English cigarettes. She looked at her watch. Then she took one of the cigarettes to smoke and put eight or nine into her empty case. And time passed. She walked back and forth along the windows. The curtains were of yellow silk looped up in crisp curving folds to frame a view of the small river that lapped the walls and of the fields and hills beyond the river and the misty horizon far away and the high sky that now was clouding over again.

At last Yves came. But he came with Daphne, and he was so absorbed in his business with her that he really did not notice Isabel. Daphne did, but she only smiled faintly. "Not a great deal done," he said, going straight to the writing-table and opening a drawer. Then he hesitated for so long a time, staring down at the open drawer, his free hand poised over it, that Isabel thought he was at this late date on the point of changing his mind about showing his book. But his funny hesitancy passed; his hand went down with decision and took out a thin sheaf of paper. "No, not a great deal done, but perhaps it will give you some idea of the plan of the work —this is the English version, not completely, finally revised—you will find roughnesses in it, I am sure, but—" Daphne put out her hand for it encouragingly; after a moment he parted with it. It was really a manuscript, handwritten. She went a bit grey. "That chair is quite comfortable," he said, "and there are cigarettes—you smoke, I know. . . ." He frowned at the littered breakfast tray, glanced at Isabel, and jerked his shoulders as if to shrug her off for the moment.

"But mayn't I," said Daphne, "—mayn't I take it up to my room? I'm simply the world's worst concentrator—Miss Regan knows," she said, giving Isabel another smile, less faint, more true, because Isabel knew very well how unaware she had been of every kind of bustle round her—clattering typewriter, ringing telephone, squeaking swivel chair—when she was reading even the dullest manuscript, "and I want to give this my very best attention. It does look interesting," she went on, lifting one closely written page as if she could not wait to see what was happening on the next.

"If you like," he said; "only I wanted your honest reaction, and

I'd hoped to learn a great deal from just the expression on your face as you read. . . ." Daphne gave Isabel a brief glance, despairing and gay; they were almost friends again, sharing a viewpoint and a joke. "But, as you please."

"And may I go now and start at once? I'm so eager to get into it."

"I'm flattered," he said, smiling.

"A wonderful first sentence," she cried, and escaped.

He stood at the graceful table, staring downwards, and Isabel hopefully began to think that perhaps he knew how silly he had been. But if he did, he was not going to admit it.

"Well, you've rocked the boat badly, at a time when I particularly didn't want it rocked," he said bitterly. "Everything's gone wrong. It's most unfair. It's spoiled everything. Everything's gone wrong!" He cut short his nervous phrases with an impatient gesture, smoothed his brown hair, and sat down at the table to scowl up at her with exasperation and pleading, quite as if she were his prosecutor, his defender, and the bar of justice, all in one. But she could not care about his troubles, which she guessed—from what Henry had said, and correctly—might be only a love affair gone awry and money needed to avoid scandal. "You see, you've no idea," he went on as debonairly as he could. "I'm in a most awkward pickle in Paris —I had to come here for money: always a delicate subject to bring up with our dear Mathieu—and then in you walk, by my own arrangement— God!" He put his hand out to the open tin of cigarettes and once again hesitated, frowning at it. But he took one, after all, and lit it with a small gold lighter and smoked for half a minute or so in silence. "God!" he said again, staring at her, and his blue eyes were bleak with hatred of her. "What's to be done?" He sounded really at his wits' end.

"What have you been told to do?" she said coldly, unwilling to have the moment she dreaded put off any longer. But something that may have been wounded pride—because she had had to remind him of her father's rejection of her, which ought to have been first in the thoughts of everyone who knew of it, so awful and wrong it was—made her voice tremble.

"Yes, that's the point exactly. I must get you out of here today. But that's all I'm going to do; I warn you of that right now. I've got enough troubles as it is—you've no idea! Everything's gone wrong—everything! Why, why, why did you have to come here like this, without warning? I could have managed it, told you the sort of appeal to make, and so forth, and I *would* have, if you'd given me the smallest chance— Yes!"

"That's very kind of you," she said unsteadily. She had thought herself prepared, but she found she was not. Hearing it put into words was simply an altogether different thing from expecting to hear it. She felt profoundly shaken. "You take it all so easily. . . . I don't think you understand how—how sickened . . . and revolted . . . and *appalled* it makes me feel—" He frowned up at her. "It doesn't seem strange and unnatural to you at all that my father refuses to have anything to do with me?"

This plain speaking embarrassed him, sophisticated though he was. And he looked perplexed as well. She took the letter out of her pocket and threw it at him. It sailed to the floor, and he leaned to pick it up. "I don't think much of the system!" she cried out. "These heads of families that can get their dirty work done for them, who stand so high and untouchable and give their orders and wash their hands of it and never find out what the world is like because their servile relatives shield them so obediently from everything unpleasant. . . ."

He looked up from the letter, the three spiky lines on thick white paper. "This must have hurt you a great deal," he remarked. "He might have put it more gently. . . ."

Her outburst had done some good. He looked at her now as if he saw that she was human. There was no kindness in his eyes, but there was something that she thought was better than that: there was understanding. There was thoughtfulness. He ran his fingers through his thick brown hair. "Well, there it is," he said after a moment, dropping the letter on the desk. "That's that."

"But it's not fair!"

"Oh, fairness—" he said wisely and vaguely.

"I mean, it's not right!"

He shrugged his shoulders.

"Don't you care whether a thing is right or wrong?" she said furiously. "Don't you care at all what sort of dirty work you're told to do? Do you just hold your nose and wade in? Or don't you even have to hold your nose?"

"Why be so harsh with me?" he said, getting up and coming round to sit on the edge of the table, smearing out his cigarette in the ashtray as he came, then folding his arms as he leaned back, ankles crossed. He was calm and attentive now. "What's the good of all this fury? Heads of families, high and untouchable, as you said. He's a law to himself here, and in any case you have no real proof of your claim, have you? And I shouldn't think any legal claim, in any case. There's nothing but a moral obligation, and if he chooses to ignore it— That's the way it is. It's all very unfortunate. Henry has behaved unforgivably, putting you in the way of a rebuff like this. To do him justice, I don't think he'd have done it if he'd known what would happen. But it's happened, and there's nothing to do but accept it."

"I don't agree."

"There's nothing I can do—"

"But you've nothing to do with it!" she said, going round the table to take another cigarette from the tin there. He turned his head to see what she was doing, but did not otherwise move. "That's what I've been telling you! It's nothing to do with you; you're only a pair of tongs that he's manipulating—do you like to be a pair of tongs?"

"Not particularly," he said carelessly, watching her.

"Then stay out of it!"

"Oh, gladly! As much as I possibly can! But tell me this, what do you want? Are you asking that he dismiss you himself, in his own person; is that it?"

"I'm asking not to be dismissed! I'm refusing to be dismissed!"

"Nobly said; but what do you want, what are you hoping for? What do you think he owes you?"

"I think," she said, moving towards the fire—illogically, not meaning to make use of it—because flames flickered there and she had no match for her cigarette, "I think he owes me a living . . . but I should refuse to take it from him now. And I think he owes me affection and a little caring what happens to me, which can't be bargained for. . . ."

"Well, there you are," he said.

"No, all I want, I guess, is not to be treated as if I had no right to want anything—I mean, as if I were being dishonest and unclean in expecting something. Only I don't expect anything any more. . . . I don't know. I've got to think it over."

"I don't precisely see why," he murmured, moving at last, taking his little gold lighter out of his pocket. "Forgive me, but I don't exactly see the point of that. . . ." He came a few steps towards her and clicked the lighter into flame, and she moved a few steps towards him and took a light from it—and then she realized from a sort of smiling subsidence and relaxation in his posture that he had misunderstood that natural response of hers. He took it to be the surface symptom of a deep, unconscious yielding in her, a giving up, a shift to docility. "And it seems so foolish in any case to want something from the past, when there is life to be lived now. . . . You have so much already," he said glibly. "You're young and intelligent and extraordinarily beautiful. . . ." That shook her a little. No one had ever called her that before, not even Miriam, and in spite of his glibness he seemed to mean it. And it had for some reason special weight, coming from a cousin. "You have all that to make a life with. Isn't it enough? All this, all of us, we're your hindrance, we're the only thing in your life that other people could look askance at. We link you to a sordid and shameful beginning. Why should you want to stay here?"

"Listen to me," she said, feeling the relief of being able to speak openly to someone who was bound to be interested, "please listen, try to see—" But, after all, she could not put into words the despair and uncertainty of her childhood. She was too much in the habit of silence. She could not display her sores to anyone.

He leaned against the table, arms folded, ankles crossed, thick brown hair catching the sunlight in glints of gold, blue eyes narrowed attentively, waiting for her to go on. He was wearing a fine silk shirt and crystal cuff-links and a grey suit that had only been worn enough not to seem new; his shoes were hand-made; his idle hands were smooth; he smelled of good wool and good tobacco; he drove a Rolls-Royce; and when he needed a little extra money to help himself out of a difficulty, he could come down here and get it.

He saw that she was not going to continue, and he said, "No, it was a great mistake to come here; you see that, don't you?" And she began to hate the very sound of his voice. It was light and resonant, and it buzzed against her ears as annoyingly as a fly. "What you must do, for your own good, is go far away and forget the whole unfortunate connection and make a life of your own for yourself. Isn't that the thing to do?"

[63]

"In Paris, you mean? As your secretary?" she said scornfully, and he looked alarmed.

"Hardly. No, that's out of the question now, isn't it? The talk there'd be! You wouldn't like it any more than I should. And there'd be no future in it for you. Whereas in London . . ."

She stared at him, and fear grew in her. "So you don't mean to have anything to do with me either?" He studied the tip of his burnished shoe. She smoothed the harsh wool of her skirt and was aware of a thinness in the heel of her stocking where a shoe that was not hand-made rubbed as it ought not. She thought of her flat purse and all her belongings in three large shabby suitcases upstairs. "Do you mean I can starve, for all you care?"

"Oh, come," he said. "You've said it was none of my affair."

"That wasn't. This *is!* I left a good job to take this one with you, but now my place has been filled, I can't go back to it! You can't change your mind now! I've got to have a job! I've got nowhere to go!"

"Well," he said, "of course I mean to find you something else. . . ."

"I don't trust you!"

"And there's this," he said, tapping the letter, which was lying where he had dropped it on the desk. "He apparently intends to make some provision for you."

The meaning of the moment thrust itself against her with a dull pressure that brought not comprehension, but pain. She shrank back from knowing that she no longer had anything to look forward to, that it was all over. She could not accept that finality. But the pressure did not lessen. "I don't want it!" she cried wildly. "I won't go! I have a right to be here! He has no right to send me away like this! I won't go, I won't!"

"Which only means that you will be removed by force. He doesn't want you here. And I'm not going to be saddled with you either, that's flat," he said with cool decision. "Now, be a good girl, do."

She could not look away from him. She was hardly able to believe that he had so completely failed to understand her reason for coming as to be capable of dismissing her with such a phrase. But she had not been able to put her great private hungers into words before, and she did not futilely try to do so now—nor did she any longer want to try. She only wanted him to know how fiercely determined they had made her.

"Oh, no," she said, her eyes still fixed on him as she hunted for the threats that would touch him, "oh, no . . . oh, no. When I get to Paris I'm going to camp on your doorstep day and night!" He turned away with a little gesture of distaste for her exaggerations. She lowered her voice to a level of deadly promise that almost slipped into the tremble of hysteria, so desperate she was. "Oh, yes! You'll have to have me arrested to get rid of me! And then I'll tell anyone who'll listen what you've done to me, you two. And before I leave here, everyone in the place is going to know what I think of this wonderful Duke of theirs—and *he's* going to know what I think of him. And you're never going to be rid of me—never, never. I'll be round your necks all your lives, I promise you—"

Without warning he lost his temper completely. He had begun to pace, but he had seemed well in control of himself, annoyed but essentially untouched. Now suddenly his face was still and pale with rage. "Yes, round my neck," he shrieked. "It's not fair! Round my neck like a millstone, you filthy bastard—"

He stopped because the door had opened. She was too much numbed by pain and shock to care much who it was that had heard those words said. But when her father spoke she turned blindly towards him, looking for comfort where she had always hoped it would be, and she found it. "For the love of God, Yves," he said, quietly amazed. Compunction had brought him there. He had not changed his mind, but he had wavered a little, he had wanted to see that all was going well, that the hard intruder was taking her dismissal philosophically, and he had come in time to hear the one word that could make him doubt himself. He put his hand on her shoulder in a very kind fatherly way and pressed her towards the door without himself moving. "Never mind," he said; "go to your room." And she went.

Ten minutes later he knocked on her door. During that ten minutes her defiance had collapsed, as defiance will do when someone offers sympathy. When the surrounding hostility weakened in one quarter, the strength of her feelings had poured out through the gap and lost itself in gratitude, and she could resist no longer—she could only wait for what might happen next.

He came in hesitantly and stopped just inside the door, and he did not know what he was going to say. It was a strange situation that he found himself in, one that he had never anticipated for himself, and he had not yet decided what he meant to do about it. He may have expected to find her in tears, and her habit of impassiveness may have disconcerted him. At any rate, though he looked as haughty as ever, he hesitated before speaking. He glanced at her as she stood by the window, but remotely, as if she were a lay figure propped there, then he looked at the room as though he had not seen it for some time and was really interested in it, and very likely that was the case. He took notice of the speckled red curtains, the quilted coverlet to match, the fire flickering and hissing under its pale stone hood in the corner, the suitcases stacked by the wardrobe, the top one open. Then he looked at her again, searchingly this time, and the reds and browns of the room blurred and he seemed to loom over her, larger than life and fantastically distinct.

"Well," he said at last, taking his time, "perhaps they might bring you your lunch here. My sister will be lunching with us, and I should not like to have her meet you without some preparation. . . ." He looked away as he spoke, and so it was necessary for her to do more than nod her head in answer. She cleared her throat, but could not find her voice and had to nod. Hearing no answer, he glanced at her, and she nodded again. "Perhaps dinner, too," he added, and she nodded once more, wonderingly. Then he looked away and said, "If a thing's true, it really shouldn't bother you to hear it said. And if it's obviously not true, it shouldn't bother you. Should it?" He thought about that. "Well, never mind." He put his hands in his coat pockets and faced her again, saying with exasperation, "Have you really no place to go?" She shook her head. "Have you lost your voice with all that shouting? I heard you through two rooms as I came." She did not dare to smile; people do not always like to have their jokes laughed at. Nor did she feel like smiling, except from the surprise of it, and to please him. "Well, I can't put you out into the cold. There are impossibilities. . . ." He thought it all over, and she waited. Then he went on slowly, but with the effect of a pounce. "There is nothing permanent in this . . . no capitulation. You are not here for the rest of your life."

But those words made real the prospect of a solid immediate few days or weeks there, and that counted for more with her than any vague rest of her life. "I know," she said breathlessly, and he stepped back into the passage and began to close the door.

"Actually," he added kindly, as if, the difficult task accomplished, he had already relaxed with relief into his normal sociable self, "it's the best room in the house—for this time of year, anyway. Small, and therefore—heatable. While the rest of us shiver!" He closed the door.

In one leap of emotion she forgave him for everything—because he had come to deal with her himself and because he had dealt with her on the whole so gently. She saw how natural it was that he should be suspicious of her motives, since she had dropped down on him without warning in the company of a cousin whom he apparently did not quite trust. If that seems an easy forgiveness, it must be remembered that she had come prepared to love and be grateful for crumbs, and all the painful events of the morning and the day before had only made a kindness of any sort loom the larger. She thought him at that moment the best man that ever lived, and she felt warm and safe in her little room, the best room in the house, which was going to be really her own for a day or two, perhaps for a week or two, and perhaps, if she was very good, for even longer.

The plain, dark maid brought lunch on a tray, smiling shyly as she looked for a place to put it. The household was already reflecting the slight change in Isabel's position. Isabel asked her name; she said that it was Louise. She was glad not to be distant any longer, not only because she had a friendly heart, but also because the change meant that her master was no longer being displeased. She built up the fire before she left; and since the sun by then had begun to slant through the window, Isabel was very snug. She was for the time being safe from the threat of being jobless in the winter world, an unwanted outcast forced to make a fresh start from nothing.

She saw that her father possibly had even more of an excuse than her mother for disliking her, or at least disliking the idea of her. When a boy of sixteen has a child by a girl of twenty, he may feel proud of having conquered her; on the other hand, he may feel that he is the one who has been conquered. It was possible that he remembered her mother with hatred and loathing, in which case how could he be glad to see the child her mother had given him?

Against that, however, she could put the fact that he had no other child, nothing of himself to leave behind in the world, which ought to interest him in her whatever the circumstances of her beginning, once he had got past his first half-conscious revulsion. But these thoughts began to make her uneasy; she felt less safe when she mixed her mother into it. She wanted this to be a meeting of father and daughter, with mothers left out of it, with the past left out of it. She thought instead about the bad luck that had brought her here in Yves's company and so had disastrously linked her to Yves in her father's mind. Then she felt safe again, because that had been merely fortuitous, accidental, therefore unimportant in the long run. It could be got over. The truth would prevail.

When Louise came for the tray, she brought a message. "M. d'Ayz requests that mademoiselle have the goodness to come to him. . . ." Isabel did not want to go. People who have said ugly things become ugly and fearful in the memory. But now she was anxious to be docile, to make no trouble for anyone. "M. d'Ayz suggested that mademoiselle come down the other way," said Louise when she saw her preparing to go.

"What other way?"

"Through here, mademoiselle," she said, opening the panelled door into Daphne's room. "It is quite all right, no one is there. . . ." Isabel followed her through Daphne's room and through two other rooms that were completely bare of furnishings to a door that opened on another little spiral stairway. It went up into darkness and down into darkness, and the landing was only a slightly wider triangular stone step; one felt like someone boarding a bus in motion. "It will take mademoiselle down to the room where she was this morning," said Louise. "I will leave the door open for light. . . ."

"Thank you," said Isabel, and she boarded the stairway and groped her way cautiously down.

She had thought herself quite calm, but all the mingled tremulous symptoms of fear or anger played through her as she emerged on the flowered rug and saw Yves sitting at his writing-table. Her heartbeat quickened; she felt hollow and weak for an instant. She was startled by that; it unnerved her. "There you are," he said, twisting round only to establish her identity before facing front again. She was able to approach him unwatched, and she tried to regain control of herself. The western half of the room was in shadow; the eastern half was still crossed aslant by delicate diagonals of sunlight that brightened the gold frame of the painting above the mantel and made insipid the leaping fire on the hearth below. It was a beautiful room and a beautiful time of day, and the fire did not think it important that she was illegitimate, nor did the winter or the afternoon.

"I'm so very, very sorry," he said before she came in sight, and though the tremor of shock played through her again, she felt at once much better, more sure of herself, because he had apologized. "What an unforgivable thing to say! I lost my temper. I've got so fearfully much on my mind just now," he added, rather more lightly, but that only made it seem as if he felt so real a remorse that he wanted to shuffle past the pain of it as quickly as possible. She paused by the table. He smiled up at her sidelong and said, "In point of fact perhaps you ought to thank me for saying it, however, because it has softened his hard heart a little. He has agreed to let you stay here till some other acceptable arrangement can be made. A concession!" he said, and laughed, looking down at his hands flattened against the top of the desk. "A great concession!"

"Yes, he told me," she said rather proudly.

"You've seen him?" said Yves, very much surprised, looking quickly up at her, and after a moment, "What did he say?"

"Just that."

"Has he . . . he has not decided to acknowledge you?"

She said, not knowing why she was confiding in him, but probably doing so because he was the only one to whom she could talk of these things, "I don't think he ever will."

"Why do you say that?"

"Don't you agree?"

He smiled, still watching her intently. "Oh, yes, I'm afraid I do, but"—he shook his head—"you were of such a different mind before. You were going to insist—"

"I was cornered and desperate," she said quietly, and he blinked. She was really calm now, quite unafraid of him, and she knew why. Her father was no longer a dark, cold mystery to her. "I'm sorry I made such a scene."

"Oh!" said Yves magnanimously, forgiving her.

"Some other acceptable arrangement, you said. . . ."

"Yes. He says I must find you a job if I don't mean to employ you myself. . . ." She felt rebuffed, and she wanted to cry out that that was the least of it, that she did not care whether she had a job or not, if everything that she had really come for—a sort of welcome, a little kindness, some show of caring what became of her—was to be withheld; but her mother's caution kept her silent. "It was some little time before he could grasp that aspect, so to speak, of your complaints—he does not think quickly—but when he did, that was his decision. Salaam! The rest was all vague scolding and grumbling; you know, very difficult to make head or tail of. Ranting and raving. He still thinks I planned it. He has a suspicious nature. . . . It is not," he added thoughtfully, "probably good for any man to live as he does."

She thought of the maid who had brought breakfast in sulky silence and lunch with a smile—because of an indefinable difference in the tone of a command. "You mean, it makes a tyrant of him."

He was puzzled. "I meant, it circumscribes him; you know, it narrows him. . . . He does not know how the world works. On the other hand, he's indolent. Slow. If you are very good and don't ask any unpleasant questions or make any awkward demands, you may be here forever—or until you are tired of it. Because he is so inclined to take life as it comes. So long as you are a good girl— I would not, for instance, if I were you, show him yourself in your fishwife guise, as you did me— No! Don't mind if I tease you—I tease everyone." He studied her, smiling. "Do you know, I can't help feeling that all your recalcitrance really began because I so rudely called you a bean-pole, for which I again abase myself in apology."

"Perhaps so," she said, flushing again.

"But you *are* a bean-pole, you know, so perhaps I may be forgiven a small slip into truth."

"The ice," she said lightly, "is just a little thin along here. . . ."

He was startled. Then he laughed politely—or placatingly—as he turned to the papers on the table and glanced at his watch. "And in the meantime, do you want to work a little on this famous manuscript of mine? It might amuse you, keep you from dying of boredom in this mausoleum. . . ." She had no great desire to refuse; in a way it appealed to her as a way of earning her keep a little, while she was still an unwelcome guest. "Yes?" She lifted her shoulders slightly. "It will occupy you—you will have time on your hands, I fear. Well, then. Will you make a fair copy and then on it indicate any changes that you think should be made in idiom, diction, grammar, all that? Miss Small has already been kind enough to intimate that my command of English is not all that it could be." He was irked by that, perhaps deeply wounded, but he spoke gaily. "I'm driving her back to Paris. I ought to make her take that dreary train again. But I have to go, anyway. . . ." His face grew sullen. "Oh, well . . . we shall see," he said to himself, sighing.

"A fair copy by hand?"

"No, no, there's a typewriter somewhere in that cupboard—I think one of the lower doors. . . ." He took a cigarette from the tin on the table, smiling at some joke that passed through his mind, and then, unaccountably, he began to blush. It was painful to see his complacent face becoming slowly suffused with red. He tried to ignore it and to make her ignore it too; he occupied himself fussily with lighting his cigarette and then with the drawers of the table, pulling them out, pushing them in. "As a matter of fact, there's more of it than this— I began a revision when Henry wrote he was sending Miss Small, and this is as far as I got, but there's the first draft somewhere. . . ." He pushed back his chair to pull out the wide, shallow central drawer and stirred through the papers there, his cigarette in one hand; then he put the cigarette between his lips and used both hands for the papers, squinting through the smoke. "Or have I left it in Paris, like the addlepated idiot that I am? No, here it is. You will see how it joins on. . . . There's paper in that same cupboard. That's that. All clear?" He looked up, defying her. But his face was almost its normal colour again.

"Yes, all clear, thank you."

"Good." He stood up. "I shall leave you to it, then." He made an easy little stretch and yawn and looked at his watch. "Time to go."

"Now? You're leaving now?"

He nodded.

"And how long will you be away?" she asked, wanting to know how much time she had for the task assigned her.

"Till I've found you that other job." He looked back from the door and said mockingly, "Shall I try very hard?"

She moved her hand in an indecisive gesture and did not look at him.

[71]

"You do not wish me good luck?"

"Are you leaving at once? Because I should like to say good-bye to Miss Small." She said that because she thought she ought to; she was not at all sure that Miss Small wanted to say good-bye to her. It sounded polite and poised.

"Of course," he said. "I'll tell her where you are." And he went.

He must have met her on his way, because she came in while Isabel was still standing by the table thinking of what had happened, or trying to think of it, trying to make thoughts out of what seemed now a breathlessly swift boat-ride through twined powerful contradictory currents that had carried her an immense distance in an unbelievably short time. The morning seemed hundreds of miles away.

Daphne was wearing her light-blue suit and her severe little hat, and she shook hands and briskly said good-bye and was gone again in another minute. There had been kindness and anxiety in her eyes, but the formality of farewells was something that she had been brought up to respect without question, and she had dutifully kept them formal.

It seemed to Isabel afterwards that a farewell to a whole great segment of her life had been said, and she felt rather lost and forlorn. She missed Yves, too, oddly enough, and hoped that he would come in once more to say a last word or two, because she could talk to him, as she could talk to no one else in the house. It was not that he was unshockable; he was, on the contrary, easily shocked, like all egotists. And it was not that he was tolerant; he was, on the contrary, narrow-minded in the extreme. The standards and conventions of his class were the only meaningful standards and conventions in the whole world for him, and he despised her for her origin, which she seemed to wear for him like a mark on the forehead, and was contemptuous of her for her poverty, and feared her because she threatened to be a nuisance and hindrance in his pleasant life. But he had no high wall of dignity round him; he was easily approached.

He did not come in again, however, and after a while she decided that they must have left for Paris. The room was now all shadow. The fire glowed red. Through the windows the clouds in the eastern sky reflected the pinkness of a winter sunset. The country stillness was complete. It was a lonely time of day and a lonely time of year —winter-time, night approaching, a pink-stained sky.

She could not settle down to anything. She paced the floor, looking down at the creamy rug, enormous and fine, patterned in delicate lozenges of flowers, pink and rose and turquoise; she turned from her pacing to look half-heartedly for the typewriter in the carved walnut cupboard, opening drawers and doors, but soon gave up the search because the light got so bad. There was a shaded oil lamp on the table—the electricity did not go beyond the drawing-room at the other end of the wing—but she was not sure how to light it. She went to stand by a window, and she stood there for some time looking out at the landscape darkening in twilight. The stillness depressed her. She felt forgotten. And whenever she thought of her high hopes of three days before—and she thought of them again and again—her spirits sank lower. She stood again in the little flat with dark early-morning fog pressing against its windows, drinking tea that tasted strange in her mouth, refusing the porridge and kippers and toast that Betty, whose mother had believed in solid breakfasts, urged on her, too excited to eat, her secret expectations glowing in her; she walked again through the murmurous clamour of Victoria station; she heard again the sound of winter evening traffic in Paris and a clear little quacking voice in a telephone receiver giving her news that made her exult over her good luck; and she could hardly believe in the state of mind that had allowed her to think that her uncertainties would end with the journey. She had only come, it seemed, to the beginning of a long uphill road, and she despaired of climbing it.

The room filled with shadow; light lingered outside. Her hands and the tip of her nose were cold, and every movement that she made to warm herself sounded loud in the silence. She thought with longing of the seclusion of her own small, warm room, but she could only wish she had gone there earlier. She could not go there now, because she feared being seen as she crept upstairs to hide. But neither did she want to be discovered here, all forlorn and forgotten in the dark. Self-consciousness magnified her fear of other people's observant eyes into a paralysing dread and made what she had come here to find seem hardly worth what she was having to pay for it. If there had been a city street outside, she would have been tempted to go out into it and disappear forever from the life of her reluctant father—who came into the dark room at that moment through the glass doors of the terrace.

She stood very still against the curtains, hoping that she would not be noticed, but when, closing the glass doors, he turned at once to open the door of the little spiral stairway, her sensation of relief had all the flatness of disappointment. The stairway, however, was filled with so solid a darkness that he decided against attempting it without a light, and came strolling past her down the length of the room to the chimney-piece. Her breathing quickened, her pulse hurried, and she looked quickly away from his silhouette against the red glow of the dying fire, lest he become aware that he was watched. A match flared; a candle-flame grew slowly large; he came back towards the stairway, carrying the naked candle unconcernedly in his gloved hand, his dark, austere face serenely preoccupied. She could no longer hope not to be seen, and he did see her, but he was not perceptibly startled, and he did not seem to care at all that he had been watched unbeknown to himself.

"What are you doing here all in the dark?" he said.

"Nothing," she replied, hideously embarrassed.

She had tried to say it casually, but he must have heard a note of misery in her voice, because the expression on his face changed to a mixture of impatience and pity. He studied her for a moment or two, frowning; then he said, "You arc going to be so bored here."

She answered the implication. "There's no place I would rather be."

"No friends anywhere?"

She thought of Betty and Miriam, but she knew that Betty's affection was the dutiful loyalty one feels towards someone one lives with, nothing more, and that Miriam's was too easy to count for much. Neither of them would have died for her, and she would not have died for them—that was how she measured friendship in those days. "No," she said.

"And no other relatives?"

She caught her breath and said, "My mother is dead." Whatever that news made him feel could only be guessed at. Gazing absently down at the candle he held, he merely listened. She went on at last, "My mother died last August. In childbirth. She married three times."

[74]

That startled him; he looked up. "Three times!" he said, amazed, shaking his head. "But then you must have half-brothers and sisters. . . ."

"No. I have only . . ." He was so obsessing a presence that she had to stop to count. ". . . only three living relatives that I know of."

He looked sharply at her and sharply away, jerking his shoulders slightly, as if he were resenting the brush of a burden against them. She did not blame him for that; she was a burden even to herself just then. She did not admire herself at all, begging for pity, acting out pathos.

"Oh, it's hard," she cried out abruptly, "—it's hard to want something so badly that you have to take it even when it's grudged to you. . . ."

He let that pass with a wry reflective movement of his lips. It was not a successful appeal. It seemed to reach him, but also, in some obscure way, to disgust him, as he was willing to let her see.

"I'm sorry," she said despairingly. "I don't know . . ." She meant, I don't know how to please you, how to win you; but of course she could not say that to this aloof, suspicious man.

"All I wonder is, what you'll do with yourself here," he said, moving on towards the stairway. "It's the dullest place in the world. . . ." Then he swerved back towards the fire.

"I'm going to work on the book," she said, meaning to show him how little she wanted luxurious idleness. But that was the wrong thing to say, too. It did not offend him, but it awakened thoughts that made him scowl as he walked on in his aura of warm light and shifting shadows to the fire, where he found another candle, this one in a holder, and lighted it with the one he carried. "Have they gone?" she said, suddenly terrified that Yves was still in the house and that her position was not so secure as she had thought it.

"They? Oh, yes," he said, leaving the lighted candle on the mantel and going once more towards the stairway, and he added deliberately, "Thank God."

Her hands were behind her, clutching the thin, sleek folds of the silken curtains; at her back was the cold, blue winter night.

"Do you want me to go, too?" she called after him. "I will, if you want me to. Tonight, if you say so. I'll go. It's no use. . . ."

"Oh, for God's sake let's leave it as it is," he said wearily, not pausing in his slow stroll towards the stairs. "I'm tired of argument.

I told you before, I can't put you out into the cold. If you have nowhere to go, you must stay—for now, at least. Leave it at that. And you have a right to be here. It's no favour. . . . And since I'm rid of him for a while, I can put up with you, I suppose, if only you'll not be difficult and . . ." He went on talking, but his back was to her and his voice was a dwindling, unintelligible mutter.

When she thought he had finished, she said again, "I'm sorry. . . ."

"All *right!*" he shouted furiously from the door of the stairway, and then he made her jump with astonishment by laughing aloud at himself. She had thought him set for good in anger and quite incapable of laughter of any kind. The suddenness of it shocked her into seeing him briefly not as a vagueness of fatherhood but as a person alive in his own right, made him human and co-existent for a moment, a separate human being with a steady heartbeat of his own and his own private view of the great world and his own desires and longings and memories that had nothing to do with her —but only for a moment. "All right," he said again, more gently. "All right. . . . And I've still my poor sister to prepare. . . . You might dine here."

It was a beautiful room, exquisitely civilized, and she did not want to be difficult again, but now that Yves had gone, it seemed a desolate place, isolated as it was by many dark, cold, unfurnished rooms from the daily life of the house.

"In my room?" she suggested hesitantly. "I should much prefer it."

"In your room. . . ." He shook his head and shrugged his shoulders over the possessiveness of that. "Do you know your way by these stairs?"

She guessed that he did not want her to use the other stairway because she might then meet his sister before his explanation was made, and since she rather dreaded meeting that sister, who was a countess, she was glad to do as he wished. "Yes," she said, "I know the way."

"But be careful. They are terribly steep," he said, and then he disappeared round the upward curve of the stairs. The light of the candle glowed a moment longer on the smoothly fitted stones of the wall; then it disappeared, too.

After which she stood for a while brooding over the interview, regretting her part in it, which had been cowardly and insincere. She wished that she had been braver, simpler, more forthright, and therefore, perhaps, more attractive, telling him plainly what her experience of loneliness and not really belonging anywhere had been and how little in the way of an acknowledgement would satisfy her, pushing boldly past the barrier of his anger towards Yves and his prejudice towards herself, forcing him to see her point of view and understand her motives, which were selfish, certainly, but not mean, not revengeful, and not hostile to him. And, in fact, everything would have been different if she had been able to do that—merely different, however, not better. Less painful, perhaps, less far-reaching in consequences, undoubtedly less violent, but not, in the long run, better.

But she knew well enough that she could not have behaved in any other way. She did not want to assert herself and force him into concessions; she did not want to dominate him. She longed as much to be obedient as other daughters seem to long to be free. Whenever there was the faintest assumption of rightful authority in his manner, she was profoundly content to submit, hoping that in time her willingness would strengthen the bond between them, the bond that had to be there, however tenuous it was at this stage, because they were father and daughter.

And so, having introduced herself into a household already precariously balanced in its tensions, she contained herself in docility, and the effect of her arrival was dangerously postponed. And the effect, when it came, was different.

Three

THE NEXT MORNING WAS CHEERFUL, all blue sky and red sunlight and hoar-frost, with sparrows chirping and roosters crowing. Her breakfast was brought at the hour she had named the night before, and she was primly dressed and ready for it. When she had eaten, she started downstairs, pausing nervously half-way to look out of one of the narrow windows at the village cheerfully sunlit, steep roofs steaming, chimneys smoking, an old brown dog wagging his tail benignly as he stood regarding the scene and approving it, a black-stockinged little girl in a blue dress with a shawl over her shoulders running into the bakery, an old man coming out of a cave doorway and spitting on the cobbles and then wiping his mouth with the back of his hand. She descended again, step by step, and the downstairs passage came into sight. By chance, the tall Duke and his tall sister were standing there in cold morning shadow, talking quietly together. They stopped talking and looked up at her.

The mood was new—workaday, sober. The guests had gone, the normal routines had returned with one slight change, and the expression on his face showed his final feeling about the change. It was wry and resigned. He had turned a corner in his life, and was not sure that he liked what he saw, but knew that there was no turning back just now.

He wore breeches and gaiters and the old brown coat again. His sister was dressed for riding, too, in a black habit. She was tall and thin, in her middle thirties, and somehow not formidable at all, though a countess. Her soft grey-brown hair was arranged in waves to frame a bony, vulnerable face; her eyes were a profound clear blue, humourless and kind. She stared at Isabel in utter astonishment, evidently not prepared for the resemblance, although obviously warned of something unusual, and she almost annoyed her brother by glancing at him to confirm it. She seemed an innocent and gentle sort of person.

There was also the dog, the large black poodle. Three pairs of regarding eyes were difficult to bear. Isabel seemed to herself to be growing extra arms and legs like a spider, and to be stretching out as well, like Alice when she ate the wrong cake. She caught her heels clumsily on the treads, saw unclearly, and heard the roar of silence.

She stopped on the last step of the stairs. The Duke said pleasantly, "Well, we shall meet at lunch," and moved away towards the door of the great hall. His sister smiled uncertainly as she turned to follow him. The dog dubiously wagged its tail.

Isabel watched them go.

They met at lunch. He sat thoughtfully remote; his sister was hesitantly cordial. And they met at dinner, and at lunch and dinner the next day, and the day after that. And the point at issue seemed to sink out of focus to become submerged and blurred in moods and sensations—the rural stillness; the winter cold; the loneliness; the isolated life of the castle with the vital currents of village life eddying strongly below its walls; the ancient rooms; the good food and good wine; and the great open fires, infinitely fascinating to Isabel, who had never known anything but hot-air registers and steam radiators and gas fires before. Staring into a fire on an open hearth, she seemed to look along deep alleys in time to the oldest time of all and to feel the unchangingness of it, the presentness of the past, because winter was outside and the living fire was keeping her warm, as it would have done in a cave or on a hillside in Greece or in the castle itself in the days when its Duke did his riding out in armour. At such moments she felt that words were beside the point, facts were all that mattered, and they would matter just as much as if they were never put into words by anyone. She was for a while a little drunk with moods and sensations.

She learned afterwards that he had explained her to his sister as a distant relative whom Yves had come across in his travels, which was surely not an explanation that it required a day and a night to invent. Yves was right about him; he did not think quickly. On the other hand, he did not have to think quickly. No one ever tried to press him in that house, except Yves, and even Yves had to wait for his answers.

Isabel waited too. He was determined to dislike her. He earnestly tried to be cold to her. He stirred up his suspicions, when they began drowsing off, by reminding himself that her motives were still unknown and probably disgusting. But at the same time, funnily enough, he was continually slipping into friendliness. That was the behaviour most natural to him. It was always his impulse to be as comfortable as possible with people. He really detested Yves, it appeared, but even with Yves he could on occasion engage in pleasant casual conversation. That was his strength as well as his weakness. In fact, it was not really a weakness at all, because he could like and enjoy without caring a jot whether or not he was liked in return. He did not smile in order to win something; he smiled because he felt like it at the moment. And so, before long, he was pleasantly and gaily conversing with Isabel as if she were a normal sort of guest for him to have—and then, suddenly remembering what she was and what she might be, he would interrupt what he was saying at lunch or dinner to give her a rather irrelevantly expectant stare, blank and indignant, that made her very nervous.

His sister's attitude was more puzzling. She knew without being told that Isabel must be her brother's illegitimate daughter, but she was not dismayed by that. Instead, she seemed actually inclined to be pleased. She was kind from the beginning, and she subdued her cordiality only to harmonize her conduct a little with his. Isabel felt the queerness of that without wanting to have it explained, because she was afraid it might be explained out of existence, and it was too pleasant to be sacrificed. But she did not altogether trust it, it was too impulsive, too unthinking, too unexpected; and in that she was wise.

She met them at first only at lunch and dinner, where she always sat facing the sideboard, her back to the fire, with the Duke at the end of the table to the left and his sister to the right, the negative and positive poles of a temperate hospitality. It was not what she had hoped for, but it was, she saw, a good deal more than she could reasonably have anticipated.

Neither was it the life that she had looked for, the unimaginable life that she had tried to imagine behind the pale, lovely walls of the pictured castle. Her most steadfast conception of it had involved vulgarities of hothouse roses and crystal chandeliers and gleaming marble floors, the splendid background of a life of leisure and gaiety. She found cares, duties, and tasks. The Duke did not employ an agent for the estate; he managed it himself. In the mornings, as a rule, he rode out on horseback or went farther afield in his car, which was a large old black touring-car; in the afternoons he occupied himself in his office in a corner of the stable yard with the yet duller tasks of book-keeping and letter-writing; and often in the evening he went there again to meet a tenant for further discussion of some question that had come up. He was always tired at night. His most familiar gesture, as he came into the drawing-room before dinner, was the pressing of finger-tips against his temples, slanting his eyes to relieve the strain of long hours of paper work.

It was not really remarkable that he found Isabel's presence a rather welcome change, and he would have had to be a very stupid man to go on for long mistaking the good will that she so strangely felt towards him at that time, but for a while he did. One evening he talked to her quite as he had talked to Daphne, looking bored, but giving her sudden involuntary glances of amused interest whenever she abandoned caution in despair and spoke her mind. But overnight he regretted *his* abandonment of caution, and the next day, happening to overtake her at the head of the stairs, instead of saying good morning he said, "Tell me one thing." She turned at once and looked hopefully up at him, doubting her ability to convince him of anything, but anxious to try, but she doubted a little more when she saw his dark, gloomy face, which was already distant with disbelief. "For how long had you been in communication with my cousin?"

"Not at all!" she answered eagerly. "Honestly, not at all! I didn't even know he existed till Mr. Dolphin—that's who I worked for before—mentioned him. Honestly! I came here not knowing, just suspecting a little, and only suspecting at the last moment, but not really knowing, and not planning anything—honestly."

He stared down at the toe of his boot, moving it in and out of a shaft of thin sunlight that fell through one of the stairway windows. "Lady Macbeth," he remarked at last.

"You mean, protesting too much? But that's because I don't feel believed. Honestly, it was all chance. . . . But it wasn't Lady Macbeth, it was the Player-queen in *Hamlet*. . . ."

"So it was," he said, turning away as he laughed so that he would not be laughing with her. But she saw why he had made the mistake; perhaps he did, too. He had in his mind the idea of a woman urging a man on to dark plots; and she began to fear that nothing would ever get it out of his head. She waited for another question; he frowned and rubbed his upper lip. "So it was," he repeated, starting absently down the stairs. "Oh, by the way," he called back as he passed out of sight round the curve, "you should be more out-of-doors. Shouldn't you?"

She took that as an invitation to explore and was grateful. "Thank you very much," she said loudly, because his footsteps continued, carrying him out of earshot, and she meant it, but he laughed rather dryly as he went on down the stairs, taking her thanks as sarcasm—but enjoying the sarcasm. He was a self-sufficient person, much too sure of himself to be touched by her sarcasm.

And so she went sight-seeing round the castle. But it is an awkward thing, sight-seeing alone; it is fatal, really, to keeping one's footing in modern times. One lacks a point of reference—a guide's recital of the facts, however misinformed he may be, or someone else's impression of what dimly impresses you. She saw it first alone, and sometimes she seemed insubstantial to herself as she walked through the substantial but non-existent past. She was real for herself only as the daughter of all that grandeur, and because she could not see that daughter as Isabel Regan with a head full of memories of Wichita and Liverpool and London, she knew there must be another finer Isabel within her to be awakened by these glimpses of old riches. She walked about here and there more than half trying to bring to life that proud and fascinating creature—but trying in vain.

There were three courtyards that she learned, four altogether, but the fourth was beyond the stables and coach-houses and storage sheds, and she never had any excuse to go there. The first courtyard was the one served by the cobbled ramp of the entrance, the one overlooked by her bedroom window. It was smaller than the others, and irregular in shape, wider at the south end, narrower at the north, with a piece taken out in addition by the projection of dining-room and drawing-room. It was paved with large squares of stone that were often white with frost when she looked out of her window in the morning, and from that velvet pallor of frost the opposite façade rose pale to silvered roofs and blue sky, all silent and still and very beautiful. The third was the cobbled stable yard, which smelled wonderfully of horses and hay, and which echoed sometimes with the cheerful noises of workaday life. Between them was the deserted main courtyard.

This was the part of the castle that was shown to tourists. On the north side was the high retaining wall of the garden; on the other three sides were the elaborate façades built during the Renaissance, colonnades and galleries surrounding the perfect circle of a gravelled drive, within which was a great circle of lawn, at the centre of which was a well sheltered by a carved stone canopy upheld by four stone nymphs. The canopy was an airy affair. The nymphs almost seemed to be holding on to it to keep it from floating away, it looked so lightly balanced on their up-raised hands, though it must have weighed tons. And they could still smile after bearing it on their curly heads and lifted hands for almost four centuries. Isabel came through the dark chill of the archway from the first courtyard and saw it sunlit, and it looked to her like the heart of perpetual spring-time, a flowering of stone as pure and perfect as white lilies, and she was enchanted by it till she saw that the well had been fitted with a heavy oak cover and was no longer in use. Then she felt hurt; she suffered for it; she wanted to turn time back and give the well its old employment again and the nymphs their important purpose. But she thought it was the barbarian Isabel in her that made her feel like that, and she tried to drive the idea away. She turned slowly, looking around.

To the north, above the retaining wall of the garden, she saw the pollarded tops of lime-trees high against the sky and the narrow plumes of poplars glistening in sunlight with a few old leaves flickering on their bare branches. To the south was the stairway of the main entrance. It was a fantastic stairway. It began on a rather modest scale with a narrow arch sculptured in leaves and fruit and flowers, and then swelled into a triple cascade of shallow curving steps that came together in a single broad step at the dark, high door. She left the well, crossed the withered lawn and the drive, and started up the steps, feeling like I don't know what far-away princess in a dream of ancient times unaware of her trailing brocades on these gentle gradual steps, but certainly not feeling like herself, Isabel without a name of her own, in harsh wool and square-toed brogues that rubbed the heels of her feet wrong. It was winter; the air was sharp and clear; there seemed nothing between her and the past except the membrane of her own obtuseness. She stood very still and tried to remember standing there a hundred, two hundred, four hundred years before, and felt herself observed, and turned and saw the Duke looking curiously in her direction as he sauntered across the courtyard towards the archway into the stable yard. She felt caught out and guilty, not so much because she stood on his stairway, but because she had been trying, in a manner of speaking, to pick an apple from his past. He only lifted his hand in a little gesture of greeting or permission and walked on.

But she found she could not continue her imaginings. She felt an outsider and uneducated; she did not even have the facts of the tradition to use as a foundation for reveries. When he was out of sight she touched the crumbling stonework of the nearest balustrade with critical fingers and left the stairs for the well again, to which she now gave the hostile stare of a provincial tourist, no longer taking sides with it, as a daughter of the house should do. But still it troubled her.

Another thing that touched her, but with a different sort of wistful appeal, was the stable clock—because she could rarely hear it strike the hours, and never succeeded in getting a glimpse of its face. It had a dim, blurred, jangling note that did not penetrate, but let itself be carried by the wind and turned by any obstruction. Even in the high garden one could hear it only if the day was perfectly still; one could never hear it in Yves's room and rarely inside anywhere, except as a ghostly sound down the chimney of a room, a thin, disembodied note telling a time that never was. It was a sound that was already preparing to carry a great load of memory; hearing it then was a kind of premonition of looking back through the darkness of war years to sunnier, more innocent days of peace, when private troubles, close and real, were what counted.

The more she saw of the castle, the more she longed for what she could not somehow get—a feeling that she belonged there. She had expected to slip into her setting like a hand going into an old glove, but everything held her off, isolated her, thrust her back within the boundaries of her difference.

The wing that was lived in was the oldest part of the building, but also in many ways the newest, because it had always been occupied. Daily use had worn out everything that could be worn out, and it had then been replaced, and changes in taste had remodelled the rooms over and over. The panelling in the great hall that looked so old had been put in just before the revolution; the parquet floor upstairs had been there only for about thirty years. Only the shell of thick stone was really ancient, that and a very steep breakneck stone stairway that led down to the kitchens from the pantry at the east end of the dining-room. Over that stairway a set of wooden stairs had been built, with easier rises and broader treads, that made the old stairway look impossible for the human foot, but its worn concavities showed how thoroughly it had been used. She thought of kitchens she had known, the brown fusty basement kitchen in Liverpool, the little wooden kitchen with the linoleum floor and kerosene stove in Wichita, and felt like an alien, a tourist, incapable of assimilation.

The bathroom was especially inimical. The plumbing had been installed in the nineteenth century, and the bathroom was extraordinary. It was a room more than twice as large as the room of the water-closet; there was a fireplace at one end, and at the other a tall black oak linen cupboard; and in the centre on a broad dais, was the enormous bath of red-veined marble, with gleaming ornate marble pillars reaching to the ceiling at each of its four corners, and with gilt brackets for candles on each of the pillars. One could feel unspeakably grand and elegant, reclining in that bath by candlelight, deep in hot water, while a good fire on the hearth hissed and crackled and sent soft waves of light rippling across walls and ceiling and the red velvet curtains drawn together at the windows; one could also feel as Isabel did, unspeakably out of place.

Arnaud was butler, steward, and housekeeper all in one, and he was very pleasant to her, as indeed all the servants were after the master of the house ceased to be hostile. Arnaud took her down to see the kitchens one day and introduced her to Claude the cook and her sad widowed daughter Roxane, who never appeared abovestairs, but carried on below-stairs a lively social intercourse with people from the village, among whom they queened it royally. There was also the plain dark maid called Louise and a rather prettier dark maid called Félicie, and there were the two footmen, Gilles, who served at table with Arnaud, and Joël, who seemed to be Arnaud's left hand for dirty work. It was not a large household. The only

[86]

usual sounds indoors were the ticking of clocks and the busy rustle
of fires; outside there were sounds of life and activity only in the
stable yard. She sometimes heard children's voices from the other
side of an overgrown brambly hedge at the north end of the garden
—there seemed to be a path behind the hedge connecting the village to the farm-yards and fields west of the castle—but she never
saw children anywhere within the walls. Their kind of life, turned
towards the future, careless of the past, was not the life of the castle.

But she was not bored. It was a quiet place, and she was unsure
of herself, uneasy, and often discouraged, but she was not bored.
And when her father by slow degrees began making friends with
her, her life grew positively exciting.

She finished copying Yves's manuscript, which was an unexpectedly sober and studious piece of historical writing, all brave
with footnotes and scholarly evasions of finality. It was not his sort
of thing at all, and she wondered what sort of report Daphne had
made on it. It seemed decidedly meritorious and quite interesting,
but it was only well begun, no more, and the English of it was
amazingly stiff and awkward.

Late one cold grey morning, as she was trying to uncover the
skeleton of one complicated construction to see where it was out
of joint, she heard noises from the spiral stairway in the wall by the
glass doors. She screwed her head round and waited rather breathlessly. The door opened; the Duke appeared. He had changed for
lunch from riding-clothes to brown tweeds, and she thought he
looked very comely.

She no longer saw her own face when she looked at his, because
she knew him now and could see how well his face expressed him
and so how completely everything in it belonged to him, how in-
divisibly the portrait of his personality it was: serene forehead,
sombre brows, pensive eyes, ironic mouth, and all. Her sense of the
resemblance lingered to warm her heart with the knowledge that
what she was had come from him; but when she looked at him she
saw only his good humour and self-sufficiency, his zest and contradictory indolence, his pride, his thoughtfulness, and her own private
ideal, as she had recently discovered, of masculine beauty. She was,
in fact, just then a little bewitched by his face; she loved to watch it.

"Roundabout," she said shyly, meaning a roundabout way to go
to lunch.

"I got carried past my stop," he said, laughing. "I lost count. No, I was up," he said, interrupting the wiping of his fingers on his handkerchief to point vaguely upwards, "and once on those damned steps one may as well stay on them to the bottom unless a door's opened somewhere. . . . Well, time for lunch, I think." He tucked his handkerchief in his pocket and looked distastefully at hands that seemed quite clean again. "Come along and I'll explain to you that stairway you were so puzzled about. . . ."

She was puzzled now by the reference, but she left her task and followed him very gladly out on the terrace and along its splendid length to the door at the far end, though it was cold outside and she had no coat on, only a fairly thick suit. But she understood what he meant when they came round into the stately hall where the fantastic stairway continued its curves in a new arrangement upwards.

"Have you seen Chambord?" he asked, pushing open one leaf of the great outside door.

"No. . . ."

"You've never seen, you've never heard of the famous double spiral on which one man may go up and another down at the same time without ever meeting? What a pity! Half the point will be lost on you. You see, my ancestor . . ." He paused, and something that was perhaps only simple reconsideration shadowed his face. Then he shrugged his shoulders and went on equably, ". . . our ancestor thought very little of that notion," and her heart glowed, and she looked quickly away to spare him the wave of love flowing from her, as if it might swamp him if she directed it with her eyes. "He was a more social nature than Francis I, or perhaps not! . . . At any rate, he chose to contrive, or have contrived, a stairway on which people were certain to come together, and at rather close quarters, too. Here it is!"

They stood at the head of the lovely cascade of shallow steps, great colonnades on either side, and cold grey sky as ceiling. "Is there any truth in that at all?" she asked happily.

"What other possible explanation is there? Look at it. Imagine a dozen ladies in spreading skirts"—he indicated them—"emerging here, all at their ease, exclaiming over the sweet springtime, then descending and all coming together in a crush in that bottle-neck of an arch!"

[88]

"But it's lovely," she said after a moment—it was all she could think of to say.

"Oh, yes, lovely," he said ambiguously, pulling the door to behind him and starting down the steps. "So you have lived in the United States, have you?" he continued very casually as they crossed the withered circle of lawn—something had been said about her residence there on the night before.

"Until I was fifteen, in Wichita and New York," she answered in the same tone of voice.

"And where is Wee-chee-tah?"

"Wichita," she said, amused that he could do what so many people do, hear a new word pronounced correctly and promptly repeat it according to their own system of pronunciation.

"Wee-chita."

"Wichita."

"Which-ta," he said, really trying.

"Good enough. It's in Kansas."

"And Kansas is in the United States of America. Good enough. I am informed," he said, laughing all to himself.

He continued to laugh and make jokes at lunch, but he came late to dinner and was tired and thoughtful, ignoring her. The next night they were quite on family terms again. Arnaud lived with his wife in the gate-keeper's apartments at the foot of the cobbled ramp; his wife was the one in charge of the rooms that were shown to the public. She cleaned them once every week or so with the help of a couple of women from the village, and she was the one who guided the visitors through. Isabel came upon her in the guardroom, a stout woman all in black, as waxen pale as Arnaud himself, and was told a number of lurid tales about the room that made the assistants laugh, and so she did not believe them. But that evening, in the drawing-room after dinner, the Duke assured her that they were all true. "But why did her friends laugh, then?" Isabel asked.

"To hide their pride," he said. "They were pleased to see you so much impressed."

"But truly I can't believe—"

"Cain't?" he said. "What is this cain't?"

"Caan't," she said by accident. "Cahn't."

"Ah, the layers peel off," he said delightedly; he had all along surmised somehow where *cain't* came from. And she laughed, too, and forgot what it was she could not believe, because the poodle, Céphise, was let in from her after-dinner airing, and she came to each of them in turn to be welcomed. She touched her nose to her mistress's hand and wagged her tail before Isabel; but to the Duke she gave her most emotional greeting, weaving towards him like a spent arrow, head drooping, tail low, flattening herself before him at last so that he had to lean to touch her curly topknot. It was what she had done the first time Isabel saw her, but now it did not seem servile.

Her soft fur was cold to the touch; and it smelled of clean winter night air. "Oh, look, she's smiling at you," Isabel said, and Céphise really was, smiling as a human smiles, a little curved wrinkle at each corner of her mouth, and her eyes soft and bright. "Oh, Céphise, you're smiling!"

"She does not smile for me," said Jeanne de Varaisne ruefully; "faithless animal. . . ."

"You're her bread-and-butter," said Isabel, "he's her cake."

"Cake?" he said, much amused, but he gave her one of his considering looks, wondering about the motive, the character, the experience that lay behind that choice of words, and his blue eyes were aloof and calculating. Yet it was not strange that Isabel gave a greater weight to the friendliness, at this stage, than to the distrust obviously drowsing beneath it. She felt that she deserved the friendliness and that it therefore had a better foundation than the distrust, and so would outlast it. He finished by smiling at her, suddenly and engagingly, I suppose because she seemed to hang so breathlessly on his decision. Then Gilles came in to murmur a message, and the Duke got up.

"Come here, Céphise," Isabel said when he had gone, "come to me," but Céphise only wagged her tail twice and went off to plod round the room in search of the correct place for a nap. "How did you happen to give her that name?"

"My brother gave it to her," said Madame de Varaisne with a wan smile. "A little joke and a little compliment . . . and a little tease. . . ."

Isabel was interested, but she did not see that; she had returned to her book. Perhaps she thought the explanation complete. Perhaps it was.

Isabel went from the fire, with its hot, hissing intricacies of glowing caverns and busy flames, to a table where there were magazines and books scattered at random, *L'Illustration* and *Figaro* and *Punch*, and *David Copperfield* and *Le Lys dans la vallée*, and a large book bound in red velvet that she had noticed before. There were photographs in it. "Pictures," she said, closing it again with insincere politeness.

The Countess looked up. "A family album," she said apologetically; "not very interesting, except to—" and she caught her breath. "You would be interested, perhaps. . . ." She put her book down.

It was permission. Isabel carried the album over to the sofa and sat down beside her with it, opening it by chance to a photograph of three stern little boys much of an age, all wearing white—white knickerbockers and bloused belted white tunics—with black four-in-hand ties and black stockings and shoes. Two were dark, one was fair, all were obviously related. They leaned against a stone wall in stiffly casual attitudes.

"My brother, Barnabé, and Yves," explained Jeanne. "Barnabé is another cousin. . . ." There was an awkward, uneasy pause. Then she laughed a little and said fondly, so fondly that Isabel was rather embarrassed, as by an accidental glimpse into a friend's private life, "Yves always says he had a stone in his shoe when that picture was taken, and that's why his face has a pained look. . . . But I don't know. It was an uncomfortable thing to have one's picture taken, the eyes of one's parents on one. . . . Look at me," she said, pointing to the photograph of a little girl in white who looked as if she were seeing a ghost. "Turn," she commanded comfortably. "My father. . . . The only picture of him with moustaches. My mother did not care for them. . . . A house-party before the war," she said, pointing to a sunlit gathering of ladies in straw hats set very straight on their heads and trim, pale, pear-shaped dresses ankle-length, with gentlemen here and there like dark leaves to set off the blossoms in a bouquet. "A shoot." Gentlemen in knickerbockers and vaguely Tyrolese hats, carrying guns. "Turn. . . . My mother and Aunt Sylvie—Barnabé's mother—and just the arm and shoulder of her husband, you see?" She laughed again. "He was so disappointed. . . . He was a very wealthy man, he manufactured a remedy for headaches, but a very nice man, and the picture was quite accidental. . . . Here he is again, alone." A short, stout, bearded man with an intent, spectacled stare, standing with one foot at right angles to the other and both hands behind his back. "My grandparents. . . ." Two very old, handsome, white-haired people seated on a bench with trees behind them and dappling shadows at their feet, both scowling impatiently at the camera. "She was my grandfather's cousin; you see the resemblance. . . . My parents in Italy, just after they married. . . ." She smiled peculiarly; something amused her; there was some unkind joke that those two shy, solemn young people in the picture did not share. "A birthday party. . . . My brother on the right: the only one in profile—you see? He is staring at the girl on the other side, with whom he was in love—at nine years old! And she was eighteen! It was a fact well known to us all. But he was always falling in love, and quite openly, without shame. . . . And it was never unrequited," she said, amused again, but differently, indulgently. "Even that girl of eighteen, she gave the first dance to him, at the ball, because he was so devoted, she said; and how the others raged! . . . Turn."

There were other girls that her brother had loved; there was Yves slouching in English clothes after his first term at Oxford; there was Barnabé on horseback looking worried and trying not to show it; there were her brother and Barnabé dressed for tennis; her brother smiling, and Barnabé stiff and stern and a little blurred.

"My husband," she said gravely, pausing over a picture of a short, broad man who was holding up his hand protestingly and laughing. "And here he is again, when he did not know he was being taken . . . but it is no more like him than the other. . . ." She considered those two pictures for a long time, and then she looked away. "It is late, Isabel," she said. "Céphise?" Isabel carried the album back to the table. "Shall we go up this way?" said Jeanne, going towards the little stairway behind the tall, thin door in the north wall. Drawing-room, dining-room, and pantry met there in a complication of doorways and arches. "Come, Céphise," she said, with sad laughter in her voice as she spoke the name, and Céphise stood up, stretched out her front legs, stretched her back legs, and then came plodding cheerfully across the room to lead the way up the dark spiral, her nails clicking on stone.

Isabel found her room brightly illumined by firelight and very warm. She was not sleepy. She sat down in the shabby wing-chair by the fire and put her feet up on the curbing and for a while thought herself as contented as a purring kitten; but it was actually only an assumption of contentment that had spread softly and deceptively over her. She had been treated that evening for the first time as a member of the family, therefore it went without saying that she was happy. It was unarguable that she was happy.

She gloated over the events of the evening for some time before she began to realize that she was really miles from feeling blissful about them. In point of fact they troubled her, and she could not tell why. Her aunt had been very kind to her, which ought to have been a positive step forward, but it was not. She had become vaguely aware of new strains and veins in the character of that mild, sweet-tempered woman, and it had been like finding a new flavour in a familiar dish and not being sure whether the effect was pleasant or unpleasant. And all that age of balls and house-parties and children made the present life of the castle seem a once-bountiful river dwindling inexplicably to a trickle in arid sand. The old names and gaieties had no associations for her, they had awakened no sleeping response, they rolled now like brisk, meaningless marbles through her thoughts. She bent forward to fold her arms on her knees and cradle her head in her arms, feeling queerly desolate.

When she looked out of her window the next morning, she saw the grey Rolls standing in the frosty courtyard, and she knew that Yves had returned. It caught her off guard; she had to struggle upwards, it seemed, through a great depth of dreaming to meet this bleak daybreak of reality. He must have found suitable employment for her, therefore she would be invited to leave; and the relationship she was cultivating would halt its growth at the point it had reached. She wanted to run and hide.

Then she had to know the worst at once, and she went straight down to him. But when she met him, she could not ask questions, she could not go near the subject, she tried not even to think of it, lest her thinking of it bring the thought to his mind.

She found him standing at the table looking at the work she had done on his manuscript. He was wearing the brown leather coat that he wore for driving, and his leather gloves were still in his hand. "Good morning," she said. He looked up and looked down again, leaving her with the memory of a half-caught glimpse of what might have been a smile. But she was sure of a certain friendly awareness of her in his manner that had not been there before— and also of a depression that had nothing to do with her or with the manuscript, though the sight of the manuscript certainly did not please him. "You must have left Paris very early, or driven very fast," she remarked. He lifted his smooth brown brows as answer and turned the page, to find the next as black with written emendations as the first had been. He made a face. She felt a little sorry for him. "It has seemed to me," she said placatingly, "that you would really do better to write more colloquially— I don't think you know how good your spoken English is. If you would write as you speak—"

"But one can't write a serious historical work in colloquial English!" he protested. There was a sound of running footsteps approaching. Only Louise of all the household ran in that upright, modest, seemly fashion, with heels scuffing along the floor at every step. She came in out of breath. "The fire," said Yves. The fire had gone out, but it was newly laid and needed only a match touched to it. Isabel had an indignant desire to speak, but she did not. Louise was returning to the door. "And bring me, please, something to eat—coffee, toast, something, anything, quickly." Isabel looked at him involuntarily, doubting him. The fire, not his breakfast, ought to have been the afterthought. But he was staring again at the blackened page. Louise departed, breaking into a run as soon as she was on the other side of the door, and Yves took off his leather coat and tossed it, with his gloves, on a delicate yellow brocade chair. Then he went to pick it up again. "I've brought you a present," he said, taking out of one of the pockets a flat black tin of English cigarettes and dropping the coat once more. "When a theft is inevitable, why not save the thief from further blackening his soul, or her soul, by—" But when he opened the tin that he had left on his table before, to give point to his remark, he saw that the bottom layer in it had not been touched. "I see. . . ." He looked discomfited; he frowned. "But whose cigarettes have you been smoking all this time, then, since you haven't been smoking mine?"

"The rest of my own, and some of my father's."

"He has acknowledged you?" he said mockingly, confidently.

"We've not gone within a hundred miles of that truth," Isabel said, "and I never shall, till I'm invited to. I only said that because I wanted to hear myself saying the word for once."

"How touching."

"Is it not? But one tries in vain to keep one's touching aspects a secret always."

He smiled undecidedly. Louise came in with a tray. "By the fire," he told her, "and you might bring another cup."

This was friendliness indeed, and Isabel was half tempted to ignore the hardship for Louise of another run to the distant pantry, but she said, "I don't want coffee, thank you."

"Never mind," he said, waving Louise away. He sat down. "Ah, the threadbare linen of Ferronçalles," he murmured, laying the napkin across his knees. "And the good simple food of Ferronçalles. . . . I dined last night on salmon from Scotland and reindeer steak. . . . Sit down. Over here. I can't talk to people unless I can see their faces. I want to tell you something about myself."

"What an unusual man you are," she said, sitting down in the chair on the other side of the hearth, facing him.

He smiled.

"I want to admit to you that I am rather spoiled. Is that so unusual?" he said, beginning to eat with a certain rude, absent-minded gusto that reminded her of the Duke. "But perhaps it is. How impossible to keep oneself out of the ruts of life!"

"Not that you mind," she said maliciously. "You know that you occupy your ruts with a difference."

He really seemed to miss the malice of that, which was amazing. "Well," he said, making a deprecating gesture, and then he looked at her seriously. "I think you understand me a little. . . . And in my turn I understand you."

She felt that he did, that he saw clearly how she was trying to distract herself and him with a side-show of impudence that was getting her nowhere, how she was foolishly trying to evade a fact that she ought to face at once, because it had to be faced. "That doesn't speak well for you," she said with bitterness. "But I suppose you've come across a good many like me in your varied life."

"Oh, why dislike yourself?" he said, genuinely concerned. "You are what life has made you; *you* aren't to blame for what life has done, and I think in any case there is much to admire, perhaps. Be

[95]

a friend to yourself," he said vehemently. "Always be a friend to yourself."

There was silence, and in the silence the snapping of the busy fire and the chirping of a sparrow on the sunny stone ledge of a window. Then the bird flew up and its shadow flew aslant across the floor. "Did you find me a job?" she said.

He set his cup down with a little clash and stood up, wiping his lips with the napkin and then dropping it carelessly into the butter and the marmalade. "You may breathe again. I've been far too busy with my own affairs to give that matter any attention at all." He picked up his leather coat and began putting it on. "And now I must go to His Grace the Duke, who has been waiting for me all this time in that little hole of an office, arranging his precious evidence. . . . No, he will simply have to put up with you a while longer. And why should he not? Surely he can spare me that, at least. . . ." He pressed his thin lips together pettishly, like a hurt child.

"You've already seen him?" she said, and her heart sank.

"Briefly."

"You talked about me?"

"No. I had other things to talk of. You must arrange things for yourself. You must fight your own battles. I have no time for them."

"I didn't mean that—I just wondered if he'd . . . said anything."

He understood her and looked at her resentfully. "So that you could prepare to obey? So meek, so docile! But, with *me*—"

"I know, but I told you why that was," she said, flushing. "I was scared. But I've never wanted to make trouble for him. I didn't come here for that."

"But you were willing to make as much trouble for me as possible. Well, of course, he is a duke," said Yves with a sigh, and he seemed to speak his simple thought, without irony. Dukes were to be respected.

"It isn't that," she protested. "I wouldn't want to make trouble for him, in any case. Why should I?"

"If he seduced your mother—"

"But I think she probably seduced *him*," said Isabel boldly.

He stared at her. "You embarrass me! Such ideas should not be in your innocent head," he said, and he really did look uncomfortable, which disconcerted her as much as did his steady, speculative stare. "You are odd," he said suddenly. "You make me wonder what your life has been, your experiences. . . . You are—how old?"

"Twenty-one."

"And capable of such notions?"

"I interest you," she said, oppressed.

"Yes, rather. . . . It's strange, as a family we've produced rather fine men on occasion, but never before a beautiful woman. . . . Never before. . . . All you need is a little more confidence, a little more assurance. . . . Well, you need not stop here; if I want you I can send for you. But don't forget your cigarettes," he said, handing her the black tin with a little mocking bow before going off in a great hurry.

She set the tin on the desk again and walked back and forth in the room along the windows, her arms folded, thinking the thoughts that Yves had unintentionally put into her head. He had made her seem to herself a spineless worm, crawling and submissive when she should have been proudly demanding; and he had made her distrust her instincts, which is a distrust that makes the earth dissolve under one's feet. He had brought with him the odour of Paris—society, busy gaiety, and serious accomplishment —and it had made her wonder what on earth she was doing here, where no one ever came, and where she had no future. His compliments had been as unsettling as his contempt. She had an obscure fear that he might be making fun of her—the idea of beauty can turn on such a hair's edge of difference. Miserably uncertain, doubting and despising herself, she walked back and forth through the long rectangles of sunlight until she alarmed herself by putting her fists up to her temples in a gesture of despair beyond endurance. Then she tried to compose herself; she took a cigarette from the case in her pocket and lit it, and looked out at the view of fields and hills beyond the river, quiet under the winter morning sun. Finally she opened the glass doors and went out on the terrace.

It was a cold day, but the terrace caught the thin warmth of the winter sun and made the most of it; and the sharpness of the air brought reality back into the world.

While she leaned with folded arms on the balustrade, a sheet of paper floated past her face at a slant and was drawn inward by a draught to land on the stone floor. It was a fine, clean rectangle of white paper. She picked it up and turned it over and saw a rambling, confused, incoherent drawing, not so much one drawing as many drawings mingled, delicate sketches drawn with the light point of a very sharp pencil.

Then she heard a mutter overhead and the noise of a sash window closing. It sounded as if the paper had blown out by accident and to someone's annoyance, and so, expecting it to be come for, she walked with it towards the farther door. Vaguely in her mind, in that small part of it unoccupied by her thoughts of herself, she had an idea that some young architect or artist was being shown about by Arnaud's wife, because most of the drawing consisted of unrelated architectural details. But she heard a noise behind her and turned.

There came into sight through the glass doors a strange creature, a short, strong old man with a smooth, hairless face and something odd about his sweetly smiling mouth, dressed like a servant in hoary black and coming towards her with a servant's deference, holding out his hand for the paper as he fixed on her the apologetic gaze of the most speaking eyes she had ever seen—limpid, brown, innocent—and alive and responsive in a way that made words unnecessary. "Oh, you have it!" they said. "Thank you! Who are you? Never mind, I see that you belong here. It is all right." He took the paper from her, bowed his head, and went back the way he had come, and she somehow could not offend those vulnerable eyes with idle questions.

In himself he was not frightening, but she was in a state of mind where anything unexpected is upsetting, and she turned again and walked on towards the farther door, feeling a resurgence of undefined doubts. She went through the anteroom into the hall, and out on to the cascade of shallow steps, cold to the bone now that she was away from the sun. She could see her breath in the still air.

Yves and the Duke were coming through the stable-yard archway, walking well apart and out of step, muttering at each other as they came. She went to meet them, and all her doubts had vanished utterly. She had a sense of such security and ease that she could have laughed aloud at what she had just then been feeling. She believed in her instinct again, she knew that she had come here to make a beginning from which she could go out into the world as people should go, with something solid and safe behind them. Her future was not here, only the foundation stone. But she had been right to come, and she was right to stay—if she could manage it.

They all met at the canopied fountain, and Yves said consolingly to her, "Never mind. I have pleaded hard for you, after all, and his instinct of protection is well developed. It is his weak point." He spoke so lightly that she was sure he had received some help with his problems; the strain had lessened; he had resigned himself; he saw his way clear now. She turned blankly to the Duke, who moved his hand impatiently and frowned. She realized that he had indeed brought up the question of the job in Paris, which meant that he was still anxious to be rid of her. She had expected that, but it was still a blow. "Your claim on him—"

"I make no claim on him!" she said miserably.

"But you have one," said the Duke slowly, clasping his hands behind his back and staring thoughtfully downward. "I admit it. I do not mean to evade my responsibilities in this—"

It was a sentence that was going to end in "but," and she did not want to hear him say it. "But I make no claim; do you understand?" she said, staring at him till he looked up and then meeting his eyes with all the honesty and forthrightness that it was in her power to express; and Yves laughed. But the Duke turned away, withdrawing into himself.

Then Yves called, "Good morning!" and Isabel glanced over her shoulder to see Jeanne de Varaisne in her long black habit coming through the other arch, with Céphise eager beside her.

Céphise broke into a gallop, reared up on her hind legs before Yves, and rested her front paws lightly against him, laughing up into his face. He was annoyed. "Yes, good dog," he said, and Jeanne said quickly, "Down, Céphise, down, down— Yves, I am astonished; when I saw your car, I could not believe, at that hour— How long will you stay?"

"I don't know," he said, brushing himself.

"And, Mathieu, you were to meet me at the Grêles—"

"We can go now," said the Duke. "Oh, I have something for you," he said to Isabel, taking a letter out of an inner pocket and handing it to her. It felt warm for a fleeting instant. "And I have a horrible confession; it came yesterday, and you must forgive me for forgetting it till now— Oh, sorry, was it important?"

"No," she said, "and it's taken its time getting here, anyway." It was ill-directed, and it had been mis-sent here and there; the envelope was all marked up and shabby with handling. "I think it's from Mr. Dolphin. . . ."

"Oh, yes, Henry Dolphin," said Yves to the Duke, with a sidelong glance at Isabel, "to whom you owe so much. . . ." The sharp irony hung in the air. It seemed dangerous to stir a finger.

Then the Duke said, "Your nose is red and your hands must be ice. Take my gloves." He pulled them off and handed them to her. She did not look triumphantly at Yves, but she would have liked to. This a little made up for her father's desire to see her go. She was always ready to make the most of favourable trifles.

She put one worn, faded glove on. It received her hand with hollow warmth; and then she pulled it off. "But you'll need them," she said, "if you're riding out."

"So I shall!" he said, and he burst out laughing—odd behaviour, but she understood it. He was laughing at futility, enjoying it. He could at moments look down at himself as if he were a child playing childish games and fondly love that child. "Go inside at once, then," he said, taking the gloves that she held out to him, "and sit by the fire and read your letter. . . ." It was so kindly said that she had to glance at Yves and make sure he had heard. He had heard; he was watching with a curious expression on his face. "Jeanne?" said the Duke.

"In a moment?" said Jeanne. He walked away with his long, slow strides. "Yves," she said anxiously, "how does it go with you?"

"I shall have to sell a Cézanne and the Seurat," he said. "At least."

"Oh, what a pity!"

"What do you know of it, how have you heard?"

She hesitated, and Isabel moved away and began to make much of Céphise, who was still suffering from the rebuff that Yves had given her, but she only pretended not to listen. "Cécile wrote me."

"They are all laughing at me," he murmured gloomily.

"No! Cécile did not."

"It's funny enough."

"Yves, if I might help, as much as I can—" she began, but he interrupted her quite fiercely.

"It would not be enough. It would not help at all. Don't irritate me!"

"And *he* cannot help you?"

[100]

"Not enough," he said. "The Seurat will certainly have to go.
. . . He is waiting for you."

"Yes. . . ."

Céphise heard that and grew tense, but she was too courteous
to pull away. "All right, go then," Isabel said, letting her go.

Jeanne went off towards the stable yard with Céphise trotting
beside her, Isabel walked with Yves towards the house, across hard,
withered lawn and noisy gravel and under the arch to cold, hard
stone. She hunted uneasily for something to say, and noticed again
a row of pointed windows at the south end of this courtyard. "Is
that a chapel?" she asked.

"It was," he said. He appeared to be quite unconcerned by his
recent rudeness to Jeanne. "I thought Mathieu had forgotten how
to laugh. You are clever to make him laugh."

But she did not want to discuss that subject with him; he might
quickly spoil her pleasure in it. "I was standing on the terrace after
you left," she said to divert him, "and a paper with drawings on it
floated down, and a very strange old man came to fetch it. Who
is he?"

"Ah, you have met Cousin Barnabé's servant! What do you
think of him?"

"Does *he* live here? Barnabé?" She was astounded.

"All his life, almost. But he is a recluse now. He sees no one.
Many years ago, poor chap, he had a great blow . . . and as a result he has retired from the world. . . ." They went into the intense chill of the entrance hall and through to the passage. "He
lives in the top-story rooms above the terrace and takes his exercise
among the chimneys and lanterns. . . ." They turned to the right
past the staircase and through the empty rooms. "He sees only the
family, and however much you make Mathieu laugh, I do not think
he will ever introduce you to Cousin Barnabé."

That hurt her, as it was meant to do; that foolishly hurt her. "Do
you see him?"

"It is of course one of my chief reasons for coming here, to spend
an hour or two in pleasant conversation with Cousin Barnabé. . . .
What did you think of his servant? Did he make your soul crawl?"
Yves asked with sudden passion.

"No," she said, surprised. "Why should he?"

"He never speaks. He has something wrong with his palate. He can make only uncouth sounds, and so he chooses to make no sound at all. And he has never grown a beard. He is a monster," said Yves. "What do you think of a man who lives retired from this lovely world, with only a monster to serve him?"

They had passed through the bare rooms and were entering his study, where silken curtains were festooned in folds as pure and crisp as if fashioned of beaten gold, where sunlight fell across the creamy, pale-flowered rug and glittered on little ornaments. The fire was leaping high. "I pity him," she said.

"Yes, I pity him too. . . . I pity all recluses. . . . I do. Though at times," he went on, taking off his coat, and speaking almost in a whisper, "I could envy them!" He laughed softly.

He was not speaking to her, but on impulse she said to him, standing with her back to the fire and her cold hands tucked under her arms, "What is this trouble you're in? A woman?"

He turned to look at her in astonishment, and his handsome face flushed again. "What sort of upbringing have you had, to ask such a question? You make me blush for you," he said, but then he laughed, and she helplessly laughed too.

"I only wanted to know."

"And so you only asked. And would you be not at all shocked if I answered, Yes, a woman, and it is her husband that acts for her in these threats and demands?"

After a moment she said, "No, that shocks me."

"That it does not me," he said daintily, taking and lighting a cigarette. "They see their chance and take it, that's all, as anyone would—as you have done." He clicked the lighter shut, dropped it in his pocket, and leaned back on the edge of the table, his ankles crossed, his arms folded, frowning down over his shoulder at his bescribbled manuscript.

"And that's not fair; that's a filthy thing to say!"

He looked up quickly. "I wasn't condemning you, Isabel—it's the way of the world," he said, surprised. "But it's as true of you as of anyone. Chance may have brought you here, but you've been doing your best to take advantage of that bit of luck ever since. Even if you're still a bit too much the youthful idealist to make your demands in terms of hard cash, that doesn't make you any the less an opportunist."

She sat down in the chair where she had been sitting earlier that day, feeling blank and cold and tired. She saw what he meant: one could be just as greedy and grasping about love as about money. "Yes," she said. "Quite true."

"Because, if you really want nothing, you would simply go away." Then he laughed a little, not unkindly. "Funny. Even at this distance I can feel your resistance to that notion. You grip the floor with your toes, I think; in an instant you become a leech, clinging and clinging—how is it one makes a leech let go? A pinch of salt, isn't it?" he said, coming to sit in the chair opposite hers. He crossed his long legs and waggled one foot idly and looked perfectly relaxed and easy. "Salt on a bird's tail to make it stay, and salt on a leech to make it go. Fiction and fact. What I ask myself is, Wouldn't you feel a bit prouder of yourself as a wild bird tempted with baits than as a leech clinging where you aren't wanted?"

She had no time to resent that pleasant description of her; it was the last four words that caught her across the heart. "He still doesn't want me here?"

"Of course he doesn't want you here. He has been begging me to take you off his hands somehow, to take you back with me to Paris and find something for you there—he doesn't want to see you starving and homeless, he feels his responsibility, but he would like very much to see you happily established somewhere else— Did you expect something different, my poor Isabel? Does this hurt you? Did you think you had won him over? . . . You don't understand the man at all. Even if you could awaken paternal feelings in him —and that would be difficult enough in itself. . . ."

He smiled a rueful, musing smile. "I've known him all my life; we grew up together, he and I and Barnabé were like brothers. I've seen him falling in and out of love all my life, and he has a strangely simple heart in such matters. . . . He went into each affair completely, whole-heartedly, holding nothing back—and then emerged from it intact when it was over for him, laughing at himself for having been so absorbed, totally disregardful of consequences, untouched by them. I think that makes him far more a libertine than I am," said Yves with a faint blush once again colouring his large forehead. But his eyes were steadfast, and his buzzing voice did not waver. "Is this too plain-speaking for you? But you ought to realize, and soon, what you're trying to deal with. How can such a man accept or even understand fatherhood when it's thrust on him twenty-one years late, long after any emotion that may have existed has been quite forgotten? You have probably been thinking of him, or of the idea of him, all your life, Isabel; but he has not been thinking of you. . . . But that's only a minor part of it. That's the least important, almost. If that were all—! If he were only himself, unwarped, untwisted, it might be possible to come to an arrangement with him, a fair and sane arrangement, without much sentiment, but fair and sane. . . ."

"What are you getting at now?"

"I shan't say another word," he said quietly. "Just use your eyes, and use your head. Let that reasonable mind of yours digest your observations. Look at this room. It's a lovely room, is it not? I furnished it. It's a large and prosperous estate, and well managed, too, and look at the way he lives, look at the clothes he wears. . . ."

There passed through her mind a few crooked images—Barnabé the recluse shut away from the world with a strange old man; Jeanne de Varaisne stubbornly mourning a fat man who did not like to have his picture taken; her father's sociable nature and solitary life. . . .

"Yes," said Yves, watching her steadily, but the faint inevitable colouring of triumph in his voice, which only acknowledged her response to his words, made her turn away in blind revolt.

"It's not true; nothing you've said is true!" she cried. But what it was that was not true, she did not know. She did not look at it, she did not want to see it. "He does have a heart, he does—a far better heart than yours; and he's honest and brave, he tells the truth and faces things; and he's kind! He is! Far, far kinder than you; I think you're only jealous of him, hinting such things behind his back! Jealous of him!"

The expression of patient attention on his face did not change. "Perhaps I am," he said gravely. "And perhaps I am only disturbed to see that you are falling in love with him, Isabel, as no daughter should ever fall in love with her father."

She stood up. He stood up too, warily. And she struck him across the face as hard as she could with the heel of her hand and went from the room with her wrist so achingly numb from the force of the blow that she feared she might have sprained it. She was at first too much appalled to be affected; pacing swiftly and indignantly along through empty rooms that echoed her footsteps, she thought of his words as flung stones that had luckily missed their aim. She did not see that they were not stones, but a poisoned mist that could not fail in its purpose, till she met Louise in the passage and found herself blushing to the eyes for no reason at all.

Louise noticed the blush and stared curiously. Isabel ran past her to the stairs, taking by instinct the newel end of the steps, and so tripping on one of the hollowed edges and scraping her knee badly. But she stumbled on upwards and into her room and closed the door.

It is a very terrible thing to discover that slurring lies and wicked misconceptions can have any weight at all; and nothing can give one a greater sensation of helplessness than the pressure of their unjust weight. She felt penetrated by the ugly wickedness of the world. She hated life so much that she had to hate herself, too, because she was alive. But this black anguish did not last very long. Hardly aware that she had got past the worst of it, she was soon examining her knee, which had bled, and her stocking, which was all ladders, and then the natural thing to do was to bathe her knee and change her stocking, which done, she looked at her watch and saw that it was getting on towards lunch time.

Her wrist ached now and felt lame, but it worked. Henry's letter crackled in her pocket. She took it out and sat down by the comforting fire with it, putting her feet up on the low stone curbing. Then she began to feel defiled all over again by what Yves had said, and it seemed in some queer way that she would bring Henry on the scene of this ugliness if she read his letter, and so she had to put off reading it a little longer, till the turmoil of her feelings had died down again like a retreating thunderstorm.

Getting a letter was an event for her then, and she felt a little extra bitterness towards Yves because he had spoiled her pleasure in this one. Henry had written it by hand, and from his flat in St. James's Street, not the office. It was short and peculiar. "Dear Miss Regan," it said, "Miss Small's little excursion evidently proved as exciting for her as I had hoped—she is blushingly mum on every aspect of it but the professional one. Meanwhile I am being driven quietly mad by your successor, who appears to have a defective windpipe—she says ahem at me all day long, and half the time it means nothing. How could you? Seriously, I rather miss you, really. But quite apart from that I hope I haven't got you into anything that may prove awkward? Don't feel bound to stay. Dear Yves doesn't deserve it. If the situation doesn't shape up, come back and we shall find something else for you. Yours, Henry." There was a postscript. "I mean this." And in a separate line below that, "I really do." And below that, "Oh, God!"

It was all Henry in one of his oddest moods. He could dictate fluent, charming, amusing letters that said exactly what he intended to say to old friends and familiar enemies. But she had watched him often enough tie himself into knots, inexplicably, over other letters—to friends who had offended him or to literary women he was briefly rather taken with. This was not the same sort of thing, but she supposed that writing to an ex-secretary for whose present difficult situation one was responsible would not be easy for any-one, least of all for him. It sounded, in fact, like a desperate fourth draft condensed out of other versions and sent off in haste on the theory that it would have to do because he could do no more. For hours afterwards he must have re-read it in his thoughts and turned cold. But whether the signature had been calculated or a slip of the pen, she could not tell.

It took her far from the castle for a welcome few minutes; she saw things more clearly afterwards. She saw in Yves's ugly accusa-tions not only a revelation of his decadence but also a plain desire to drive her away. He had always wanted to get rid of her. Now he more particularly wanted to get her out of the castle and away from his cousin, as if it displeased him very much to see how close and pleasant her relations with the Duke were becoming, as if he felt himself being crowded out of a place he thought his own, and did not like it, and so was resolved to change the situation somehow.

His new enmity was alarming enough, and his suggestions had had their effect—not his insinuation about her feelings, because that was too mad and bad even to be thought about, but his hints of avarice. She was haunted by the shabbiness of everything. The fabric of the very chair she sat in was threadbare over the arms. But Henry's concern made her feel less friendless and unimportant, and his slighting reference to Yves had put Yves in a larger per-spective that made him shrink in stature. And she could summon up a picture of the Duke—his gaiety and humour, his warm kind-ness, his sincerity, and the respect that his servants felt for him—

that reflected a light almost noble on the austere habits of the house. Holding that picture before her as a shield, she was able to return defiantly to Yves's room. He had to be shown at once that he had failed.

She approached the study too briskly to hear anything but the sound of her own footsteps, but as she opened the door and saw him at the table and said, "Have you decided what you want me to do now with the manuscript?" she knew that her voice was falling in air already in motion with voices, and she looked to see who else was there, and saw her father standing by the fire. He was in no pleasant mood. He looked harassed and irresolute, tired and angry.

Yves gave her a pale glance. There was actually a visible bruise on the side of his jaw. "Oh, you might make a fair copy of this, if you please, incorporating your emendations— I find your handwriting quite barbarous. . . . That is, if you can use the typewriter? Is your hand recovered?"

"Have you hurt yourself?" the Duke asked grudgingly.

"She has swatted an insect with her hand."

"An *insect*?"

"What she thought was an insect."

"Oh," said the Duke, startled. "Well, come to lunch."

Yves left for Paris soon after lunch, and Isabel rejoiced that he was gone. As soon as the Rolls had roared away down the cobbled ramp, she went to the estate office in the south-east corner of the stable yard. She found it to be a dusty, dreary room of moderate size, with no view but of the stable yard itself, heated by a round black stove the chimney of which went out through a window that had been masked with sheet-iron. It was furnished with a desk, a table, a few chairs, and some file-cases. Above the table hung a large square faded map, which the Duke and another man—a tenant, she supposed—were studying as she came in.

They turned, and their expressions were the same, the mindless look of people who have not yet succeeded in bringing their thoughts to meet the interruption. It was odd to see the same look on two such different faces—one gnarled and brown, all shrewd wrinkles and obstinate lines; the other dark and wearily handsome. Then impatience came into the Duke's eyes, and amazement into the eyes of the other man, whom she had not seen before, and who had not seen her. He glanced frankly from her to the Duke, and then he looked annoyingly wise. "Don't let me interrupt—" she muttered, feeling that her coming had been a serious mistake, and they turned back to the map and continued their conference, which did not last long. The old man departed with a last inquisitive stare as he passed her; the Duke made a free gesture with the hand that held a cigarette and waited, frowning.

It was hot and stuffy in the room, and the air was blue with smoke. She blinked and said, "I've been wondering—isn't there something I might do for you here?"

"Oh?" he said, astonished.

"Surely there's something—"

"Haven't you work to do for my cousin?"

"But that wouldn't take much time. . . . He's gone back to Paris, you know."

He did know that, but he said, "Has he? But not forever. He will be back." He sighed. "He will be back."

"I thought there might be something I could do for you here. . . ."

"Did you?" he said from the depths of one of his dark, inattentive humours—but she had never before felt herself so closely studied.

"Something useful. . . . There's surely something. . . ." He moved his shoulders uncomfortably. "Anything at all, anything humdrum and tiresome. . . ." He shook his head. All her emotion broke free. "Oh, but he's been so appallingly unpleasant—please! You don't know how I feel! I don't want to work on his book— I don't want anything to do with him! Mr. Dolphin said in his letter, 'Come back if things aren't pleasant,' and God knows they aren't; only I don't want to go—but I will if you tell me to. All you have to do is tell me to go, and I will. I mean it."

"If I should say, Now, and have the car brought out to take you to the station? Now, this minute?"

"Yes," she said, feeling suspended over dizzy space.

He laughed, and she plummeted an inch or two to solid earth. She did not know at all what he was thinking. He sighed and yawned and rubbed his hands over his face, and then he gave her some work to do, some very tedious, discouraging work. It was the itemizing of a thick stack of receipted bills on the proper pages of an account book. She strained her eyes doing it because she felt she ought to copy accurately not only the figures, but also the shapes of the figures, so that the account book would be in a uniform style, and it was finicking work, learning to make graceful, long-tailed nines and stroked sevens and fours in which the L-shaped bit came exactly to touch, but not to overlap the straight stroke. The sun went down red in the west, and he pumped up a couple of lamps and lighted them, and they added their fumes of hot metal and oil to air that already smelled of dozens of things—dust, old paper, smoke, barnyard, wool, musty wood, old leather. Horses' hooves and footsteps and voices echoed outside in the cold dusk.

At last he said politely, "Have you enjoyed yourself?"

She closed the book on the unentered bills and got up to put her coat on. She did not like to answer Yes, and she could not truthfully have said No. He put out the lamps and opened the door, and they went out. He locked the door behind him. The night was cold and clean; there were stars in the sky. As she walked beside him through the arch, she said abruptly, "Did you ask him to take me to Paris?" and her voice reverberated against the stones—"Paris, aris, aris. . . ."

They came into the central courtyard, a pallor of colonnades roofed over by a rich blue sky brilliant with stars, and their footsteps were now soundless on dead grass. "I did, yes . . ." he said indecisively. "I suggested that. You don't seem to care for the idea. He didn't, either, to be frank."

"Turn me out if you like; but not in his custody, if you please. I'd rather starve than have anything to do with him. I'd rather starve. If I can't stay here, if I'm such a loathsome thing you can't bear to have me here, I'll go; but not with him, not with him—"

"Oh, do stop this," he said irritably. "You're only tired and—and silly. So am I. Don't make melodrama. And don't quarrel with him. Don't lose your temper again. Control yourself. And don't be hysterical; it's so boring."

"Please," she said, choked by despair. She could not seem to take the right tack with him ever. "Oh, please. . . ."

"Please what?" he said, stopping by the well. He was a tall shadow of substantial darkness in the starlight, nothing more. Beyond him, far away and high above, the frail, dark plumes of leafless poplars were delicately traced against the rich blue sky. "What do you want?" he said less sharply.

She looked round at the pale colonnades, the dark blurs of windows, the high, strong rooftops that had sheltered the same family for so long, that had lasted so well. "Just to stay here for a little while."

"A little while?"

"Just a little while. Till I . . . till I get to know you a little better. If you don't mind."

"A worthy ambition," he said ironically. "Admirable, in fact, but—" He thought it over, and she waited, feeling that his mood was changing and that there was some hope for her, after all. "But why not, then? We're all agreed. Because I rather like to have you here, myself, Isabeau, Isabel, when you're good."

"I could fall on my knees," she said. "And I will be good."

There was silence, and then he laughed, which was not exactly the response she had expected, but she did not exactly feel rebuffed by it. "Oh, some day," he said, "some sad day you will learn not to be so open, so incautious . . . and then again," he went on, moving on, but walking very slowly, "in some ways you are not open enough. I think you know what I mean, what's on my mind. . . ." But she did not. After waiting for an answer, he said with some hesitation, "What I mean is that this is surely not your only refuge in a difficult world . . . an obvious and natural refuge, yes, I'm not denying that, but surely not the only one?"

"It isn't a refuge I want—"

"No, no, no, that isn't what I mean. I realize you did not come here in flight. But have you felt no—no curiosity, no interest in— Not that it would have accomplished anything," he added quickly and, it seemed, conciliatingly, as if weakly—by his own standards— trying to prevent her from saying what he did not want to hear. "The family's dispersed, years ago. The men of it never came back from the war, and the mother's dead, and the sister married and went away . . . perhaps you've been in touch with her."

"No," said Isabel, beginning to understand. "I never wanted to know them." He stopped and waited. "I knew my mother," she said, "and so I've never hoped for anything from them. I knew what they must be—they made her."

"I see," he said coolly, doubtfully.

"Oh, you don't! Oh, I know," she said, her voice rising in bitterness. "You despise me for not being loyal to her, and generous, but you don't know. . . . Would I have wanted to come here if I had loved her? Except to revenge her somehow? . . . But not to be friends. . . . She hated me, and I hated her, and I can't say anything good about her, there's nothing good to say!" But that denial reproached her at once, sharply, and she mumbled with remorse, "No, there are a few good things to say; but I won't say them. Don't laugh!"

"It isn't very comical, you know."

"But you were going to laugh."

"God help me, I was," he said, walking on again. "But I understand, now. It's all right. Never mind. There is no need to talk of these things again. I don't want to know any more." They entered the cold hall and went through to the passage, where the hanging lamp by the staircase was lighted. It swayed slightly in a draught, swinging the shadows of its brass grillwork over stone floor and walls. He took her hand and turned it palm up and held his own, palm up, beside it. "Honest toil," he said, "or so they call it. . . ." Both palms were darkened with the fine black dust that collects on papers. And both palms were alike, long and narrow, with long fingers and long, tapering thumbs. She did not look at him. "Odd, isn't it?" he said. "Heredity. . . ." And then he put his hand on her shoulder and pushed her lightly towards the stairs. "Go and wash."

Four

ISABEL ANSWERED HENRY'S LETTER late that evening, sitting by the fire in her room with a block of paper she had got from Jeanne de Varaisne, and she found it difficult because there was so much that she could have said and so little that she wanted to say; she had to pick her way past immensities with every sentence. Finally she covered two-thirds of a sheet with half-truths, folded the envelope of his letter and tucked it into the envelope of hers, so that he would see why he had had no answer before, and went to bed to lie uneasily wakeful for some time.

Once again she felt that she should be happy, but was not, and the trouble was that everything was counterbalanced, good things precariously taking the weight of bad things, kindnesses serving, with nothing to spare, to keep her from being oppressed by cruelties, anxieties annulling the force of joys. Even Henry, far away in London, had his place in the tangle of stays and counterweights that spared her the heaviness of enmity but also deprived her of the solid support of good will. When she slept, she dreamed of standing tense and motionless, longing to run, but afraid to move, in a room overhung with swaying solidities dangerously interlinked, so that the parting of a thread might start a shift in balances that would bring everything crashing down on her. She did not sleep well.

The next morning, when she went into Yves's study for the first time since his departure, she found on a corner of the table the black tin of cigarettes, his little gold lighter, and a note that said, "For Isabel." Finely picked out in bright enamels on the side of the lighter was a tiny replica of the coat of arms of the house. It was clever of him to hit upon the one peace offering that could have tempted her. He had said unforgivable things, and she did not want to have anything to do with him, but she had the lighter in her hand before she could think, and once it was in her hand she imagined using it in the future when she was out in the world again, and people would say, What a pretty lighter! and she would say, Yes, isn't it? My cousin gave it me. . . . She said aloud, "Oh, how pathetic you are," and put it down again.

The amended manuscript lay on the table; the typewriter stood ready beside it; on the hearth the fire was laid and ready to be lighted. She did not quite know what to do with herself. She had resolved to work no more on Yves's book, to separate herself completely from his affairs; she had even looked forward to the displeasure he would feel when he next came back and found himself deserted by her, with everything just as he had left it. But the morning stretched long and empty before her.

The top drawer of the table was open an inch or two; and it resisted when she tried to push it neatly shut. She opened it farther and found a sheaf of paper wedging it—another manuscript, apparently—and she remembered then his hesitation over this drawer when Daphne was there, and wondered if he had wanted to show this manuscript, too, and why he had decided not to. She sat down to put the drawer in order so that there would be room for the manuscript, and read the first twenty pages of it with some curiosity. It was a novel, or part of a novel, written in short, elaborate sentences and rich, breathless phrases chiefly punctuated by triple dots. It began at a ball; there were swarms of people, all particuled and far too elegant to bleed if cut; it was difficult to remember their names. But the hero seemed to be a man called Edouard, and he was adored from afar by a young girl called Clarissa; he was pursued round trees in tubs by a beautiful woman called Solange, and he was talked about by everyone. No one at the ball could talk of anything but Edouard. From group to exquisite group the reader was carried, and always the talk was of Edouard, his irresistible charm, his perfect taste, his remarkable indifference. The consensus was that he had a greater capacity for love than any other man of anyone's acquaintance, but that his armour might prove to be impregnable. Everyone agreed that poor Solange was to be pitied, and Clarissa retreated to a balcony to think triple-dotted thoughts about her hopeless young ecstasy, and Isabel pushed the pages together and found a place for them in the drawer. It was hard to believe that clever Yves could be responsible for anything so fatuous. But the corrections of errors—there were a good many—in the typescript were certainly in his handwriting; and his hand had hesitated over the open drawer as if he had been making a difficult choice. She shut her eyes to remember that moment, and conviction grew in her. She was astonished and gleeful and triumphant. Forgetting that he remained the same man, with his achievements of the past, the possibilities of the future, however many such trivial discoveries she made, she felt that she had somehow got the upper hand of him because she had seen a ridiculous aspect of him that he must be unaware of.

She looked again at the lighter. It was the most casual, impulsive sort of gift possible. She thought he would scarcely remember having left it when he came back, if he did come back. Then she looked at her watch. And finally she went to put a match to the fire.

After lunch she got her coat and overtook the Duke in the great quadrangle of the central courtyard. It was a cold, raw day; heavy, purple-tinted clouds hung low in the sky; but he was in a genial humour, and he said cheerfully in imitation of Arnaud's wife as she joined him, "The main courtyard of the Château de Ferronçalles. . . . Here on a hot morning many years ago Francis the First drank water from the well, observing that it was better wine than any the vineyards of Ferronçalles had yet produced . . . and here, some centuries later, a young lady offered to kneel. . . ."

He left the sentence in the air and turned on her a sharp look of interest and amusement, expecting to see some signs of embarrassment, because it is embarrassing to be reminded by day of things one has said in the dark, but she only answered, rather doggedly, "I meant it."

"That's right," he said, laughing; "don't be cowed."

"Why is the well no longer used?" she asked hastily. "Is it dry?"

"Not dry, I think. It was filled in long ago, as a sort of gesture of locking the barn, you know. . . . The Duke of that day disappeared," he said, pausing by the well and looking up at its carved canopy with an expression of ironic admiration, aloof, critical, and resigned, on his serene face, "and one morning a month or two later someone noticed that he was bobbing about in the water below, poor fellow! Well, they fished him out and buried him, of course, and no one knew if he had suicided or been pushed, but after a while a feeling began to grow that he had been pushed, and since they could not discover who had pushed him, they decided to punish the well. And so they filled it in, or so the records say, but I doubt that they threw in more than a token of dirt—think of the quantities of earth they would have had to haul to do the job properly!" he said, thumping the wooden cover with his fist, and the thump dislodged something—a bit of rotten wood from the cover or a flake of stone from the sides of the well. After a second or two she heard a small distant splash, a small hollow, lonely sound. "Myself, I think they abandoned it from laziness; the water sank too low in it; they were glad of the excuse. After all, there were three other good wells besides. . . . The one in the kitchen, have you seen that one? A miracle of a well, always the same, whatever the weather. Someone drowned in that one too, but there was no talk of filling it up; it was too convenient to be filled up. . . . She is Arethusa, this one," he said, touching the nearest of the four stone nymphs. "But, to work, to work." He walked on.

"I spent all morning on that manuscript," she said abruptly.

He glanced quickly and inquiringly at her; then he thought about it for a moment, rather grimly; finally he said, "Good."

"No, it was only because I had nothing else to do. I didn't want to, and then I thought, What does it matter, obliging him a little, in spite of everything? So I did. It was just to occupy myself."

"I warned you that you would find it dull here."

"I am *not* bored! Only the mornings are long!"

He said, staring straight before him with an expression that had something ambiguous in its gravity, "I suspect that you are no more and no less bored than I am." Then he changed the subject, and she was sure he had been joking, because he was always so busy he did not have time to be bored, and besides, how could he be bored when he lived where she wanted to live, and legitimately, too?

But on another day, just before lunch, she climbed the crumbling stairway recessed in the retaining wall at the north end of the main courtyard to walk in the withered garden, and through the lime-trees she saw him coming back from his ride far away along the edge of the forest, and he was making that poor old horse gallop. She thought something had happened till she saw him pull the

[116]

horse up; the rest of the way he came at a walk; and when he got closer, she saw that he was idly smiling, as if he had enjoyed the run. She went down to the stable yard to meet him, and the man who came to take the horse did not seem surprised to see it in a sweat.

"Do you ride?" said the Duke, as they walked back through the courts.

"I've never been on a horse," she answered absently, pondering over this revelation of secret restlessness that cast a new light on him. There had been something forced and reckless about that gallop. Watching it had made her nervous, and the remembrance of it made her nervous now.

"Too bad," he said. "And this is scarcely the time to begin—the ground is so hard!" He drew a breath to say more and changed his mind.

"That old horse can gallop," she said.

He laughed and kicked at the gravel of the drive that circled the lawn. "Ah, well, it gives one an appetite for lunch," he said wryly. Emerging from the second arch, he looked up at the blue-and-grey sky. "It's going to change—the weather."

"How can you tell?"

"One smells it, or feels it—I don't know."

"Does it matter?" she asked anxiously.

"What? Oh, no. Let it rain, snow, blow, hail—it's just that I'm observant of the weather. Habit, I suppose."

He seemed to think it odd in himself, and it was odd, because he was not, she realized then, on thinking it over, observant of other things or of people. When it was important, he could notice, he could study expressions and responses; but it seemed to require someone's firm opposition to his will to awaken that kind of attention in him. For the most part, unopposed—and he usually was unopposed—he simply went his way enclosed in his own mood, whatever that happened to be—and it was never, it appeared, quite so placid a mood as she had believed.

He was good-humoured at lunch, but he changed as the afternoon wore on in the overheated, evil-smelling office, full of dusty papers and recurring tasks; and at dinner he was rather gloomy. Jeanne had had a letter that day from a nephew of her husband's, the present Comte de Varaisne, who was still a schoolboy, which she thought very witty and clever; she brought it to the table and showed it to her brother, who looked at it and merely said, "Silly."

"No!" she protested. "Show it to Isabel."

"He did it only because he can't spell. A cheap trick."

"No!" she said, but he was already tired of teasing her and he let the letter sail to the white cloth between his plate and Isabel's. It was one of those riddles or puzzles, I forget the proper name, in which every possible word is represented by a drawing, and the tiny drawings were very quaint and vivid.

"It's awfully clever," Isabel said. "It's awfully clever."

"Isn't it?"

"He must have been feeling gay that day."

"Oh, gaiety's an excuse for anything," said the Duke; and thinking of his playful humours, she agreed with him, but she did not know whether or not he meant it.

"Is it?" said his sister pensively, and a sudden gust of wind attempted the chimney and retreated, and smoke puffed out into the room. The Duke turned slowly and gave it an absent, indignant look and turned back. Isabel laughed a little, but he did not notice; he was deep in thought again. His sister gave her a doubtful glance of inquiry.

"A rude chimney," Isabel said.

"Yes, isn't it?" said Jeanne soberly, and she went on to say that it had always smoked when the wind was from a certain direction and that her father had had installed a patent damper, which had not helped at all—which had, in fact, made it worse. But when they sat drinking coffee in the drawing-room after dinner, she returned to the other subject with an air of grave philosophical interest. "I have sometimes thought," she said, tucking her evening shawl, which was of fine, lacy black wool, very warm, round her bare arms, "that gaiety might be the spiritual equivalent of poverty, for it makes the heart, at least, travel light through the world, clinging to nothing. . . . And so perhaps Yves's gaiety . . ." She spoke, of course, to her brother, but she had not forgotten Isabel's presence, and that was a measure of her acceptance of her illegitimate relative.

"And so at last you have seen that he needs an excuse," said the Duke darkly, and Isabel looked at him with vague alarm—he seemed in so much the wrong mood for this kind of discussion.

"No, that's not fair," his sister said; "I don't think he does. But there it is, if he does."

"It is only the reason one might want to try to find one." He sat low in his arm-chair, holding his cup and saucer at about the level of his chin, his shoulders hunched, his long legs outstretched, with ankles crossed. Only one lamp was lighted, and that was behind him, but he faced the fire, which illumined the strong, sombre contours of his face clearly.

"If one is not affected by the charm of someone—" his sister began.

"He can be very pleasant company."

"But—" she said, and she hesitated, like someone who has tried a door that cannot possibly be locked but that will not open. Isabel was very much troubled because she could not see what Jeanne was getting at or what he was resisting. "But—"

"And I am not concerned with his morals. Meaning by morals what worldly people always mean," he said scornfully.

"But, should you despise—"

"I'm not despising anything. But light heart and empty hands are one thing, light heart and a Rolls-Royce and a house in Paris stuffed with treasures are another."

"Yet he holds those things so cheap, not really caring for them except for the pleasure in them. He is generous. He has so many friends."

"Not gay, really, but careless. Not debonair, but nonchalant," said the Duke, and he went on in the same breath, "I wish this subject had never been started. This is one of those times when one drifts in small currents and goes too far and then is too listless to work back and undo the error. . . ." He sat up and leaned to put his cup and saucer on a table and then sat back in the same posture as before. But now he was no longer listless; he was collected in an iron humour; his dark face was savagely stern. "I cannot admire Yves, and my ways are my ways—leave them alone."

The moment hung briefly like that, mysterious and menacing in its silence and its dull pressure of unspoken thoughts, and then it turned, and Isabel saw that there might be something wrong and that he might at times bitterly detest his life as he led it and yet feel powerless to change.

She saw the possibility, but she was far from accepting it as a truth. Such people—misers, I mean, people in the power of money —seem like harmless curiosities from a distance, inexplicable and funny, but with a perfect right to their own queer ways. Yet when one comes close to them one feels them as people not of odd habits but of dark compulsions, and their ways become frightening, as the processes of thought of a lunatic are, because, like lunatics, they are out of reach of logic, eerily closed to reason, and with strong passions uncontrolled except by a mania. They cannot be argued with; they cannot be changed. She could not believe that of him. No one spoke, and the brooding moment did not swing again, but hung in suffocating stillness. She waited—as for the only possible relief from tension—for the opening of the door to let the poodle come clicking gaily in after her airing, her hazel eyes bright, her dark fur smelling of the clean, cold, night air.

"Where *is* Céphise?" said Jeanne.

Isabel jumped up. "Let me fetch her; she comes to me now. . . ."

She went through the dining-room into the pantry, where Gilles was putting glasses away in a cupboard. From the stairwell in the corner she heard laughter in the kitchen below and then Félicie's shy voice in protest and more laughter. "Has Céphise come in?"

"Not yet!" said Gilles, looking in all simple sincerity aghast.

"Never mind," Isabel said, "I'll get her in," and she left the pantry by its other door to go down the long, stone-paved passage, round the corner past the great staircase, and through the hall. But when she opened the outer door and whistled into the windy night and listened, she heard no sound of clicking paws trotting across the stones; so she went back to the wardrobe in the hall and took one of the coats from it to hang over her shoulders, choosing by chance a heavy grey one with a short shoulder-cape that the Duke often wore.

The wild, cold wind swooped over the rooftops; it smelled of stone dust and winter. The night was very dark. Isabel walked towards the stable yard, where Céphise loved to go, whistling and calling her name, slipping her arms into the sleeves of the coat and her hands into its pockets when she heard no response. And as she passed the canopied well she remembered, with a total comprehension of the truth that she had not felt when she heard the story, that a man had drowned in it, either taking his own life or being thrown in against his will to die a cold and choking death. A few hundred years ago he had often walked this frozen turf, dressed in the fashion of his time, as she was walking now, sometimes idly, to take the air, sometimes on business, sometimes alone and worried, or alone and happy, sometimes with a companion, talking casually of this and that; and all the while that nearby well had been waiting for him as his destiny, waiting for his troubles to become desperate, waiting for his life to become unlivable. . . . She felt a horror of that blur of pale stone dimly visible in the darkness. . . .

The wind thrust down and lifted and swirled, making a great hollow rush of sound in the night; and surrounded by blowing rural dark, she thought of the lights and busy traffic of London to the north, and the flat near Covent Garden, and Miriam reading Shakespeare with pathos, and Betty washing up methodically in the kitchen, and in the morning up the two long flights of carpeted stairs and "Good morning, Miss Small!" and the telephone ringing. Before that it had all been wretchedness and uncertainty, dependence and obscurity, but she could not see now that it had been anything but a mistake to move on from that pleasant ignorance to this queerness. What was there here to countervail a low, hateful mother with wrinkled stockings who picked her teeth in company and laughed at her when she cried? There were only people in retreat from the world for one reason or another—Cousin Barnabé the recluse up there among the dark lanterns and chimneys; Jeanne de Varaisne in permanent mourning; and her father—the last warped remnants of an ancient family. She thought how odd it would be if she should ever feel grateful that she was her vital mother's child, and then she shouted urgently, "*Céphise!*" and Céphise had heard all along; she had been hovering in the black archway to the stable yard, waiting to be confirmed in her strong suspicion that it was only the wind making a noise like her name and that she was not wanted at all. She came now at a gallop, very sorry to have been so stupid; but she had not really understood, had thought she heard, but could not be sure with this terrible wind, and perhaps after all was it not a question of going indoors? She stopped a few feet away, wagging her tail, ready to turn back. "Come along with you!" said Isabel severely.

Jeanne was alone in the drawing-room. "My brother had to leave us," she said, her fingers stirring in Céphise's topknot.

"For the office?" said Isabel, puzzled that she had not seen him go.

"No, no, to sit for a while with a cousin who lives with us, who is a little upset this evening—don't be frightened," said Jeanne very softly, and dismay gathered in Isabel at once. "He is quite harmless almost always. . . ." That was not a reassuring phrase. Isabel sat down in the Duke's chair, which was closest to the fire, tucking her feet up, shivering now that she was near warmth, hugging herself, shaking back her blown hair. Céphise turned round twice and lay down in the shadow of the sofa, twisting herself in a pliant, comfortable double curve. After a minute of silence, Jeanne closed her book on her long forefinger and said with resolution, "Forgive me."

"What for?" said Isabel, afraid.

"I tried to use you this evening, perhaps you noticed, and my brother saw that, and he may in consequence feel a little unjust irritation towards you. It would be only human. It was a mistake, and I am sorry." She looked at Isabel with her blue eyes of a deep purity in her delicate, bony face. "You see," she said apologetically, "I have often seen what a difference it can make in people to have a child, a son or a daughter—it can make frivolous men turn serious, and sad men hopeful, seeing that formidable thing, a child of one's own. . . . And he has changed so since you came, and so I suppose I thought he could be made to change a little more, if he could be made to see himself for a moment through the eyes of someone who had some right to judge, who was concerned. . . . That was what I was trying to do, do you see? Did you notice? . . . I will not pretend that I was not utterly overwhelmed to find that you existed, and full of pity for him and for you, for this difficulty; but you are so like him that I have become glad to think he will leave something of himself behind in the world when he dies, however it came into existence. . . . I am clumsy. . . . I did not mean . . . Well, I hoped that if he could be made to see how his ways must look to someone new to them . . ."

"But I see nothing wrong with his ways!"

Jeanne's thin eyelids drooped over the brilliant blue of her eyes. "I am not disloyal," she said. "Loyalty can see a fault and long to have it mended—for his sake only, not for mine." She opened her book again.

"Oh, please, let us go on speaking frankly, I beg of you. Please—

it is people who go in rags and live on black bread and water and grudge the fuel burned to cook the food, all to save a penny here and there—they are the ones who have gone wrong—"

"You haven't seen him change, you haven't seen him draw back into himself year by year. . . . It is not what he is now that worries me, it is what he will be in ten years, in twenty years. . . . No, he was right," she said, returning to her book; "this is one of those nights when one says too much on impulse. . . . I have so wanted to talk of this with someone; I never thought I should ever be talking of it with his daughter."

"Have you not talked of it with M. d'Ayz?"

"With Yves? Yes, a little. . . . Oh, it's sad, it's sad. . . ."

"What is sad?" said Isabel defiantly.

"That they are not friends any more," said Jeanne, turning her head to look at the fire, so that her clear, pale profile was outlined against the shabby dark-blue velvet of the sofa. "That's what oppresses me so, the sad changes. . . . They were inseparables as children, he and my brother and Barnabé; they were all three my dear big brothers; and now— Oh, it is very sad. . . . When my brother had just come into the title, his uncle, Yves's father, who was his guardian, used to worry that my brother would be a waster—he had such ideas, you know, race-horses and yachts—and sometimes I've thought it was his uncle's warnings, given from experience and too seriously, pounded in, you know, too hard, that took root in his young mind and grew and grew. . . . I don't know, except that it was so slow and gradual a thing. A slow withdrawal from society, a gradual retreat. . . ." She set her book aside and began twisting her pale hands in the black ends of her shawl, still staring into the fire. "And sometimes I feel that he dislikes Yves because he is jealous of him . . . because Yves has the kind of life he wanted for himself and was afraid to take. . . ."

But the fire burned richly, pouring out a generous warmth to meet the warmth from the fire at the other end of the room, silhouetting untouched logs at the front against a great busy golden flickering of luxurious flame. "Is there so much money, then?"

"Not perhaps for yachts and race-horses, no, I grant you that— not if the estate is to have what it deserves; but for a gracious normal life in society, yes!" She leaned forward and gazed accusingly at Isabel. "I never dare bring my maid when I come here, not any more; I never dare bring friends with me. . . . Yves is braver than I; he does, thank God, or my brother would be a hermit entirely and forget how to meet people—but the silent anger, the resentment! Once he would not appear at all, for the whole three days of the visit! I could not myself face that. . . . Two things, my dear Isabel. My grandfather got into difficulties once; it was a famous crisis; until Uncle Gondebaud—Barnabé's father—came to his aid. Second, my grandmother would not feed the beggars that came. We used to give them things behind her back. . . . Do you see? Experience and heredity, and all those stern warnings of my uncle, who knew what he talked of, and being left an orphan so young, burdened with great responsibilities, taking them all too seriously—do you see? Good God, he will have all Barnabé's money when Barnabé dies; it's all in Uncle Gondebaud's will; a great fortune—I see it making no difference!" she said with horror. "Will there be these great fires ten years from now? Will these rooms be habitable, or will they be bare and dusty like those others? Before you came, we rarely lunched together; he took his lunch on a tray at his desk, and he would come to dinner so unused to conversation that we ate in silence. . . . Well, you can see how the change encouraged me, so that I tried to hasten it so unwisely. . . ."

After a while Isabel looked up, tried to smile, and said, "It's late. . . ."

"Yes, it's late." Céphise heard that and got up and stretched herself, first her back legs, then her front legs, and then, while her front legs were still extended and her head was low, letting her high rear and slowly wagging tail subside, so that she crouched ready to go. "At the moment what I feel is only how glad I am that you are here," said Jeanne shyly. "And—be patient. Be patient." She stood up; Céphise stood up. "Come along. He will not come back here tonight." Isabel got up and followed her to the little stairway. Through the archway into the pantry Arnaud was visible, sitting on a high stool with his hands in his lap, waiting. "Good night," she said to him, and he stood up quickly and said good night, smiling.

In Isabel's room the red-speckled curtains were drawn, the bed was turned down, there was a lump at the foot of it that meant a stoneware bottle filled with hot water, and the fire was burning well. But she left her door ajar and sat down on the edge of the bed, feeling all rubbed wrong. She had to make a new end for the evening somehow; she had to reassure herself with another glimpse of her father's serene face, which was never in this world the face of a man unbalanced in any direction; and she had to smooth away any anger that he might feel towards her. She sat attentively still, listening for sounds, while the fire dipped and bent uneasily in the changing draught and the wind flung itself against the window and fell away. Something in her attitude teased her with a reminder of something similar in the past, and she identified it after a moment—she was sitting as she used to sit in London lodging-houses before the days of the flat, with soap and sponge in her hand and towel over her arm, listening for the unlocking of a door so that she could make a run for the bathroom as soon as it was vacated. She shook her head. She had all the wrong memories for this kind of life.

At last she heard doors opening and closing in the room that Daphne had had and in the corridor, and she got up quickly and went to her door. The Duke paused when he saw her. "Is he all right now?" she said in a whisper. "Barnabé?"

"Oh, yes," he said at once, but he also took pains to speak very quietly, "quite tranquil. The wind made him a little nervous, that was all." He was carrying a lighted candle in a silver candlestick, holding it carelessly tipped so that wax dripped down the side, and he did not look angry with her, only tired.

Then she said an unpremeditated and ridiculous thing. She said, "Yves's life is ostentation and vulgarity!"

His eyes widened, his mouth dropped open. He stared. Then, very thoughtfully, he put out a finger and traced a line down her nose to its tip, where he pressed hard for a moment. Then he took his finger away. "Sleep well," he said, and walked on, and he was laughing.

It snowed the next day, hard small flakes that collected like white dust in the angles of the buildings and in the cracks of the paving and the sallow grass of the lawn; and she found in the cabinet in Yves's room an elaborate set of notes for the history that were not in his handwriting. She had finished copying the manuscript for the second time and was looking for a better place for the typewriter than the crowded lower shelf, where she had found it—and quite frankly amusing herself, too, by examining the oddities hidden away in the cupboard—when she dislodged a small shabby portfolio and scattered its contents on the floor; and there were the notes. His handwriting was slashing and close and excessively slanted to the right; this writing was small, rounded, neat, and clear. The paper was yellowed at the edges and crisp to the touch, and the ink had faded a little.

She had soon decided that he must have arranged the novel on purpose to catch her eye, hoping to amaze her with his genius, but ready to pretend that he had never meant her to read it if she was not amazed. But this was different. This had obviously been tucked away and forgotten, and she looked the pages over with an increasing deep-seated sense of shock, not so much because of the dishonesty involved—and there was dishonesty whether the labour was hired or stolen—as because she had never come across anything like it before, and so did not know how to take it. Cheating at school had been different; that had always made her uncomfortable; but that had been the affair of children.

These methodical notes, with their carefully sketched arguments and corroborating quotations, made her feel queerly ashamed of the inept sentences that she had taken such pains over. She felt humiliated in her own person. Before she returned the notes to the portfolio, she got up and collected the two typescripts that she had made, the old one with her corrections on it and the copy just finished, and took them over to the fire and burned them, stirring them with the poker till they were quite consumed. Then she put the table in order, laid the original manuscript on the cleared surface, and set the portfolio on top of the manuscript. She wanted him to know that she knew, but she did not mean to speak of it ever, to him or to anyone. But she was soon tempted out of that resolution —to her regret.

That night the temperature rose, the next morning was grey and drizzly, and when she came out of the office in the evening, the air was misty and mild, and lighted windows were reflected in golden smears across the wet cobbles. It felt like spring, and she said so, feeling an unexpected upsurge of good cheer such as she had not known for some time.

"What of that?" said the Duke.

"Spring is spring," she said positively.

"Season of hard work and much worry."

[126]

"But, spring."

"Why," he said suddenly as they passed under the black, dripping arch, making his first reference to that tiny conversation at her door —"why, I've been meaning to ask, why ostentation and vulgarity?"

She could not think what to say for a moment. Then she said, again without premeditation, "He gave me his gold lighter. I wish you'd give it back to him."

He laughed in a puzzled way and said, "But I could only give it back to you. Why don't you want it? Is it ostentatious and vulgar?"

"I don't know."

"Don't know what, which?"

"I don't know."

"Oh, but why hurt his feelings? He wanted you to have it, if he gave it to you. Or shall we throw it down the well?"

"I don't much like that well. . . ."

"Don't like our pretty well?" he said, pausing in the humid darkness to lean against its damp stone rim as if it were a balustrade overhanging an attractive view. "Oh, because of the dead one? I don't think it's haunted." He thumped on the cover as before, but this time nothing fell. "Hullo down there! . . . Here, don't be silly," he said, reaching out to catch at her arm as she moved away. "Are you afraid of ghosts?"

"I don't know," she said.

"The things you don't know, Isabeau, Isabel!" He was silent for a while; and drops of moisture gathered together and grew heavy on the edges and underside of the stone canopy and dropped to the wooden cover, marking time's passing. The stone nymph nearest her faintly glistened, dimly pale in the dark, cold and wet and rough to the touch. Then he said, "But you must not let yourself dislike my cousin. That's foolish. A waste of time."

"You dislike him."

"What are you setting yourself up to be, my shadow, my echo, with no mind of your own? Come, now, Jeanne's very fond of him; he has a great many friends; what of them? No, he's human, a human being, driven and drawn . . . only a little more unaware than most, I think, of how others would see him—but I don't know, it's a shock for anyone, that glimpse through someone else's eyes, that snapshot of the prison from the meadow outside . . . only really from the window of another prison, I suppose, difficult though that is to comprehend. . . . Do you know the epitaph Régnier made for himself? I've often thought it would do very well for Yves. . . .

> 'J'ai vécu sans nul pensement,
> Me laissant aller doucement
> A la bonne loi naturelle;
> Et je m'étonne fort pourquoi
> La mort osa songer à moi,
> Qui ne songeai jamais à elle.'

That expresses him quite remarkably well, I think . . . except that *la loi naturelle* is not, as great Victoria's poet has pointed out, always *bonne*."

"And that's a prison?" she said angrily. "That *is* a meadow! A pleasant playground!"

"No, it's a prison too," he said sensibly. "It must be. It's bound to be. If it were not, he'd be more than human, and that I refuse to believe. . . . But, of course, if he never feels the pinch of it— and sometimes I think he doesn't. . . . Oh, Jeanne is quite right, that is his great charm, his carelessness. A shallow heart, quick forgetting, a clean slate every day. . . . Oh, yes, one could live comfortably enough with him, if— But then, again, a more feeling man, a deeper nature *could* not— You see?" he said, but not to her, except as the representative of another hearer, the familiar companion of his solitude, detachment. "There you are. The vice of the virtue, the virtue of the vice. And so, an endless mean contest, endlessly renewed. . . ."

He had not been feeling very merry to begin with, and now he had talked himself into real gloom. The contempt and detestation that he felt for Yves had never been more obvious. But envy was not enough to explain it. "What did he do to you?" she said, but as soon as she put the question she felt it miss its purpose; it was a hook of the wrong shape, the wrong design, for laying hold of the information she wanted. He hardly had to evade it. He shook his head, absently; he was far away, out of reach, drifting downward in inchoate struggle to familiar resignation.

There was stillness, close sounds of dripping, but behind the sounds a large nocturnal stillness. He laid his hand on the cover of the well and said as if the idea truly and profoundly comforted him:

" 'Là est le bien que tout espirit désire,
Là le repos où tout le monde aspire. . . .' "

His hand rested lightly and lovingly on the wooden cover of a cold, dark depth that had been a man's grave a few hundred years before.

What is there to say to people in that mood? Words of encouragement or disapproval have no power over someone who has lost for the moment the joy of life. She wanted to distract him, to turn his thoughts from the centre of darkness they stared at so uselessly, but the ancient walls, enclosing empty rooms with stone floors worn by the light footsteps of people long since dead, the silent grassy courtyard, the strong rooftops that sheltered silence, all this closed her mind in, too, and made her feel that life itself was empty and sad. The dark windows once had been bright with the soft light of many wax candles, and torches had flared and fizzed in the mist, and the night had been filled with voices and there had been music for minuets—but all those happy dancers were dead and gone to dust now; there was no more music. She stood in the dark, silent mist of a later age, deserted by joy.

She turned towards him urgently. "What has he done to you? What is he doing?" she cried. "Because I can make him stop! I know something about him he wouldn't want known, and I'll tell him I'll tell unless he stops!" There was silence as before, but it was a different silence, refreshed and made new by a new emotion, and for an instant she was foolish enough to misinterpret the quality of it and think him impressed by her offer and grateful to her. "Don't worry, I can make him stop!" she repeated. "I'll tell him that unless he does I'll tell—"

She was bewildered and appalled when he moved suddenly in the dark and took her by the shoulders and rudely shook her, saying fiercely, "Be quiet, you filthy little blackmailer, hold your tongue!" He shook her as she had seen startled parents shake bad children, trying to shake wickedness away before it could stick, but it seemed to her that he was the one who had basely hung the deed on her in the first place, which horrified her as much as his violence did. She pulled away from him; he let her go. "Don't say such things, do you hear?"

A great cold calmness fell over her. "I thought," she said in a voice that did not sound like her own—"I thought for once I had someone on my side who'd not just think the worst at once—that's not fair," and then she turned and ran for the shelter of her own room, but through some fourth dimension, seemingly, beyond sound, beyond pain—she was aware of cold darkness blowing against her face and then aware that it had stopped, but she hardly knew that she had stumbled and fallen on the wet, cold stones of the next courtyard till he was beside her helping her up to her feet again. The lighted windows of the old east wing were golden in darkness, blurred by mist.

"I see," he said. "Of course you wouldn't profit. You would be doing it for me. That was stupid of me. But it wasn't a nice idea."

"All right, it wasn't a nice idea," she said wildly, brushing her skirt.

"Have you hurt yourself?"

"No!"

"I'm very sorry. I was very stupid."

She walked on.

"Oh, God!" he said behind her, but he did not try to overtake her again.

The fire was bright in her room; there was hot water in the copper can beside the wash-stand; but she lay down across her bed, face down, her head in her arms, feeling extremely miserable. Some twenty minutes later there was a knock on her door. She did not move. The door opened with a squeak and a creak, and the Duke said, "Are you ready for dinner?"

"I don't want any dinner," she said.

There was a moment of indecision; then she judged by the sound of footsteps, the cool clink of metal against marble, the rasp of a match, and a brightening of the red light that seeped past her arms, that he had come in and lighted a candle. He said firmly, "Now, get up at once and wash yourself and put on your nice blue frock and come down."

"Is something wrong?" said Jeanne from the doorway; sounding all alarmed.

"No," he said. "Everything is quite all right. Go down; we shall be with you very soon."

"Is there something I could do?"

"Nothing," he said. "Run along." Her footsteps and the click of Céphise's paws retreated; he went on in a much quieter voice, "Now

I've misunderstood you twice. That should be enough for a lifetime, don't you think? . . . Are you crying?"

"No."

"But quite unforgiving?"

"No," she said, rolling over and sitting up on the edge of the bed and pushing her hair back from her face. "It doesn't matter, I guess," she said drearily, but when she looked at him and saw how really unhappy about it he was, how really concerned, she put her head down on her knees and found herself making grotesque grimaces to keep from sobbing aloud.

"I've meant to tell you before how sorry I am I was so unkind when you came," he said slowly and seriously. "It was a sad homecoming for you. But, you see, I was so sure he'd brought you to make some sort of new trouble for me. I couldn't believe him when he said it was all chance, pure accident . . . but I found I was also incapable of believing that there was malice in you. . . ."

"A homecoming?" she said, looking up.

He was leaning in the doorway, his hands in the pockets of his dinner-jacket, watching her thoughtfully. He smiled. "The home of your ancestors?" he said. "Isn't it?"

"And now you hate me again. . . ."

"I don't, I never did! I only mistook you. How could I hate you?"

"My mother did."

"Did she? Yes, so you said. But that's different," he said, and his voice had changed, it had become duller and flatter, as if his enthusiasm had failed to follow the discussion round this corner. "Parents must love by instinct or not at all. They are the last to see their children as people—lovable people or detestable people. Never expect a parent to give you your just deserts in the way of affection."

She scarcely knew that she was happy; the lightness and warmth that had spread over her seemed more like springtime itself than balm for a narrow wound; but she dared to say, "Not even a father?"

He laughed with her and made a face. "I must guard my tongue now. But I would not hope for too much from him—as a father."

"Because . . . because he's so young?" she suggested diffidently.

"That certainly adds to the difficulties all round, doesn't it?"

"I know," she said eagerly.

He was silent for a moment; then he said, "But you must not hate him. I mean that."

After a puzzled moment she saw that he had returned to the subject of Yves, and it was for her like waking from a dream to the grey troubles of daylight. She had walked on roses for a while; now she stood on hard earth. "Oh . . ." she said dully and dubiously.

"Because whatever there is between him and me has nothing to do with you; remember that. And hating is a dangerous thing, dangerous for you. . . . So don't take sides, and wash your hands, and come down to dinner at once, because I am ferociously hungry."

"If I am very quick, may I go on despising him?"

"Oh, God, I'm no peacemaker, that's plain."

"Except for yourself."

"For myself? Oh! Friends, then?" He held out his hand, and she put hers in it. "But don't—" he began, and then he cautiously decided not to go on, laughed instead, shook his head, and went out, pulling the noisy door shut behind him.

On the whole, however, it had not been a happy incident, and her triumph and elation did not last long. She had really shocked him with her impulsive offer of help, and in retrospect she could see it only through his eyes and be as dismayed by it as he had been. The thought of it subdued her whenever she saw him because she was sure the thought of it was always in his head too, shadowing the pleasure he took in her company. Besides, she was at last becoming convinced that he was not really interested in their relationship, as she was, and never would be, as she was. It seemed to be not only distasteful to him, but boring. Yves was right, it had happened too long ago, it had meant too little at the time. And so she began to give up—give up hope of discovering in herself the hereditary discrimination and niceness that would have impressed him, give up hope of awakening in him the paternal instinct that had slumbered too long undisturbed.

For a day or two the air was kind and it was hard to stay tamely indoors. She went outside one morning, just to take the air for a moment, and found herself upstairs in the guardroom before she knew that she had moved, and from the guardroom she went into the state apartments, with their faded fragments of wall-paintings and frescoed ceilings, clean and cold and empty now, and then out on the gallery to look down at the sunlight and shadows of the central courtyard. While she stood there, Arnaud's wife, in

black gown and cap and shawl, came from under the archway lead-
ing the first tourists of the year, who had paid their four francs each
and followed her with eyes quick not to miss anything. One was a
man alone, small, slender, and dark, by the look and sound of him
an Egyptian or Persian; the other two were women of the district, a
mother and daughter, it seemed. The women were shy; the man
asked questions. Arnaud's wife listened benignly but went relent-
lessly on with her set lecture in answer: "Here we see the great well
of the Château de Ferronçalles, which has been in existence for
more than six centuries. The stone canopy, supported by four
statues, each representing a figure in mythology associated with
water, was completed in the sixteenth century; a hundred years later
the well was filled in as a result of the death by drowning of the
then Duke." She turned decisively from the well towards the cascade of steps; her little flock, two nice sheep and an active little
goat, moved with her, looking back over their shoulders, however,
at the interesting well. At that moment Isabel saw the present Duke
coming through the farther arch from the stable yard. He saw them,
then he looked up by chance and saw her, and he moved his fingers
in greeting before turning back to give the strangers time to disappear.

Her smile died away. She had looked at herself for a moment
through the eyes of the tourists and had felt their envy, and then
she had imagined them with the knowledge of the truth and had
felt their envy go. She was truly just as transient as they.

The next day was grey and cold, and that night it rained a winter
rain, with gusts of wind from the north-west shaking the panes of
the windows and flinging rain against them with a slap and a thud,
and it was pleasant to sit by the fire after dinner and hear wild winter outside. Jeanne had some village affairs to discuss with her
brother; Isabel sat back in a deep chair and idly listened and less
idly watched.

He always looked very handsome by firelight, and remarkably
young. It seemed no wonder, after all, that so young a man found
it impossible to accept a grown-up daughter. The miracle was that
after his first moment of rebellion he had managed to be so uncon-
strained, so natural, keeping his distance without being distant, and
never infringing on her independence. She realized abruptly how
angry any real assumption of authority, peremptory and brusque,

would have made her, because he had actually done nothing to earn that kind of obedience, and how embarrassed she would have been by any tenderness, because she hardly knew him. She had once hoped for both, but now, watching him by firelight, she drew back from the thought of either. It was best as it was.

Jeanne began a more general topic; she had finished the book she had been reading; she said it was very interesting and strange, and urged Isabel to read it. "What is it about?" Isabel asked, and she said, "It's difficult to say, very strange and odd, about being lost and cold at night, and the past opening before one, a great ball . . . a ghostly story. . . ."

"Are there really no ghosts here?" Isabel inquired, and the Duke looked at her curiously.

"A dank duke from a well, for example, dripping along the corridor shouting for vengeance?" he suggested.

"Mathieu!" said his sister. "Don't say that; she will think of it when she is alone in the dark."

"You've just ensured that she will," he said, amused. "Are you frightened, Isabel?"

"No, you must not be frightened," said Jeanne earnestly, "because there has never been a ghost here, never. . . ."

"Which is odd," he said. "That Duke ought to walk, I think. So should that lady who leaped off the balcony into the river. So should that poor little twin who was overlaid by his nurse. There must be ghosts! We are simply a crass race insensible to them."

"Oh, no," said Jeanne. "Great-aunt Angèle would have found them out if there'd been any. She would run from the noise of her own footsteps, Isabel; she was of a truly abnormal timidity. When she went to bed, she would barricade the door. She locked it and barred it and barricaded it. Oh, she had all sorts of queer ways, Great-aunt Angèle. She washed her hair, which happened to be very thin, every day. And if she was awake at midnight, she would get out of bed and ring a little bell."

"I didn't know that," he said, interested. "She'd ring for someone?"

"No, just shake this little bell in the air. Her maid told me, and I heard it a few times myself, when I was sleeping in the room next to hers."

"And why did she do that?"

"I haven't the least idea in the world. But she did it."

"I didn't know that. . . . That's as mad as Cousin Thibaut and the earwax."

"What was that?" Isabel asked.

"You don't want to hear what that was."

"Please," said his sister, her hands on her cheeks, "let us forget that Cousin Thibaut and the earwax ever existed. He had a plan that it was useful," she said to Isabel.

"And so he set about collecting it," said the Duke.

"No, that is really nauseating," Isabel said.

"Indeed it is," said Jeanne. "His little spoons! No, say something quickly, take it out of my mind! Oh, Céphise!" she said to her dog, who had just been let into the room, wild with joy because she had got wet and had been towelled, which made her feel new and fine. She galloped about with such sudden swerves and halts that she wrinkled the rug, so happy that no one could bear to quell her, though her roughness was worrying. She quelled herself after a while and sat steadily panting and looking from one to another of the group, her eyes bright and attentive.

"Remember Great-aunt Pauline's dog?" said the Duke.

"Poor little monster! A pug," said Jeanne to Isabel, "and Cousin Thibaut was convinced that it was possessed. Possessed by an evil spirit, I mean. It was absurd, that poor little dog."

"He used to stand outside a room and refuse to come in till he was promised the dog was not there."

"And Great-aunt Pauline would put it under her shawl or lay a cushion over it and say, All's safe, come in!"

"Which accomplished nothing," said the Duke, "because no one believed anything she said. She was a pathological liar." Isabel looked at him quickly and disbelievingly, but he was staring at the fire, amused by his memories of his relatives and quite oblivious of the impression of them that he was giving.

His sister said thoughtfully, "Pathological?"

"Congenital, then. Habitual. It's all one. She couldn't tell the truth to save her life."

"Father used to say it was her nurse punishing her so for faults, so that she was afraid to tell the truth."

"But his father had the same nurse, and he was as bold as a lion with the truth."

[135]

"Much too bold," said Jeanne, laughing. "But it was different for a boy. Grandfather was outrageous," she explained to Isabel, "a perfect tyrant, and outspoken—! He gave his own nicknames to everyone; I mean, he invented them for himself; it was a thing he did. . . . Me he called—no; I won't tell."

"No, don't," said her brother kindly, "because it wasn't true."

"Then I don't mind telling. He called me 'fat-legs.' Oh, I wept over that."

"Which pleased him enormously," said her brother, "as you should have realized. He never chose his nicknames for truth, only for hurtfulness. It was his method of ruling, and my God, it worked as well as any other. 'The silent, wise man'—and poor old father never dared open his mouth except to utter a theory, one of his theories, one of his causes and consequences. . . ."

"Poor old father!" said Jeanne with comfortable resignation. "He could not even have his moustaches!"

"Poor old father!" said her brother, sighing.

They went on evoking and dismissing grotesque fragments of people; the past grew thick with faces, and all the faces were queer in one way or another—cruel, mean, mad, false, fearful. . . . But the fires burned low, and Joël was sent in at last to mend them, and then the Duke sat forward in his chair to look round at Joël, who was bending over the other fire, and said, "Never mind, bank it up; we shan't be here much longer. . . . It's late," he said, and his sister stood up quickly, her eyes avoiding Isabel's eyes. Isabel flushed. Céphise got up and stretched and stood wagging her tail slowly, waiting. In the silence Isabel heard the wild noise of the winter rain outside. The evening was over.

But Jeanne went first up the stairs, and the Duke said to Isabel quietly as they followed, walking cautiously up the ill-lit steepness of the small stairway, "Are you still troubled by that—that—" She stopped, he came on, found no room, and stepped back. "Sorry. . . . Because you've seemed a little sad since then . . . a little subdued. . . . You mustn't worry about it. You meant so well."

"Oh, God," she said, moving on; "I deserve that."

"What do you mean?" he asked, really amused.

She went on to the top of the stairway and saw Jeanne going down the corridor with Céphise plodding at her heels. "Well-intentioned. I honestly didn't know any better. Think of that!"

"You spoke in haste," he said, closing the door at the top of the stairs.

"From the heart. Let's face it—from the heart. Good night."

"Good night, sleep well," he answered automatically, but then he put out his hand, not to touch her, merely to beg her to wait for a moment. "Of course you are resentful—"

"Resentful?" she said indignantly. "No! I know I deserved it. I can see that, even if—"

"No, no, no, I meant, resentful of—of—on behalf of the past, the long neglect, the . . ."

He always found it difficult to mention the circumstances of her birth; that subject made him stutter and stammer as no other could do. Probably she was not much less sensitive than he took her to be; she considered herself hardened, but in point of fact the gentlest reference usually succeeded in touching a nerve; but she was not sure, with him, how much of her embarrassment was simply a reflection of his. "Just once in a while," she said quickly. "Mostly— mostly it was a comfort to me." Then she blushed, feeling that she had debased herself with that confession.

"Until he called you that ugly name."

The memory of that had been so overlaid by what followed it that she had to think to know what he meant. "Oh, you made that right," she said. "You made up for that. And he's said worse things since then," she added bitterly.

"Worse? . . . Oh, he's not to be understood. I don't understand him." His face grew serious and rather gloomy. "Well, never mind. And, Isabel my dear," he said, putting his hand lightly on her shoulder, "be as generous as you can."

She was too great a coward to let him see how that idea affected her, and her hatred of Yves rose a degree as she heard herself say vaguely, "I know. . . ." She turned away to walk down the long old corridor, past closed, silent doors, to her room. But as she went, three words echoed and re-echoed in her head, each time smoothing a little more her discomfort, till all was smooth: Isabel, my dear. . . .

The wind and the rain slapped against the window in her room; the noise of the wind was hollow in the chimney. She read for a while in Jeanne's book after she was in bed, with the covers drawn up under her chin and only one arm, in the long flannel sleeve of her nightgown, outside the covers to manage the book. The fire flickered and hissed, and she was warm, and even the sound of rain slapping against the window was a pleasant sound. But she did not like the book, which was wistful from the start. It was the good kind of book that promises its ending at the very beginning, and the ending was going to be unhappy, she was sure. She let the book go, licked her fingers, and pinched out the candle-flame, and slid more deeply under the covers. She was feeling happy, but her happiness was thin, and beneath it all the unhappiness and uncertainty of her whole life lay waiting to be aroused, as always. Whenever the slow drift into sleep began, the thin skin of happiness sank under the weight of it and threatened to break and let nightmare loose. But it did not break, it dissolved, and she was far down the dark slope, on the brink of the last soft, terrifying drop into lawless sleep, when she was startled by the opening of the door that she faced as she lay in bed, the door in the panelling. And Cousin Barnabé's servant looked in with a candle in a glass chimney held over his head, a yellow flicker of light in red darkness illumining a deformed face.

She should not have been frightened of him, and she would not have been—Yves's word for him came into her head, but she instantly rejected it—but she had been startled from sleep, and it is always disturbing to face the world while the doors of sleep, opening into the mad world of dreams, are still open; and besides, his clear-speaking brown eyes were much alarmed, and that alarmed her. He was looking for someone, and he was very much frightened. She sat up, struggling with the heavy bedclothes, and that struggle itself made her heartbeat hurry, and so increased her fear. And then, suddenly and terribly in the night silence, Céphise began barking, and she had never heard Céphise bark at night before. She got out of bed in one movement and ran from the strange creature in the other doorway, thudding barefoot down the cold, creaking floor of the dim corridor to the turning, where she met her father, still decorous and usual in black and white, with a cigarette in his hand, and flung herself upon him.

"But what is it?" he said. "Was Céphise barking at you?"

"It's nothing," she said, feeling so safe now that she was already ashamed of her wild flight. "I saw Barnabé's servant—"

"But you're not afraid of *him!*" he said indignantly.

"Only, he was looking for someone," she said.

"Oh, come," he said, confidently, disbelievingly, but he raised his head to look past her, and his fingers tightened absently on her arm. Then he put her into the tremulous red gloom and brown shadows of his room, flung his cigarette towards the hearth, and went out into the corridor again. It was an unfamiliar room, with unfamiliar corners and dark crannies between black chests and wardrobes and high, curtained bed, and her fears came marching back on her like a nightmare army swelling up impossibly large as they came, as high as the world, as endless as time. "Stay here," he said, "and fasten the bolt," closing the door between them. "But fasten the bolt," he repeated outside in the passage, sounding already far away. But she could not; she was afraid of being alone; locking the door seemed locking herself away from safety. Even when his footsteps went away down the creaking corridor, she did not shoot the bolt; it seemed such a useless thing to do. She could not help herself. She was in a state of blank, mindless terror.

It must have been the dark uncertainty of her childhood, the sense of being hated, of being unwanted and unprotected, that rose up now like a great wind out of darkness to blow out the little candle of her courage. They do not count for much, those habits of independence that one acquires as one grows up, when elemental memories of helplessness in a world of huge overhanging menace are aroused. And there were other nearer memories to enforce them, the feelings inspired by the evening's talk, the words used of Cousin Barnabé—"quite harmless almost always. . . ."

She did not know what had happened, and she did not try to think what it could be; she did not enlarge her fear by imagining possible and dreadful reasons for it. She did not have to. Panic suffocated her. She was afraid for herself, for her father, and even for Barnabé's servant—afraid in a total way, filled to every corner with fear. She stumbled through the moving shadows and dim light to the chair by the fire and doubled herself up in it, head first, burrowing into it, with her arms folded over her head, pressing against the worn leather cushion until the top of her head hurt. It was a mad thing to do, but it seemed sensible to her then, or at least necessary. Darkness crawled over her shoulders; the world behind her remained more real than the world she sought.

Then there was a polite knock on the door, and a gentle voice that she had never heard before said softly, "Mathieu?" and she began to whimper and could not stop, though she told herself in an agony of apprehensiveness that the sounds she made were being listened to, were puzzling someone and attracting him. She became two people, one whimpering, the other knowing that the sounds would bring danger in, but unable to stop them.

Then she heard the Duke's persuasive voice saying, "Come now, come now . . ." and then, quietly but urgently, "What has he got?" and then there was a flurry of footsteps on the creaking floor and a thud and the wall shook and a man screamed through clenched teeth, a horrible sound. After a while there was silence—a sudden silence, it seemed—but there must have been sounds of departure that she did not notice. She drowned in the silence, heard from the distant surface the handle of the door being shaken impatiently, and sank more deeply into dark depths of silence, resigned to whatever might come, but refusing to meet it.

Someone pulled her up from the chair with an exclamation of surprise and concern. The same chair received them both again, her nightgown was tucked over her cold feet, and she opened her eyes to see the ends of a black tie, badly twisted and wrinkled, lying across the front of a smudged white shirt.

"It's all right now, it's all right," he said, rocking her a little, as if she were three years old and he were used to soothing children who were wakened by bad dreams. The fire was low; its glowing heart had disintegrated in white ashes and charred wood. The wind was quieter. "It's all right," he said again, and there was a note of amusement in his voice that she caught and was more reassured by than by anything he said, because it was so like him. He was not just a dependable grown-up, he was himself, able to laugh at the situation he was in. And becoming aware of him as himself, out of her profound respect for him she made a move to extricate him from a situation that he thought comical. "No, no, that's all right," he said. "Only I haven't held a child since I was twenty and a god-father for the one single time. I think I do it rather well, don't you? Are you feeling better? . . . No, no, you are quite safe now, it's all right. . . . It's a long child, though, isn't it? A tall child. . . . However . . ."

"I'm all right now," she said, getting to her feet; but she felt at once that it was not much fun to stand alone, and when she looked at his face, dark and flushed and tired, her heart ached with a queer mingling of shyness and pity. "You've been very comforting."

"You've been rather comforting yourself. An antidote. Come back, if you like," he said with a yawn.

"But why should you have him on your hands, if he's like that?" she said furiously.

"I am the head of the house, after all. And he knows where he is and loves it here. I couldn't send him away—how could I? *This* has never happened before, you know, and it won't happen again."

"Is he mad?"

"Docile as a rule, but sometimes violent. Then he wants to kill me," he said, yawning again, a thorough yawn that ended in a shudder. "I'm tired as all hell and the seven devils. Excuse me."

"To kill *you?*"

"Mad, isn't it? But he is mad. If he went for his enemies—supposing he had them—he would be sane. Q.E.D. You look a bit chilly. Sit down on the hearth and warm yourself a little." He took up the poker and pushed the hot, charred logs together so that they smoked and hissed and then flickered into warming flame, and he brought an old woollen dressing-gown and a pair of slippers for her to put on. "Do you want a cigarette?" he said through another yawn.

"No," she said, and he took one for himself and lit it and came to poke at the fire again without any visible impatience.

"No, he's never wandered before—of course we keep him locked up, but he's never seemed to take any interest in leaving his rooms . . . and he's easy to read—one can see his moments of violence coming, and then a little distraction, a little conversation, usually heads them off."

"Do people know?"

"No one knows except us, the family," he said. "The others think him a hermit, a recluse—almost a saint; but that's because of his servant, the impression his servant gives, I think. They do strange and lovely things for him, the maids—they bring nosegays of spring flowers for him—for Barnabé! They feel so sorry for him, because they think he has despaired of the world, which seems a charming place to them. People can be very nice." He yawned again. "Well, how are you now? Ready to go?" She stood quite still, thinking, trying to persuade herself. There had been only him, and then only this room and him, but now there were the other rooms too, room after room to the walls, and beyond the walls the dark winter night, and morning far away. "What is it?"

"Only my room has no bolts on the doors."

He made a face and looked at his watch. "Oh, I can't wake poor Jeanne again. . . . It's perfectly safe now, you know; there won't be any more disturbances—" He looked at her thoughtfully and pursed his lips and shook his head. "No. No. And I don't blame you. I feel the same." He took up the candle and opened a door beside the chimney-piece to peer into a room there, and she felt like a guest outstaying all the other guests, a bore, a nuisance; but she could not help it. "Would this do, I wonder? There's a bed, cold as ice, I've no doubt, unaired, unwarmed. . . . I've never had occasion to sleep there. . . . Except once, when this great wreck lost its grip on itself and collapsed. . . . It needed new pins, or something. . . ."

She stood in a fine torment of conflicting desires—wanting to make a show of bravery, after all, wanting Jeanne to give her shelter, wanting not to make a nuisance of herself by objecting to any arrangement he chose to make—and helplessly watched him grope for the stoneware hot-water bottle in his bed and take it into the other room and come back to open the doors of a wardrobe and pull an eider down from the top shelf. He gave the doors a careless push to close them, but she caught a glimpse of his clothes—the grey tweeds, the brown tweeds, a dark grey suit that she had never seen him wear—clothes that knew him well. "Honestly—" she said when he came back without the eider down.

He looked at her inquiringly. "What, then?" he said, and then, still sleepily staring, he laughed at some private joke that had crossed his mind. "Say it?"

"I'm sorry to be such a coward."

"Oh, my dear child—" He shrugged his shoulders tolerantly. "Do you remember—" He stopped and pressed both hands to his head. "Now, what was it I was going to say? Oh, yes. Do you remember when you ordered your breakfast of me? That was not so cowardly. There is courage and courage. . . . Come, to bed with you, and let me get some sleep too!"

The room next door was cold as a tomb and very dark when the door was closed. Black though the night was, the single window showed pale in the blackness of the room. The narrow bed had sheets on it, and they were like ice; her feet grappled at once with the stoneware bottle, which was pleasantly warm. She heard him preparing for bed in the next room, whistling under his breath. He left the room once, came back, opened drawers and shut them, dropped a shoe; and then he came to the door. "Comfortable now?" he said.

"Yes, very," she said, managing to control her chattering teeth long enough to say that much.

"Then, sleep well, my child," he said, mocking himself as before, and he went away, leaving the door slightly ajar. She heard the springs of his bed creak as he climbed into it.

She did not sleep well. She slept, in fact, hardly at all, cold as she was, with all the dreadful night to think over now that the hurry of it was past, with all the long, lonely darkness of silent corridors and empty rooms to explore in imagination, meeting the lunatic at every corner and behind every door, and with a nearer anxiety to evade if she could, the puzzle of her almost intolerable uneasiness in a situation that was, after all, quite natural and proper. She could not understand herself.

The stoneware bottle grew cold before her feet got warm, and she gave up hope of sleep, shuddered and shivered and remembered and wondered, heard the distant stable clock send its thin note along the wind and down the chimney, telling the hours—three o'clock, four o'clock—and woke from an extraordinarily real dream in which she somehow had seen herself talking with great earnestness on a storm-darkened lawn to her closest relative, pouring her heart out in some profoundly satisfying way, telling him how completely she belonged to him and to some other man whose identity they both seemed to know, though he shook his head and seemed troubled by some of the professions of love she bestowed equally on both, seeming to disclaim it for himself with frowns and hesitant gestures. But she saw herself insist; she was triumphantly sure; and the contentment of having at last known her mind and thoroughly spoken it lingered with her for a minute or two when she woke. She lay in sleepy warmth reaffirming the dream, happy that everything was clear to her at last, and clear to them, the two; and then she felt a jolt, as of a fault in logic subsiding underfoot, because there had seemed to be two but now she could remember only one, the Duke, the man sleeping in the next room, breathing heavily, turning over now and then, once muttering aloud in his sleep.

The sense of the dream remained so strong and the truth was so undeniable that the world seemed dislocated between them, and she felt herself in the ludicrous but truly terrifying position of one standing astride a widening gap in the earth itself, not knowing which way to jump for safety. It was a waking nightmare; it had the same sort of reality as the bed she lay in, as the man asleep in the next room; it was more real than her self, which had somehow got lost in the dark. She wanted a light, she wanted the door closed, she desperately wanted morning.

But the grey gradual dawn made things no better. The room grew defined and closed her in with unfamiliarity; in bookcases along the wall gold titles on glossy leather winked palely behind glass; grey light fell on a neatly brushed hearth and a comfortable tapestry chair that she had never seen before. Over and over again, as daylight grew, she directed herself to get up and go quietly through the next room and down the passage to her own room, the safety of which was the same yearned-for unreachable goal that it had been on the second evening of her visit. She could not now, as then, quite make herself take the first step towards it. She kept waiting for a better moment to move, and morning came, she heard a door open, smelled coffee, heard the clink of china and the rattle of curtains being pulled back, and knew that she had waited too long.

A sleepy, confident voice said, "Good morning, Arnaud. . . . Good God! what a night," and Arnaud said that the wind had brought a willow tree down. "Oh, not really? Was it that bad? . . . Oh, by the way, Miss Regan is asleep in there. She had a fright last night, poor child! She ran into Cousin Barnabé's servant suddenly in the passage—she hadn't seen him before, and . . ." Arnaud grunted sympathetically. "You might have someone look out a pair of bolts for the doors of her room—they should have bolts. . . . Oh, and I want the car for nine-thirty, God help me! I could sleep another ten hours, I think. What's the news of Raymond?" he said, picking up the threads of his day as he took a sip of hot coffee with gusto, rather noisily, and Arnaud said that there had been no word of Raymond, but that was a good sign; and they fell into talk about this and that, comfortably, congenially, sharing the same point of view, though one was past sixty and a butler and the other

[144]

was under forty and a duke; and by the sounds, the younger man finished breakfast, got out of bed, and began to shave.

The conversation continued, quiet and easy, and Isabel lay on her side and listened, ready to shut her eyes and pretend sleep if anyone came into the room, but she was not relaxed, she was stiff with the strain of preparing her own escape. He had explained her presence with his customary serene assurance that whatever he chose to do was fitting and right, and Arnaud had listened in the same spirit. Once upon a time she would simply have docilely waited for him to manage the rest as well. But she had reached the extremity of self-distrust where one fears that any sort of leaning will make one crack in two, where one chooses between dissolution and standing alone. She listened for her first opportunity to make a run for it, and while she listened, she freed herself of all her encumbrances. She cast off that imaginary exquisite Isabel who had so stubbornly refused to take possession of her; she got rid of her dream of being the daughter of the house; she threw away all her expectations of the future and all her hopes and plans of the past.

"No, I'm going to have a bath," he said abruptly, apparently interrupting Arnaud in something Arnaud was doing or about to do, and she remembered—it was her first facing of it by daylight—last night's obscene struggle with a lunatic, the large, dark, murderous alarm that had filled the night.

They both seemed to leave the room; at least, silence came and remained unbroken while she counted thirty; and she got up and ran as she was, in her nightgown, her feet bare, through the next room, round the corner, and down the passage to her own room, and she seemed to run more swiftly for being at last her narrow self and nothing more, her narrow self stripped and pruned of desires.

She dressed at once; she was sedately armoured in her blue suit and stiff brogues when Louise came with the breakfast tray just as usual; but she took it brusquely from Louise's hands, which she regretted afterwards, remembering the rebuffed look on the girl's pleasant face. But at the time it was the best she could do in the way of meeting people. The effort of the smallest smile, the briefest exchange of courtesies, would have, she felt, tipped her off the narrow ledge above abysses where she stood alone. She ate her breakfast with a kind of mindless animal enjoyment, as if it were a drug that took her out of the troubled world for a while; and Louise returned to do the room and remove the tray. This time Isabel succeeded in smiling stiffly at her. But this time Louise would have understood a continuation of her unusual humour. She had heard the version of the night's events that the Duke had set forth, and she was all sympathy. She perfectly understood that the first seeing of so deformed a face would be a shock for anyone, but she urged Isabel never to be frightened of him again, because he was a saint, M. Barnabé's servant, a true saint, though he looked so queer.

"Yes," said Isabel, "I know . . ." and then she was safely alone in her own small room, alone with the cold drops of rain dripping from the stone drip-cap at the top of the window and sometimes swerving in the wind to streak the glass and sometimes falling straight to splash dully on the soaked stone ledge, alone with the fire whispering and hissing secretly to itself. She was horribly tired. She lay down on the bed as she was, but she could not sleep, she could not even close her eyes. She lay still, listening to the tiny ticking of her own watch, staring at the ceiling, for a long time, wondering what she was to do now, but coming to no conclusions.

There was a sudden rush of roaring sound outside, subsiding in a splashing noise that itself subsided before she had reached the window to look out. She saw Yves's grey car below, its sides splashed with mud, its top glistening with wet, both front doors open. Out of one came Henry Dolphin in a brown felt hat and a mackintosh buttoned up to his chin; out of the other, of course, came Yves, who had understood her, she thought, so much, much better than she had understood herself.

Five

AFFECTION AND DESIRE, even the warmest affection and the most transient desire, are as different as the two faces of a coin, but it is a transparent coin, and in certain lights the other side will shine confusingly through. But Isabel did not know that. She left her window before either of the doors of the car had been slammed shut again and hurried in thoughtless panic through the room that Daphne had had, through the two bare rooms next to it, down the spiral staircase in the wall to Yves's room, and through the glass doors to the terrace. She ran the wet length of the terrace to the door at the other end; from there she circled round into the great hall and climbed the stairs to the guardroom.

Back and forth in the guardroom she walked for a while, and she felt the better for it. Bad weather does not help troubles; fine weather makes them worse; a rich room isolates one with them; shabbiness adds trouble to them; but ancient empty rooms where melancholy events are known to have taken place almost cure them. They cannot help shrinking when they come to mingle with such a collection of tragedy.

In this room a duke had fenced for pleasure with his nephew and, stumbling as he lunged, had driven his light sword through the nephew's throat and then had tried to stab himself in his remorse; and at one of those balconied windows, on a fresh morning in June, a daughter of the house had paused for a moment to look at the weather as she chatted with friends with whom she was going to stroll the gardens and had suddenly stepped out and thrown herself over the balustrade into the river far below, for no reason that was ever discovered. In a room nearby a duchess had taken seven months to die miserably of what must have been poison, and in another the belle of her day had been forced into marriage to a senile duke who had already buried three wives and who was soon able to bury a fourth and find a fifth. All those unhappy people had had greater troubles than Isabel's, and they were dead with them, and she was still alive to deal with hers and perhaps overcome it. And overhead, moving about at that very moment in the top cells of this splendid empty honeycomb, was a man who lived a lonely inhuman distortion of life that made her almost hug her human troubles to her heart. It was better, far better, to be bad than mad.

She went slowly down the stairs again, round to the terrace, and along the terrace to Yves's room. She did not remember till she was opening the glass doors the discovery that she had left on his table to confound him. But it did not seem to matter much now, and she entered the room without pause.

Yves and Henry Dolphin were just going out of the room; they looked back when they heard the glass doors open and close. Yves's face was sallow with pallor. The portfolio and the manuscript were gone from the table. She met his eyes recklessly.

He did not speak, however, and Henry took a diffident step or two towards her and hesitated, not sure what he wanted to do. The last time they had seen each other, they had shaken hands and he had wished her good luck and she had said, "Thank you very much, Mr. Dolphin," but since then he had written her a letter with postscripts. She said, "Hullo," and he grinned and said, "Hullo . . ." He looked sprawly and faded after the dark definite French people that she had become used to seeing; he looked out of place and seemed to feel it. She remembered his sunless, grey-green office, bare and spare and a little innocent and awkward in its striving for an effect. Even on a rainy February morning, this room was sun-coloured and relaxed, easy in its elegance, gracious and spacious and golden.

Yves had gone. "It's time for lunch, I think," said Isabel, glancing at her watch. Henry held the door open. As she passed him, he said vaguely, "You're looking very well," but he added as their footsteps echoed through the empty rooms, "No, as a matter of fact you look awful."

She laughed. "I hardly slept last night," she said, and went on quickly, "The storm kept me awake."

"Was it much of a storm?"

"Just windy, you know."

"I hate wind myself," he said, and they crossed the passage and the hall in silence and entered the drawing-room, where Jeanne was still giving an amazed and delighted welcome to Yves, who soon quelled her enthusiasm with short answers, fretted beyond measure by a humour so out of tune with his own. She remembered having met Henry before, and they reminded each other of the occasion. Then she said, "My brother is a little late," and there was silence except for the thin spatter of rain on the window-panes, the rustle of the fires on the two hearths, and the sharp ticking of the gilt-and-marble clock that stood on the ebony lowboy. The two wings of the door into the dining-room were barely ajar; through the crack Isabel could see Arnaud standing at the sideboard, quietly watching some activity at the invisible table.

Then the Duke came in and caught her eye and made her a secret grimace of harassed disgust. "So here you are again, Yves," he said blankly, not bothering with apologies for his lateness, probably not conscious of it, and she watched him shaking hands with Henry as if she had never seen him in the flesh before—and that was nearly the case. He had been to her really no more than a living portrait in a frame, the portrait of a duke, the portrait of a father, to be freely admired and adored by her, with never a danger of any three-dimensional conflict or collision between them; and her dream had been to join him in a frame of her own, as the portrait of a daughter. But last night the frame had vanished—it had always been an illusion, but the illusion had vanished—and he had become as real as she was, a vulnerable beset human being, a man privately thinking and feeling, not aloof and lofty in a frame, but moving in the same maze that was bewildering her.

There was not a great deal of conversation at lunch. Jeanne asked Henry what he thought of Yves's history; he said that he had not read it yet, but professed a great eagerness to see it, perhaps on the decent principle of paying for his lunch. Isabel thought of the two typescripts that she had burned and minced into black ashes with a poker. She glanced sidelong at Yves, who sat beside her. She had no idea of doing more than she had done, but she caught in herself a hint of a desire that he should affront her again, because now she had a way of paying him back. He had flushed and grown pale again. He stared at his plate and made a modest non-committal answer; and Henry, playing the same game, as he thought, said something encouraging, to which Jeanne hopefully took exception on Yves's behalf. Henry then said more than he meant and immediately regretted it; and Jeanne was more delighted and proud than ever. The lunch was good. The food was good, the fire was warm, the service was careful. But Isabel saw Henry beginning to wonder whether or not he owed it to himself to take offence at his host's silence. It always put him a little off balance to say more than he meant.

He sat like a sack, Isabel thought; all the life in him was concentrated in his intelligent grey eyes. When he spoke, his words were sometimes underlined by a smile or the absence of a smile, or pointed by a change of expression about the eyes, but never by small exact gestures of the hand, an almost imperceptible alteration in posture, a tilt of the head, a movement of the shoulders, a sudden stillness. . . . Beside her, Yves sighed and relaxed. He had seen his way. "I want to talk to you, after lunch," he murmured. She did not answer. Her calm was wearing off; the strange panic of the morning was looming over her again, simply because everything she saw or heard or thought of brought her back to one person, who had become the measure, the point of reference, the comparison, the standard, the magnetic centre, the heart of her life; and that load of involuntary concentration was hard to carry with an even step.

When lunch was over, as they all moved irresolutely through the drawing-room, Yves came up behind her and took hold of her arm, saying coolly, "Come along. Jeanne will take care of Henry."

"I've nothing to talk to you about," she said, turning to face him in a way that freed her arm, and promptly moving on as soon as it was free.

"You've questions to ask, I should imagine. And I've answers to give."

"Not to me. It's none of my affair," she said contemptuously.

"But I said I want to talk to you," he said, and there seemed to be a smile in his light voice. "You will do as I ask, please."

She shook her head and was immensely surprised when he took

hold of her arm again in a pinching way that was meant to hurt her and did. His trivial face was tight with anger, the silly anger of weightless authority defied. She gave him an amazed stare as she jerked her arm free once more and moved away from him; and when he came after her again, his hand outstretched, she felt so indignant at being pawed about in this fashion by someone she despised that she struck his hand down and backed towards the door, past Jeanne, watching open-mouthed, and Henry, who looked astonished; and the colour was high in her face as she saw that the whole incident had been observed. She pushed the door shut behind her; it opened again at once, but she did not glance back till she had reached the outer door, and then she saw Yves pettishly trying to shake himself clear of his cousin as he cried, "But she must listen to me—she must hear me—" She went out into the cold, grey, drippy afternoon, rather sick with a mixture of emotions. The chilly air felt good; and it was good to feel hard stone underfoot and the openness of sky overhead.

"Isabel," the Duke called behind her, and she controlled a momentary impulse to run, and waited for him to overtake her. He carried an extra coat, which he dropped carelessly over her shoulders and absently adjusted as he said, "It's all too much to bear, I know, that sort of thing, after last night. But do try not to irritate him, all the same, will you? He can be so difficult. And you're in a mood to go to extremes—your nerves are on edge. And he might not take it well."

"I'm not afraid of him."

"I know that. But I am." She looked up at him quickly. He was not looking at her, he was busy with the coat, and his dark face was all one complicated despondent scowl. "And how I should have loved a little peace and quiet for a while," he said, putting the collar of the coat straight, "after last night. . . . All right. Listen to me."

"I know, I know . . ." she said uncertainly, and then she took a step backwards. "No, I've got to quarrel with him if he quarrels with me. I've got to stand alone in it. It's between him and me. But I don't want to stir him up. I just want him to leave me alone."

"I know I shouldn't interfere."

"You have every right to, of course, but . . ."

"Have I?" he said, looking at her, and his eyes grew puzzled, as if he saw in her face or felt in her manner something that he could

[151]

not quite understand. She busied herself putting on the coat that he had so carefully arranged as a cape. He said, "All right. . . . But there's one thing you might do for me. There's a man who's just come outside, an Englishman, I think. He seems to be cleaning his shoes against the steps at the moment—odd thing to be doing: was there mud inside? But he's got his eye on you. Beckon to him, give him a kind word; he looks so forlorn."

She was baffled for a moment; then she made a shrewd guess. "And that will keep me out of dear Yves's path for a while?" she said, relieved by that idea in spite of herself.

"I hope so," he said, laughing, but his eyes were tired. "I hope so. . . ." He walked on through the archway towards the stable yard and his office.

She turned and waved at Henry, who lifted his hand and came quickly towards her across the grey satin-wet stones of the pavement. "Have you a moment?" he said. "Are you free? Because I thought you might be kind enough to show me round the château a bit—I'm only here for this one day, you know; I go in the morning." Though he smiled briefly, his face remained serious, almost stern, and he fidgeted uneasily about as he spoke.

With her hand out, palm up, she indicated the archway in silence, and they went through it into the deserted, weather-beaten beauty of the central courtyard, the pale colonnades, the rippling steps, the well, the great circle of sallow lawn. It was reassuring to be there with him, he was so not in the spell of those things, they were so careless of him. "Here we see," she began rather cheerfully, "the great well of the Château de Ferronçalles," but he shook his head and said, "I don't care for wells, somehow. Let's go inside," and he stalked across the grass and up the lovely steps without even noticing them, pushing open one wing of the tall old door and continuing on up the stairs inside without taking notice of anything. "I didn't come here to see Yves's rotten manuscript," he said, climbing steadily upwards. "That was just an excuse for seeing you."

"And now that you've seen me, what's on your mind?"

"I think you had better get out of here," he said roughly.

"What on earth do you mean?"

"Don't let's ask what on earth do I mean and all that; it's such a waste of time, isn't it? I mean I regret like the very devil and all sending you here. It was the mistake of the century, and I feel responsible."

He left the stairs at the top of the first curving flight. "This is the guardroom," she said.

"I don't care if it's the guardroom or the chapel or the chief withdrawing-room for retired chimney-sweeps, I want to know what is the situation here?"

"Honestly, I don't know how to answer that. It's too large a question!"

"What was wrong with Yves? What was he trying to do to you?"

"Just trying to bully me a bit, that was all. It was nothing," she said cautiously.

"But why should he want to bully you? What's been happening? What's it all about?"

"I don't know what you *mean!*"

He pressed his lips together. Then he said, "I'll put it simply. . . . You must know that you're enough like the Duke to be his daughter, a most astonishing resemblance, I had no idea. . . . Well, what has he done about it? How has he explained you?"

That was not quite the simple statement he had meant to make; he had drawn back at the last moment from the obvious truth, afraid, she realized, that it was a sore subject for her—her illegitimacy. But her answer was the answer to everything, said and unsaid. "You don't understand how things are done in a place like this. He hasn't explained me at all, he doesn't have to. Why should he?"

"Good God! Isabel, the servants, for one thing. Do you think they haven't noticed that you're the image, the absolute image—"

"No, but you don't understand! They would no more show anything—why, he could bring in a dozen girls every one of them his mirror image and no one would even blink. Or at least they'd blink and that's all. They certainly wouldn't demand explanations. If he ignored these images, they'd be ignored by everyone; if he treated them civilly, everyone would treat them civilly. That's all."

After a moment he said, "I think I feel a little sick. I mean, that you accept that sort of I-am-the-Lord-God-Almighty arrogance and total lack of innate decent awareness of other people's natural feelings without the slightest show of surprise or indignation or— For God's sake, Isabel, where has it gone, that Sarah Siddons pride I loved so well?"

[153]

She saw that remark fly past her and did not even think, Look into it later, being wholly occupied by the first part of what he had said. "I think this is very strange of you, when he's been so civil to you and you're, after all, in his house—"

"Oh, Isabel," he said.

"Now what is it?"

He walked across the old bare brown tiles of the floor to windows smeared and a-trickle with cold rain and stood there with his back to her, looking out, tall and slack, arms hanging loose, fingers limply curled, shoulders unexpressive; but in his head his brain was busy. "It wouldn't make any difference to me, you know," he said at last. "It doesn't."

"What?"

"You know. If it's true—if it were true. It's nothing to do with you, and it's nothing to me."

"In what way?"

"Don't tease me," he said simply, and she felt sorry, but she also felt unjustly rebuked, because she was not really sure that she knew what he meant. "Shall I say it straight out?"

"No. . . . This is rather a chipped-looking sort of room, isn't it? It's had hard use. . . . Round the chimney-pieces specially . . . people kicking their heels here on rainy days like this one, gossiping about old campaigns, I imagine them . . ."

"The mistake of the century," he said, staring out of the window. "Why did I do it?"

"I've wondered why myself."

"Oh, it seemed a rather good joke on Yves, that's all. I think that was all."

"And a rather good joke on me?"

He stood very still. "I really do feel a most enormous contempt for myself," he said finally without turning.

"I didn't mean that—it was just a—a stab in the dark—"

"Very much a stab. And very much deserved." He turned to face her. He looked pale and angry.

She said, "I mean, a shot in the dark."

He paid no attention.

"But I didn't plan anything like this, believe me. I thought Yves would be mildly . . . irked . . . to find himself with a secretary who looked like a relative—possibly an unexplainable sort of relative—I didn't *think* it was unexplainable, I thought it all perfectly legitimate—oh, God. You know what I mean. I only hoped he'd be a bit annoyed—he's always been so hot on the subject of his very blue blood, forever making these casual references to the Duke his grandfather and the Duke his cousin, never letting anyone forget for a moment that he was Yves d'Ayz de Ferronçalles with a pedigree as long as I don't know what— I didn't dream there'd be this fantastic Duke to get mixed up in it. Believe me. Or that there *was* a—" He stopped, angry with himself. "He is your father, isn't he?" She shrugged her shoulders, and a sudden shiver ran over her. "And was he glad to see you?"

"Not awfully, at first."

"But is it all right now?"

She did not especially want to answer that question, but quite apart from that her mind seemed to slip and skid past it like a gearwheel with cogs missing, and she said instead, as if it were an answer, "Should people tell the truth, do you think?"

"Depends on who to. To whom. Whom to." But while he played with that, his eyes were fixed anxiously on her, his mind was all on what she might be going to say.

She meant to speak out boldly; she found herself rambling off into the complicated background of her doubts—partly because she wanted the light of his experience on that, too, but partly, disgustingly, because she was afraid he would be disappointed in her. "I mean," she said, "polite people don't talk about some things, hoping they'll go away if they aren't noticed, it seems. . . . No, it's different with *him*. . . . He doesn't talk about them because he doesn't understand them and feels quite sure he can't. . . . He's quite comfortable with everything blurred—he takes things as they are. . . . But it isn't natural for me, do you see? I haven't been myself since I came. I mean, I don't talk about things because— because I've been afraid of what people would think. . . . I mean, that they'd despise me. I mean, I couldn't go round talking about how I was illegitimate and didn't know who my father was, because then they might . . . Well, you see. But at home my mother called me a bastard a dozen times a week. And she never pretended, except as a matter of cold policy. Never, I mean, because facing the truth made her uncomfortable."

She felt the encouragement that comes when a listener listens.

There was nothing but sympathy and attention and understanding in his grey eyes. "Well, you see, I think basically I like things outspoken and clear-cut too. If they come in question at all, I mean. At least, I think I have it in me to feel most at home with plain speaking. But it's . . . obscured. . . . I've picked up a sort of half-baked delicacy, a—a teashop refinement," she protested, huddling herself in her coat with an effect of shrinking within it, "that isn't the least bit natural to me. And I just don't know what really is done and what isn't. And I'm too much a coward to risk it. I mean, what about other people's secrets? What about things you find out by accident but that are bad? I mean, that they have no right to keep a secret?"

"I suppose it depends on what you'd gain by telling."

"I'd gain, all right. I'd lower somebody I want to see lowered. . . . But that's not the point!" she said, startled. "Or at least not the whole point. The thing is, I'm not sure it *is* bad, and I'd like to know. That's the main thing. I don't feel any burning desire to tell for the sake of telling, but I *would* like to know what it amounts to. You'd know, as a publisher."

Still watching her, he shook his head doubtfully, meaning that he could hardly commit himself yet, but smiled, as if to say that he was determined to make the best of her side of it. It was the friendliness in his eyes that made her turn and walk the echoing length of the guardroom and back, her arms folded, her head bent. He liked her, and that was what she could not risk. That was what she had never been able to risk—the affection that people might feel for her. But she no longer dared to be weak, even in a quarter where strength did not particularly matter.

She stopped by another window, a dozen feet away from Henry, and said, "Are you going to publish Yves's book?"

"I doubt it," he said, taken aback. "It doesn't sound our sort of thing at all."

"I found a set of notes for it, most complete, the arguments all summarized, and all the documentation. . . . It isn't his work."

Henry laughed aloud; and she was relieved and disappointed—and so was he, though not in the way she had feared. "How like him!" he said philosophically, but a moment later he had taken out his cigarette case to make time for a little unobtrusive consideration of the matter. He offered it to her, struck a match, put the case away, and went on holding the burnt match in his fingers, not liking to throw it on the floor. "It's between him and whoever did the research, of course. . . ." He laughed again, wryly, and shook his head. There was silence, and then she heard, or thought she heard, from somewhere above, the closing of a door. She moved uneasily, turned to look out of the window, putting her hands up against the cold glass, and the long ash of her cigarette fell back against her knuckles with a soft brief brush of warmth.

"Do you want to see the rest of the rooms?" she suggested. "There's a very beautiful oriel window we can see from the gallery. . . . And there's a perfectly grotesque chimney-piece, all cupids and lilies and roses in marble, dainty and charming, and weighing, I suppose, a few hundred tons. . . ."

"I suppose I ought to," he said absently, "since I'm here. . . . I shall probably never be here again. . . ."

They went out and shivered on the gallery, looking at the window; they came in again and looked at the marble cupids; they strolled through the frescoed rooms; and he made intelligent comments and asked questions she could not answer—the answers were not in the lecture of Arnaud's wife. And at last he said, "But what's the future for you here? Why should you stay here to be bullied?"

"Oh, Yves is not here very much. . . ."

They started down the stairs. He was wiping his fingers on his handkerchief; he had been doing a great deal of touching of old stone. "But I mean to say, why stay? Your position here can't be so very— Is it? Because I must say you don't look happy, or sound happy. . . ."

"Where would I go?" she said lightly, trying in her mind the feel of retreat, sudden soft empty retreat.

"Come back to London," he replied just as lightly. He stopped on the third step from the bottom and looked at her.

But she went on down to the hall, ninety feet long, forty feet wide, with every inch of the walls and ceiling as intricately ornamented as a Victorian teapot. "This is a bit better than a bed-sitting-room in London, isn't it?" she said ironically. "And besides . . ."

"But what do you hope to gain?"

She turned furiously to face him. "Nothing!" she cried. "Why talk like that? Nothing! I'll leave empty-handed when I leave!"

He was dismayed. "But I didn't mean—"

"And can't you see that I might feel some loyalty towards him? He did take me in, he did let me stay. I can't just walk out on him and never know what happens to him. . . . I can't just creep away. . . ."

"No, certainly not," said Henry smoothly and bitterly. "You must say good-bye as you go, or he might not notice that you've gone." She looked up at him, her troubled anger lost in astonishment. "Strolling in like that without a word of apology, and not a squeak out of him all through lunch. . . . Living in this absurd grandeur, with never a care, letting you fend for yourself as best you might all those years," said Henry mildly, glancing about as he spoke. He might have been pointing out defects in the design of the room, except that his quiet voice was quite unlike the brisk, bellicose tone that he used for such matters. "Openly scowling at you when he did deign to come to lunch—yes, I saw that. But you can't talk of him without sounding so far gone in idolatry that—"

Automatically, without thinking, out of habit, she said the one thing that could have jolted him: "Mr. Dolphin!" The words seemed to echo far away to his grey-green office in Bedford Street and back, but the effect was not comical, only strange, bewildering. He turned and walked away. She was abruptly not angry with him, and she could not have said on oath whether it was because she wanted to keep him on her side or was sorry for him. But all her anger, old and new, had gone. "Those windows are locked," she said gently. "We shall have to go round if you want to go out on the terrace."

"All right," he said.

It was getting dark; the February dusk was closing in, hastened by the heavy clouds in the sky. They walked side by side along the cold, wet terrace and entered the warmth of Yves's room. No one was there, but someone had lately been there; the smell of cigarette-smoke was fresh. It was softly lighted by a splendid fire, several good-sized logs flickering and glowing on a thick bed of hot ashes. She took off her coat and dropped it over a chair.

"Madame de Varaisne promised tea in the drawing-room," said Henry. "But I expect it's too late for that now."

"It is late," said Isabel, looking uncomprehendingly at her watch. "Perhaps not too late."

"She's such a nice creature."

"Isn't she? . . ."

"Don't you think so?"

"Yes, certainly. . . ."

"I met her husband once, years ago."

"What was he like?"

"Short, broad, vulgar-looking. A buffoon. A real clown—rather embarrassing. His speciality was imitating barnyard animals."

"Really?" said Isabel, profoundly and obscurely shocked.

"I suppose it's hopeless saying I'm sorry. But I am," he said with the same air of making polite conversation.

"For— Oh . . . oh, that's all right. You don't know him as well as I do. It's not like that at all, but you couldn't know." She put her hand to her head, pressing her finger-tips into her hair. "I don't know him very well either, but he's been very good to me, and I love him very much."

"Of course," said Henry. "It was stupid of me." He watched her for a moment. "Does your head ache?"

"No, I'm just tired." She walked to the fire and looked down at its busy flames, put her back to it, and felt its primitive warmth. But it was a very civilized room that she surveyed from there. The looped-up curtains had been released; they hung in long yellow silken folds, shutting out the dark; firelight fell softly against them and traced the graceful outlines of furniture in the shadows. She said hopelessly, "And I don't know what to do. . . . I don't know what to do. . . ."

"What is it? What's gone wrong?" She shook her head. "Oh, see here, you simply must come back to London with me. Come back to Paris with us, and then come to London with me. Please come back with me. You'll be happy with me, I promise you that. You won't have a thing to worry about. I'll take care of you. . . . Oh, God, I'm making it sound like some sort of—of nefarious proposal —I meant, as a wife, you know. Oh, God!"

All London rose up behind his slack, grey-clad figure, all London and the sagging windows and discreet literary displays of the firm in Bedford Street. She almost smelled the morning fog and soot and heard the hurry of traffic. And all that was asking her, incredibly, to marry it. "Was that why you came?" she said.

"I didn't think so, but it must have been. Yes. Please. . . ."

[159]

"Oh, don't," she said, "please don't. Don't admire me, please don't fall in love or anything like that. . . ."

"But I have," he said hurriedly and shyly, forcing himself along the path of his desires. "I did, long ago. I must have done. That's what I meant—despising myself. Because I couldn't face up to it, I got panicky, like a schoolboy, all without knowing in the least what I was about. And sent you away, instead of— Oh, I loathe myself, I do indeed. Darling, you look so astonished. You knew, you must have known. Women always do know. You must have suspected."

"I didn't." The weight of the day dropped on her; she moved as if to move away from it, and it came with her, and she stopped, facing the door of the little stairway that corkscrewed up through darkness to the distant apartments of Barnabé, who was out of his mind, mad, insane, dangerous. . . . "And if I had, it isn't the same, to suspect and to know. To think of a thing and to come up against it. Nothing's real till it happens, and then one has to go back and do one's thinking all over again. And some things can't be thought about at all, it seems, except before, when they aren't real, and that doesn't do much good."

"What's wrong? If you'd just tell me what's wrong—"

"Just don't be in love with me, please, please. . . ."

"Oh, Isabel. . . ." Then he laughed dryly. "I know," he said, beginning to pace, hands in pockets. "After what I did. And after that long history of making you run up and down those frightful stairs and standing over you interrupting you when you were busy and being unreasonable and inconsiderate. That's it, isn't it? I know. Being in this most romantic château by firelight at dusk doesn't change that, does it? And those brutal things I said that day. Oh, God. . . . But it ought to be all different now, for you as well as for me. It's so different for me," he said seriously, and a door opened in the panelling of the fireplace wall and Yves came into the room, smiling.

"I heard every word!" he cried gaily. Perhaps he thought he was carrying the situation off. He was dressed for dinner, and he looked very debonair and exact in black and white, with his brown hair brushed smoothly off his large forehead. His eyes were bright with mischief. He could always ride away from his own worries for a while on the back of other people's embarrassments.

"You listened?" said Isabel.

[160]

"My dear child, if you will choose my own private study to shout your secrets in—"

"What were you doing in there?"

"But in there is my bedroom! Why should I not be there?"

"Your bedroom?"

"Where did you think I slept? Here on the hearth-rug?"

"I never thought about it," she said, marvelling at her failure to do so. She had never given enough thought to him, it seemed. She had never wanted to waste thought on him, and now he was mixed up in everything.

He looked at her quizzically, inquiringly, then he turned to Henry, who had made his face a mask but whose eyes showed his suffering, his humiliation, his rage. "My dear old chap, we must talk about this a bit."

"I don't really think it need be discussed," said Henry politely, moving towards the door. "At least, not with you."

Isabel sat down at the table and put her head in her hands. Her whole body ached with tiredness. "I don't think he heard much," she said. "We didn't shout."

"Thank you for that; you are sweet," said Henry, going out, closing the door carefully behind him, but Yves opened it at once and followed him, saying, "But on the contrary, it must be discussed, you know," and the door closed again.

She felt very glad to be alone. She stroked her forehead slowly, pushing her hair back from it. The rosy gloom had deepened, the colours of the room were as delicate as ghosts of colours, and its ornaments glinted with subdued reflections of firelight. The stillness was deep and comforting; it seemed as if Henry had taken every thought and emotion that concerned him with him when he went and had left her truly alone.

At least she did not find herself thinking of him or the strange unexpected things he had been saying. Instead, she wondered what her father would be in ten years' time if she went away; and the last inches of indecision narrowed and disappeared between her and the knowledge that she could not stay, loving him as she did, and hating Yves, whom he felt he had to pacify. He would go on as before, being book-keeper and steward to an estate and warden to a lunatic who was quite harmless almost always but now and then would try to murder him. He would ride out in the morning, spend the afternoon in his hot, dusty little office, dine in silence, and go to bed to wake to a new day like all the others. He would be serious again, he would sink back into his vague, constant meditations, he would forget the pleasure of laughter—it is one of the easiest things in the world to forget. He would forget even the sound of laughter, because the people he lived with measured their moods by his—no one would laugh unless he did, and he would not. There was no tragedy in it; he was still a duke, when all was said, and that was something; but she thought her heart might break over it, all the same.

And she wondered why he lived as he did, lonely and alone, and what reason he could have for fearing Yves and despising him, yet never hating him as one hates an enemy one has earned. But she was too tired to think; her brain would not work in that way. She could only see, with a hallucinatory clearness, the life that she was going to leave, that she somehow seemed already outside of.

She seemed to stand in the fields beyond the river, looking up at the castle, seeing lights along the top floor above the terrace where the lunatic sat at supper, and lights two stories down and to the right, where his young first cousin once removed sat with her head in her hands, too tired to stir; she stood in the village street and saw evening lights in the kitchens, where there would be savoury smells and sounds, sputterings, cracklings, vapours rising, warmth, busy movement; she floated in the cold dark sky and saw the whole great mass of masonry outspread below her, a precise geometry of stone fine in detail from afar, with other lighted windows glowing here and there, with small threads of smoke rising ceaselessly from its chimneys, small in the distance, dwindling as distance grew.

Yves came back. He was very merry; he was quite on top of the world. "And so he is in love with you," he said, giving her a glittering sidelong glance of amusement as he closed the door behind him. But there was also admiration in his eyes, and respect, and interest. "Henry Dolphin, of all people! . . . And, poor chap, he is one who has to change gears for it."

"I don't know what you mean by that," she said slowly.

"To put it another way, he is one who has to set down everything he's carrying in order to pick it up."

She thought for a moment, too weary to do anything but let her brain go where it was led, and then she said, "Isn't that customary?"

"Among the English, you mean? Perhaps. They make bad husbands, by the way, it is only fair to warn you. Because they either make the parcel so small and neat that they can carry it with other things after a while, or they set it down again and only pretend they have it. Pretend to everyone, themselves included. They are such hypocrites. Oh, you have so much to learn. There is so much you can learn from me, honestly. And now you will be told all about that puzzling portfolio."

"No." She shook her head. "It isn't puzzling. I don't want to know. You bought it or stole it, I don't care. It's no affair of mine." She pushed her finger-tips hard against the roots of her hair above her forehead and shut her eyes. "I just don't care."

He came close and put his hand on her shoulder. "What's wrong? Tell me."

"Please don't touch me!" she cried, getting up and away from him so brusquely that she tipped the elegant little chair over. "Don't *touch* me!"

"What's wrong with you? What's happened? What's wrong?" He picked the chair up. And she watched him set it straight and then sat down in it again. "What's wrong?"

"Just go away," she said, "leave me alone. I can't stand the sight of you or the sound of you."

"And now you are being rude," he said absurdly. She laughed. "And it is *not* funny! Isabel, you must not be rude to me, you must not, it's not nice!" She laughed again. He flushed. "Isabel, you are being very tiresome. And that is very foolish, in a hundred ways. It is not intelligent of you. Because, remember this, if I should say only one word to the Duke my cousin, you know, one word—"

She was ready for that. She put her hands flat on the table, leaned forward, looked up at him, and said with an intensity that would have convinced the most nonchalant soul in the world that she meant it, "If you tell him that, I will kill you. I will kill you."

He frowned, tilting his head towards her so that his forehead was more than ever prominent, and his blue eyes widened. Then his face relaxed in comprehension. "So it's true now?" he said warily. "So you would not swat the insect today for saying it?"

"I don't know if it's true or not," she said in a sudden weak ap-

[163]

peal for pity that she hated herself for making and abandoned, with an effort that exhausted her a little more, as soon as she had made it. "No, whether it's true or not, it's no concern of yours."

"Poor little Isabel!" he said, and he seemed to mean it. His face had flushed again, and he moved uneasily, like a moored boat tugged by conflicting currents. He turned his back on her at last and stood gazing at the glowing fire. She heard the click open and the click shut of his cigarette case, and then the scrape of a match against the side of a box—he had used only matches this visit, he had not replaced the lighter, which showed something about him, something nice. Then he said lightly, still with his back turned, "But you would kill me."

"Yes," she said, "I would."

"I wonder, do you have any idea what prisons in this country are like? What trials are like, for that matter? The relentless prosecution, the hostile eye of discovering justice upon you, the secrets of your whole life opened to the world while you stand where the world can watch you and speculate on every quivering change in your face— No, you mustn't say such things, all the more because you haven't the least idea in the world what you are saying."

He was silhouetted against the fire, his head bent, his forearm resting on the mantel; the only moving thing was the fluent grey smoke twisting away from his cigarette. Above him, the dim, hushed greens of the painting opened a window into a forever lost summer-time. "I wouldn't care what happened afterwards."

"Of course you'd care," he said, still not turning, which was unusual of him because he liked to see the faces of the people to whom he talked. "You must not talk like this."

It was the continuing pity and the coaxing benevolence in his vibrant little voice that she hated most. "Have I frightened you?" she asked. "Good. Then you will hold your tongue."

He turned to face her, and his handsome face was very earnest. "Isabel, I beg of you. . . . Now, listen to me. . . . Perhaps, you know, it's not so bad. Tell me—"

"You prying little monkey. . . . Stick to keyholes. Go away," she said, really longing to have him go.

"The fishwife guise again," he said, and he sat down in a small arm-chair near the fire and crossed his legs, arranging himself in an attitude of careless elegance, as if to show how inwardly easy he was. Firelight edged him and sparkled on the gold of the chair.

"Then I'll go," she said, bracing herself to rise, but she felt as weak as water and she was not at all sure that she could get to her feet.

"Stay there, please. You try to destroy every impulse of kindness that I feel towards you. You won't take warning. You behave as if I were nothing—"

"You are nothing."

"When I hold your future in my hands?"

"I warned you I would kill you. I meant it."

He smiled and shook his head and tossed his cigarette into the fire. "You meant it, perhaps, a little the first time. You've meant it less every time you've repeated it. And in any case," he went on, relaxing still more, "I haven't and hadn't the faintest intention of making use of that sordid little truth. For one thing, it makes me rather sick to think of it. For another, I don't need it."

She felt sick, too, as if a glass had been turned towards her in the dim, unsteady light to show her something horrible that was herself. "You threatened to—"

"You misunderstood me. I did not have that in my mind at all. Your guilt betrayed you, it seems." He liked the sound of that; it satisfied him; he let a pause underline it. "No, I was only trying to warn you, before things came to such a pass between us that there was no remedying our difficulties, that I do count for something in this household. We began badly. It was deceptive. You saw me commanded to remove you. And you saw me, terribly upset as I was by the suddenness of your appearance, apparently agree to obey. And so you concluded that I counted for nothing. But you were wrong. I concurred wholly in that decision, and also in the later decision to let you stay. But now I think a new disposition of you may have to be made."

She shook her head.

"Yes," he said confidently. "My cousin will listen to me. He does not despise my advice, my judgement, though he is a duke and I am the son of a younger son. If I say, Send Isabel away, he will send her away. Yes! He will! And if I say, No allowance, there will be no allowance. Yes! And then you need not look to me for help, because I have not a penny of my own. I have nothing but what he gives me—yes! You did not know that, did you? It is his house in Paris that I live in. It is his rich income that supports me. Oh, I am not negligible with him. Far from it. . . . Why do you suppose he has never married? Because I have always advised against it. There you are. He will do what I suggest. He always has. You see?"

"I see," she said. She noticed that her lips were dry, and there was a pulse beating heavily somewhere in her head. It was annoying; it made it difficult to think; it made it even a little difficult to see. There was a kind of darkness above her eyes, not in the room, but in her mind.

"Yes," said Yves, "all his little economies that puzzle everyone so—his little reputation as a miser—what is behind that? Me!" he laughed.

The darkness thickened. "And you dared to hint that he was—" She picked up the weapon at hand, a pair of very long and pointed paper-scissors, and went for him.

He was as white as paper when the brief struggle was over. He was panting; and he looked as if he were going to be sick; his lips were grey and wrinkled. The stuff of his beautiful coat was torn over a breast pocket; her left wrist was bleeding from a shallow gash; the scissors lay a few feet away on the pale flowered rug. After a moment he stooped and picked them up and took them out on the terrace and came back without them, wiping his hands on the sides of his coat without seeming to know that he was doing so. They had been pretty scissors, blue steel blades and gold handles, the gold engraved in a charming pattern of ivy leaves.

She stood intently smoothing the little torn flap of skin into place on her wrist, studying it. Without looking up from it, she said, "You ought to be crushed somehow, like a black beetle."

He cried out in a high, strange, desperate voice, "He's paying tribute, don't you see? Why shouldn't he? Don't you think he should pay for enjoying what's really mine? He's got the title that doesn't belong to him; should he have everything else as well?"

It is curious, but she recognized that as a lie; she heard it as a lie, and moreover as a lie that he had told more than once, but the significance of that for her did not become clear for some time. "A black beetle," she said, "and a lying black beetle as well."

"Listen to me—"

"Don't ever try to blackmail me," she said. "You won't have such good luck." She took out her handkerchief and bound it round her wrist, trying for a while to tie the ends in a knot with one hand, then giving up and tucking them under. When she looked up from that task, she was alone in the gentle light and soft colours of the tranquil, exquisite room. She glanced at her watch, and then she had to think for a moment before she knew what to do. The routines of life seemed strange to her; she had been outside them for a few minutes.

Then she pulled her sleeve down over the handkerchief and went out through the empty rooms, into the passage, and laboriously up the stairs, where the hanging lamp swayed and sent the shadows of its grillwork careening dizzily. She stopped on the twelfth step and tried to get hold of a memory that was stirring somewhere in her mind, tried to tease it up by hearing again Yves's high, frenzied voice, the false forcefulness of it, the hollow insistence of it. He would have made a better thing of his lie, she thought, if he had never believed in it himself. True statements have one sort of foundation, lies have another. They can both be solid; but when their materials are combined, the mixture is unstable. For one thing, she was utterly certain that the Duke would not want what did not belong to him. But there was also that note of false insistence in Yves's voice. It reminded her—at last she recovered her memory—of a little boy in the third grade at Wichita who would cry out, if he got into trouble at recess-time, that his father could lick any man in town, when everyone knew that his father, who had once won weight-lifting contests, had such a weak heart that he did not even dare spank his violent little son. . . . She went on up the stairs.

At the far end of the long, dim passage, Henry in a dressing-gown, sponge in hand, towel over his arm, was just opening the door of the bathroom; Céphise sat alertly at the next door to it, making an impatient noise in her throat, wanting admittance. Isabel went into her own room and closed the door. The fire was burning brightly, at its crest after a replenishing some time before; but the curtains were still undrawn, and there was no can of hot water. She turned back to the door and saw that screws had been ruthlessly driven into the fine panelling to fix a large clumsy bolt. The other door as well now had a bolt. She forgot what she had vaguely meant to do and shot both bolts, carefully, thoroughly.

A white light moved across the ceiling; the courtyard outside the window brightened. She went to the window and saw the powerful headlamps of a car moving through the archway; shadows lurched away from it as it came. Yves stood in the light of the headlamps, hatless and coatless, casting a broadening, angular shadow across the stones. The car stopped, Joël got out of it, Gilles came out of the house with Yves's hat and leather coat and gloves. Yves snatched them and tried to put on the coat, tried to put his arm in one sleeve with his hat and gloves in his hand, dropped the hat. Gilles picked it up and offered help with the coat; Yves swung away from him and managed to get it on by himself. He got in the car, Joël closed the door, and the gears made an ugly sound as they meshed; and the car turned in a tight circle, swaying outwards, and swooped for the sharp turn at the head of the ramp. Gilles and Joël looked at each other, moved their shoulders slightly, and went inside, unconcerned. Isabel remembered what her mother had said: *C'est un duc . . . vraiment. . . .* A duke in all truth. Or, a duke if the truth were known. It could be either. But she had believed what she said. She had believed it with all her heart. She had not lied. But Isabel's conviction was like a tree that had grown for years in a prevailing wind; it could not now suddenly lean the other way because another wind was blowing.

She had never in all her life felt so tired as now. She sat down on the bed, let herself topple sidewards as she drew her feet up, and fell into sleep as if someone had thrust her there.

First she dreamed of hammering, someone was nailing large iron bolts to the doors with heavy nails. Then the clamour was nearer and different, not hammering, something else, an enormous sound diffused through the whole room; and then the sound collected on the other side of the door and became by slow degrees someone knocking on the door, pounding on it, and calling her name.

Every bone ached as she sat up, and pain pulsated like a tiny bellows in her head, behind her eyes. The fire had become a quiet glow that reddened the room. She went to the door and pushed back the bolt; the door opened. She blinked in the hurtful brightness of the usual dim lamps. Jeanne stood there, and Jeanne's brother, her father, both in black, black harlequined with white, his white shirtfront, her white arms. "Bolts aren't perhaps such a good idea, after all?" he said pleasantly, which was a remark she could make no sense of. "Aren't you coming to dinner?"

[168]

The hurtful brightness faded to the soft bronze glow she remembered from other evenings. "I'm not hungry," she said, "I just want to sleep, if you don't mind. I'm so tired." The close, large two by the door framed small Henry far away hovering hesitantly at the top of the stairs.

"Isabel," said Jeanne anxiously, "tell him. It's true, isn't it? You know, you're very sure. . . ."

"Wait a moment," the Duke said, "let her wake up. Have you been sleeping?"

"Yes. . . . I'm so tired." Voices came distantly to her ears; motion had stopped; the passage in dim brown perspective might have been a sepia photograph of itself that she was seeing in a magazine. "I'm really not hungry. . . ."

"Mathieu," said Jeanne, "you have only to look at her—she looks just like you! Look at her!"

"You won't believe me?" he said to her angrily.

Their voices wrangled in the golden air like bluejays at sundown in autumn.

"How can I? She looks just like you! It's so obvious!"

"She looks like us all!"

"None of the rest of us are as dark, except—"

"Her mother was very dark."

"Then you know who her mother was!" she said with triumph.

"Of course I do! And it seems odd you haven't guessed; you knew the family, and there's a strong resemblance there as well," he said with exasperation. "The Miets. Henriette Miet."

"But then it *is* impossible, because Yves detested that girl."

"Oh, God. . . . Isabel, your friend, Mr. Henry Dolphin, has just . . ." In the soft bronze depth of air framed by his black sleeve and Jeanne's white arm, Isabel saw Henry turn his back and descend the stairs. The fair head sank lower and lower and disappeared. ". . . asking my consent, or approval—at least, not as head of the family, but as your father, which was startling enough. . . . I told him of course that he was mistaken . . . and that I thought you would settle such affairs without reference to my cousin. . . . He saw then that he must have misunderstood you—and then Jeanne went up in sky-rockets all over the place, and we waited for you to come down, but you did not, and Louise could not rouse you—"

He lifted his shoulders and let them fall, but remained watchful, suspended in expectancy. "He did misunderstand you?"

"My mother told me he was a duke. . . ."

"Why should she say that?" he said, puzzled, and his sister said eagerly, "There, you see! There!" and he cried out, "For the love of God, be quiet a moment and let me think!"

"A duke . . . if the truth were known," said Isabel, trying to enunciate the words clearly, but they thickened as she spoke them. She pressed her face against the hard, cool jamb of the door.

"That old story of the Italian ceremony?" he said doubtfully.

"But he would not tell that to Henriette Miet," said Jeanne indignantly. "He would not! You know that! He would never do such a thing!"

"My poor Isabel!" he said, touching her shoulder, and she turned without thought into the heart's ease of his arms as if it were a goal laboriously earned, closing her eyes gratefully against his black coat. Then she only heard his voice. The whole world became a peaceful darkness with a voice absently explaining—absently, as if other things, more important, more private, drew his thoughts away from what he said. But she did not worry about that.

"My parents, when they eloped to Italy—the marriage was not valid, because my father with his customary . . . well, never mind that. They married again, that was all. Yves found out about the first ceremony, when he was quite a child, and stupidly thought it had never been made right. . . ." He was silent for a second or two; when he spoke again, his thoughts and his words had come together, his voice was concerned. But she had hardly listened before, and she hardly listened now. She could not worry about it; she was too tired. "This must be quite awful for you," he said slowly, "my poor Isabel, my dear. I hadn't the least idea in the world that you had been so misled. I am too stupid to be allowed to live. I am a fool."

"But Yves knew the truth before he was twelve," protested Jeanne. "You know that! Because he came to you just after father died! And you went to grandfather at once, and you weren't quite thirteen, because I was ten. I remember it very well! So you see! It can't be that!"

"Then, ask him," said her brother wearily. "Don't take my word for it, ask him. He knows. We've talked of it often enough. Why do you resist so, why do you care?"

Time hung on the edge of a moment while two moments passed, then it moved again. "I don't care, of course," she said without expression. "Why should I?"

"Go down to our guest. We shouldn't leave him so long alone. . . ."

"Yes, of course."

"And, Isabel, come down, you too, and have something to eat, and you'll feel better. . . ."

Isabel touched her cheek to his hand on her shoulder and turned in a slow circle out of his arms. "I'm not hungry," she said, "not at all. I just want to sleep, if you don't mind. I hardly slept at all last night."

"Do you know where Yves has gone?" he asked quietly.

"I don't know."

"Are you all right? Would you like a headache powder?"

"I'm all right. I just want to go to sleep."

"All right. . . . Go to sleep. . . . Go to bed properly and go to sleep. . . . You knew, Isabel?"

"No, I didn't know. But I know now," she said, closing the door. She went gently over to the bed and lay down as she was, dragging the comforter over her, and the throb in her head dulled and grew distant, the room swayed up and swam down, the woodwork creaked, the glow of the gas oven lighted the shabby wainscoting, her mother said, "She belongs to no-man's land, that one," and she was asleep again.

Six

THE MORNING WAS CLEAR, fine, and clean, a lovely commonplace of white daylight, windswept and tidy; and her headache
was gone, and missing a meal made her feel rarefied and lucid. She
belonged to the fine clean day for a minute or two; she seemed
made of the same material. Then the stabbing random blows of
remembrance began, coming from this side and that, and the
wounds they made spread across her heart till all was dark and
heavy. She turned over and tried to retreat into sleep again but
could not, and at last she sat up and looked at her watch, which
was still running, though its spring was slack. It said eleven o'clock.
Her feet were cold in her shoes; apart from that she felt no discomfort at having slept the clock round and more, fully dressed.
Waking in the usual defenceless way, in fact, having to get out of
a warm bed and wash and dress shivering in a cold room, would
have been unbearable today, because her unarmed combat with remembering did not cease. She went through everything again and
again, with horror, with loathing, trying to accept it all, trying to
feel all she could feel and get it over with, but each remembrance
was still able to catch her unawares every time it returned, and it
would not stay, it was always leaving her to return with a new blow.
   Louise, who had, it appeared, been looking in at intervals all
morning, looked in again as she stood winding her watch at the
window, and came back in ten minutes' time with hot water and
breakfast. When she had eaten, Isabel bolted the door, washed herself, changed her clothes, unbolted the door again, and sat down
by the fire to wait for whatever was to happen next.
   She hardly knew herself now, she could hardly find herself in the

welter of her collapsed convictions and newly revealed possibilities. All that held her together was her hatred of Yves; and she dwelled on that, as if it were a raft in a flood. All the mysterious sense of wrongness that had shadowed the world for her had gathered together like the smoke in the Arabian tale to make the dark shape of an incubus, the incubus that was Yves. He hung on his cousin's neck like the old man of the sea, smiling and smiling, and talking, protesting, pleading in his odious voice, and pretending even to himself, it seemed, that it was a friendly bondage, but she knew it could not be that. She had seen the other side. She spread out her long, narrow hands with their long, tapering thumbs and studied them, and she saw that they trembled.

There was a gentle knock on the door; she called, "Come in!" and shut her eyes. But the poodle nuzzled her hand, and she opened them again. Jeanne had come in, dressed for lunch in a high-necked, many-tucked black wool frock with a matching jacket, a smart widow-like dress. "Isabel?" she said apologetically. "Are you coming to lunch?"

Isabel got to her feet. "No," she said, "I've barely finished breakfast—"

Jeanne smiled. There never was a more forced or a more earnest smile. She wanted very much to make it real, but the flesh has its own ways of resisting the spirit. "I see," she said, going towards the door, but at the door she paused. "Mr. Dolphin has gone. Joël drove him to the station this morning. . . . He asked me to say good-bye to you, and to say that he will write. . . . He's very nice. . . ."

"Has my dear father come back?" said Isabel, and the effort of saying it at all made her say it very loudly; and Jeanne's face wrinkled in a curious expression of pain.

"Yes," she said. "I haven't seen him yet—he has been with my brother. . . ." and she turned and went out, with Céphise clicking docilely at her heels.

Isabel waited ten minutes more, then she went rapidly downstairs and escaped outside into the glad sunlight. She met Joël in the archway. He was pulling a cart piled with wood from which he would one by one replenish the baskets beside every burning hearth in the house, carrying load after load, sweeping up, as he returned for a fresh load, the litter of bark and bits of twig that he had left behind him. And in the evening he would have it all to do over again.

She climbed the crumbling stairs recessed in the retaining wall at the north end of the main court and stared down at the court from the garden. From there, for some reason, the pale façades looked gaunt in their deserted stillness; the pillars of the colonnades seemed too thin to support a weight; the shallow curving cascade of steps was a useless relic. The whole majestic edifice was the bleached bones of a castle, nothing more. It really needed no ghosts; it was its own ghost; it haunted itself. It seemed the cradle and the tomb of much evil, and she would have liked to see sand blowing through it and lizards basking on its broken walls.

She sat on the stone coping, struck a match for a cigarette, and heard the stable clock strike once—a thin note, uncertain, compelled. She turned her back to the castle and looked to the north. She was Yves's child. It was no wonder that her cousin Mathieu had distrusted her, had resented her coming, had longed to be rid of her. It was Yves's child who had firmly forced herself on him, which was a memory that made her feel sick with shame now.

It was no good rebelling against the iron pattern of facts, but she rebelled. She had lost what she had never had, but she longed to have it back. She wanted her happy ignorance again; she even wanted her unhappy doubts. She had been safe with him as she would never be with anyone else, and now Yves had thrust himself between them and would be between them forever, and Yves was nothing. He was an incubus. He was a collector, stuffing out his emptiness with possessions. He was cousin to the Duc de Ferronçalles. Deprived of his treasures and his cousinship, he would be nothing, nothing at all. Even Jeanne had more substance than he had. She obstinately valued him for her own reasons; but he valued only what other people valued—a Rolls-Royce and fine clothes, works of art, a great name, friends in a circle envied by outsiders, a literary reputation, deserved or undeserved, it did not matter, so long as he possessed it. He was only a great flourishing cipher.

But he had a cipher's power to make a new sum out of things. That, though grossly unfair, was incontrovertible. If she could not accept the sum, she had to go away. And she could not accept it.

After a while she felt watched, turned round and looked down sidelong, and saw the Duke staring up at her. He looked grim, tired, and unhappy, and she knew that he must have heard what had happened on the night before. He beckoned in silence; she went with dread down the rough, steep steps to join him; and they went into the stable yard, where she was for the first time aware of a decided slope towards the grating of a drain at the centre; it made walking really rather awkward, but she had never noticed that before.

The air in the office was blue with the particularly nauseous smoke that comes from a smouldering ashtray; the stove was hot; she smelled dust and old papers. He began tamping out the embers in the ashtray with the end of a pencil, saying, "Well, you've roused the hornets' nest. He's told me what you did last night."

"What I tried to do," she said, sitting on the edge of the table and clasping her hands in her lap.

"No! I won't believe that! What you did."

"What I tried to do."

"Isabel," he said, tossing the pencil on the table and sitting down heavily in the wooden arm-chair, "face it bravely. He is your father. It's as disconcerting for me as for you, that you hadn't known this. It explains so much that puzzled me in you, but it . . . makes the past weeks dissolve like a dream," he said, rubbing the corners of his eyes, slanting them, which gave him a strange Mongol look, dark and tragic. "I don't know you. When you say things like that, I know you even less. What you did shocked him very much, and me as well, to be frank. . . . He is your father, and—"

She said with passion, meaning it with all her heart, "I'd rather it had been the madman!"

He looked up at her, and his thoughts struggled with some small knot of protest or frustration and mastered it as he stared. He sighed and began tapping his finger-tips in unison on the table-top. "And so should I," he said, "for that matter. Poor Barnabé's competency is not large, but it would permit a decent allowance for you—"

"I thought he had a great fortune," she said more quietly, regretting the difficulties she was making for her only friend in the world. She meant only to indicate a cessation of revolt, and his quick shake of the head in denial rubbed her wrong. "It wasn't *that*—" she said angrily, and she fell back into bitterness. "Oh, but of course it's natural you should judge me by my father. . . ."

"I'll judge you by yourself, if you give me the slightest opportunity of doing so," he said with exasperation. "Stop this—silly futile rebellion. . . . See what difficulties you've made! He was overwhelmed, appalled—he spent the night driving at random, trying to escape the horrid memory— At last he pulled the car to the side of the road and fell asleep in exhaustion. . . ."

"Good," she said, not despising him for his insincerity but decidedly taking notice of it. He looked impatient and sorry. "Habit dies hard, doesn't it? How I did try to please you! Sweet Alice. . . ." He was puzzled by that; then he gave it up, perhaps deciding it was some kind of quaint Kansas oath. "But that's how I feel. I won't pretend. I'm glad he was appalled. I wish he were dead."

"I wish," he said with an impatient jerk and hitch into a better position in the arm-chair, "that we might talk of this as we used to talk, without this silly defiance, this useless hostility. . . . Things are as they are. Can't you simply accept them?"

"I've no doubt it was a good deal pleasanter for you to have someone hanging adoringly on your words, all but swooning with gratitude at the smallest kindness. . . . What you want is a daughter."

"I don't think so, or you'd feel rather differently toward Yves now, wouldn't you?"

"Oh, my God!"

"Well, wouldn't you?" he said rather triumphantly, though very earnestly, and he seemed to feel that things were straightening out at last, that he had got at the root of the matter.

"It's hopeless," she said, regarding him curiously. "You don't see any difference between the two of you? You think I can turn round with the greatest ease and feel glad and proud to have a father who's been an incubus on your back for years and years, blackmailing you—"

"Yves told you that?" he said incredulously.

"He all but bragged about it." She felt a thin, cold tremor, involuntary, unreasonable, and somewhat frightening because it suggested depths of unexplored feeling that might get out of hand. "And I did my best to kill him for you," she said, and her hands began to tremble again.

"Was *that* why?" he said, as if he could not believe that anyone could feel murderous about that, and for the first time she really understood what it meant to have been brought up by a mother who never expected anything from the world that she did not earn with hard work.

And then she remembered the cigarettes that she had taken from Yves's writing-table merely because she felt she had been badly treated and so deserved them; she remembered the manuscript she had read because it invited reading; she remembered the use she had wanted to make of the set of notes in a strange hand. A profound wild terror of the power of heredity crawled through her.

"Why talk about it?" she said, standing up unsteadily. "No use talking about it."

He stood up too. "This air is making my head ache. I can't think. Come outside."

"I don't want to talk about it any more," she said, following him out into the fresh air. Sparrows were chirping everywhere in the mild sunlight. There were scents of hay and horses; the blue sky was serene.

"But unfortunately you must," he said, pinching a fold of her sleeve between his fingers to keep her from walking away, as she had meant to do, while he locked the door of the office. "Consequences must be faced."

She was close to the edge of hysteria again. She did not know that she was, but she was aware of a great desire to have nothing happen for a little while that would require any thought or action from her. She felt as tenuously balanced as the hairspring of a watch. "I don't want to face anything," she said, carefully trying to free her arm.

"But you must," he said sadly, letting her go and putting his keys away. She did not run. She stood very still, looking down at his wrinkled shadow on the cobbles. "Yves wants you out of here to-day. Arrangements must be made." She glanced at her watch without seeing the time and began to wind it and broke the mainspring. The winding stem turned without resistance. And all her tension was suddenly gone.

"I'm sorry," she said. "I'm making things difficult for you, a thing I never wanted to do, believe me. Don't feel you don't know me— I always meant everything I said to you, and mean it still. And if it explains about the great fortune—if you were a clerk in a shop, or

[178]

a bus conductor, or a waiter in a restaurant, I'd want to know you. And if Yves were a duke and the richest man on earth I'd still wish I'd never met him. Do you understand?"

He did not answer. He looked very thoughtful, very much interested, and slightly sceptical, like someone hearing his favourite fortune told. Then he turned his head this way and that, absently, and decided for the low wall at the south end of the yard, which overhung blue distances above river and far fields. "All the same, don't ever take things into your own hands again—in that way."

"That's as may be," she said, flushing angrily as she followed him. "Do you mind telling me how he can make you do whatever he wants?"

"No, I'd rather not," he said, disconcerting her for the second time. She had expected some expression of pleasure in response to her first speech, and she had expected him to answer her question without hesitation. They sat down on top of the wall, facing each other, two people in brown who looked very much alike and who had taken by chance the same position, one knee straight, one knee bent, hands in pockets. She took her hands out of her pockets, making an accidental thing of the change by leaning at the same time to look down at the little river, swollen and muddied by the rains, eddying sinuously against the wall far below. She faced him again in an attitude of her own, independent and wary. But it was no use. The mould of the facts had been knocked away, but the shape of feelings remained. She felt like his daughter; she loved him, admired him, and revered him; and he could scold her if he liked, and snub her: it made no difference.

"It was a great fortune once," he said. "It was a great fortune when Uncle Gondebaud made his will. But large sums went in straightening out family affairs—my grandfather's bad investments, and a lawsuit of his—even Claude got his share . . . Claude de Varaisne. . . . He propped us all up, Uncle Gondebaud, and got blessed little for it. . . . When he died, there was only enough to keep Barnabé comfortably in a private asylum, if that should ever become necessary, and there's not much more now. You understand that money's a difficulty. And at the moment Yves is quite anxious to see you starve—he's really very upset by what happened. I've spent the whole morning arguing with him, but he only got more obstinate. Finally he accused me of not caring that his life

[179]

had been threatened, which was funny enough!" He laughed. "As if I did care! As if I could! Only of course I did, under the circumstances. . . . But he is really a little more unaware than most of how the world sees him. He's always been the essence of comedy. . . . But I think I've laughed at him too much, perhaps, all my life. Laughter's no cure for other people's vanities and humiliations —only for your own. Isn't that true? . . . Well, he'll get over it, he always does; it will flicker out, his anger, and in the meantime I can easily manage a small allowance for you—"

"I don't want anything," she said, and immediately the state of her finances flitted through her mind: she had a pound note in her purse and about thirty francs left over from the expenses of her journey. She thought of being stranded in Paris, out of work, at the mercy of landladies who wanted their rent. "Perhaps a loan, till I can get work again—"

"Do let me decide that," he said, and she saw with surprise that his hands, now flattened on his knee, one on top of the other, were so taut as to be pale along the tendons. "It is abominable that he should want to send you out into the world unprotected, without a penny, whatever you've done. But he won't let you stay here—that notion enraged him more than any other. But he is adamant in all respects. He made me promise to do nothing for you, nothing whatever—a promise I have no intention of keeping. But you need not tell him that. As I said, a small allowance, perhaps fifty pounds a quarter paid through Barnabé's man of affairs in Paris— I'll arrange it as Barnabé, out of his funds, I mean, write the letter in his name, and straighten it out somehow at this end. You see, Yves goes through the books of the estate occasionally. You won't mind being a protégée of poor Barnabé? You need not. And it's all for the time being, you understand, till Yves finds a new interest. Barnabé's man of affairs will help you. His name is François Roubier. I'll give you his address before you go. I've never met him, but Uncle Gondebaud trusted him. He will help you find respectable lodgings. And if you live quietly, you should come to no harm. Can you do that? Go to Roubier with any problem? Take his advice? But, my God, you may have other plans! What of this Dolphin?"

But he laughed as he said it, and her quick shake of the head was only what he expected. "But I don't want an allowance."

"Then I shall go out of my mind with worry, I think," he said, and he looked as if he meant it.

"All right," she said, hating to say it, it was such a backing down.

He ticked it off on his fingers. "Roubier's address. Something to go on with, till the first quarter is paid. You can stay tonight in Tours— Joël will drive you there—just in case Yves should change his mind, when he feels the effect of what he's doing. . . . There's a very decent hotel in Tours; we've stayed there. . . . In the morning, if there's no help for it, I could come in and put you on the train— Yves need not know where I'm going. . . ."

It became real; and it came close. The sun was half-way down the sky, night was coming, and she would not, it seemed, be spending it in her own dear small room; tonight she would be out with strangers again in the great, cold, careless world.

"Yes, the wild bird flies away," he said, smiling a little, watching her. She looked at him quickly, not comprehending his meaning for a moment. His eyes were grave. "How I shall miss you!"

Swift, unexpected bliss filled her heart and sharpened in an instant to an edge of pain. A wild bird, he had said, and Yves had said, A leech. "Please tell me," she cried, "oh, please! I want to know. You can trust me. Why can he go through the books of the estate when he wants to, and watch over you, and dictate to you, and ride on your shoulders like the old man of the sea? Something could be done, I know it. It's all wrong. It's not fair. I know that something could be done."

"No," he said, "nothing can be done. It's not that I don't trust you; it's only that I don't even like to think of it—thoughts seem so easily guessed, sometimes. . . ."

"But I want to know, I have to know, I *must*— I can't go away not knowing; how can I?"

He looked down unseeingly, frowning, rubbing his hands slowly together as he listened to her urgings and pleadings. He did not want to tell, but he saw that he could not refuse without seeming to distrust her, which would have been more than she could have borne just then, and so he told, and she was sorry afterwards that he had, when she knew what a thin bubble of a thing it was, prickable by a word or two at no cost to her except the cost that it would be to him, because he was right—nothing could be done, except by someone as heartless, as shallow, as egocentric as Yves;

yet she felt tugged at by the temptation to act, because it would be so easy, because there was something so terrible about seeing a man in the noose of his own tenderness with the end of the rope in Yves's hands. She could free him by speaking; but if she spoke, he would never want to see her again, he would despise her just as he despised Yves, and with good reason.

He began by saying that it had happened long ago, that it was an occurrence not uncommon in the world, he believed, far less uncommon than one would like to think, and that he believed there had even been cases of small children taking the life of a brother or sister when they were too young to understand what they were doing; and she looked at him in surprise, alarmed by that beginning, which seemed to put the thing out of reach of remedies already, because it concerned children. "Yes, it will haunt you as it haunts me—not the deed, because that was nothing, it must be judged by the doer, but the long consequences. You see, Barnabé was once a very good little boy, a good friend, and kind-hearted, but he could be stubborn sometimes, as all children are, and one day he would not let my little sister play with a toy of his that enchanted her—it was a little carved wooden horse with a separate rider and tiny leather reins and little bells on the bridle that jingled, a thin little silvery sound—and he was afraid that she would break it. He was only five, but he was always very careful with his toys, and she was not yet four and apt to be a little hasty and rough. . . . She was extremely angry with him, and she sat brooding about it—she was always a tenacious child. She sat watching him as he lay on the floor, resting on one elbow, making the little horse move about; and suddenly she got up and picked up a croquet mallet and swung it at his head as hard as she could, to punish him. It was the merest chance that she hit him so squarely—she was not deft about such things. But he went over without a sound. . . . Yes, it is horrible, isn't it? But such things happen. We saw her do it, Yves and I— but we could not believe that she was really going to do it till it was too late. He was unconscious for almost five hours. We said— Yves and I—we said that he had fallen and hurt himself, we told our parents that, we were very much frightened for her, and somehow for ourselves, too. We burned that mallet, secretly, in great dread. . . . But it seemed that no harm was done. They put him to bed for a few days, and he seemed as good as new when he got up again. My sister was a little shocked by what she had done—shocked enough not to want to speak of it to anyone—and then, too, she must have felt that he had so deserved it. . . . But she soon forgot all about it, when Barnabé was up again, apparently as good as new. He was twelve or thirteen before it was thought that something might be wrong; he had moments when he could not seem to control himself, and he did not learn well, and his face was strange—stiff, unresponsive. But it passed for bad temper and slow wits—which was a great disappointment for his father—till he was seventeen and went for me one day with an axe. We are a stubborn family, hard to convince. Then his father called in specialists, and it was discovered that there was some sort of—what did they call it? Intercranial brain damage, an incurable deterioration. . . . The only thing in all his history that could account for it was the accident he had had as a child. The bad fall. The mark of that was still on his forehead."

The sun was not very warm any more, the shadows were longer. The shadow silhouette of stables, woodshed, and storehouses covered most of the yard, the rest was a close herringbone pattern of small round stones catching the sun and casting small shadows, but the west wing was in full sunlight, bone-white, dark-windowed.

"But who," she said, "who in the world could possibly blame her if Yves told that story?"

"He would only tell her, so that she could blame herself."

"But if you denied that it was true, if you told her it *was* a fall—"

"The danger is, you see," he said patiently, "that she will remember, when she is reminded."

"And you are sure that she does not remember?"

"How can I make sure? By asking her? Could I say to her, Do you remember that fine little boy, Barnabé? And do you remember giving him a terrible blow with a croquet mallet that changed him into the wooden-faced lunatic that he'll be for the rest of his life?"

Joël came through the archway for the second time pulling his cart; its iron-rimmed wheels made a great rumble on the stones; a horse whinnied inside the stable. Joël pulled the cart through the wide door of the woodshed and began filling it again; she heard each heavy log drop into it with a solid thud. "How he could want to use *that*," she said, because now she could feel only what Jeanne would feel if she knew, the weight of inescapable life-long responsibility for someone else's life-long tragedy. "How he can feel anything but . . . horror and pity. . . . I can't understand him. . . ."

"Does it pay, do you think, to try to understand people?" he said calmly. "Isn't it best just to accept them as they are?"

"But if he's my father! A liar, a blackmailer, *using* tragedy, utterly heartless, the worst kind of parasite—"

"No, no, think of him growing up here, knowing that I should some day inherit this estate and odds and ends of property here and there, and that Barnabé had a great fortune waiting for him, and that he had nothing to look forward to except what might be left of a settlement his father was rapidly wasting away. . . . I made the first offer, I thought it was so unfair. That may have begun it. And it grew, that's all."

It was always his one blind spot, the excuses he made for Yves. It was never hers. "A liar, a blackmailer, a parasite," she repeated, feeling the irrevocability of the past settle round her to draw her with it, body and soul, as it moved along its ordained path into the future. "And I can see him in myself—yes! I took those cigarettes, because I felt mistreated. I suddenly turned on him, just as he suddenly turned on me. And I wanted to threaten him with that book—that was my impulse, to blackmail him—yes, whatever the motive, to blackmail him. . . . And I wanted this castle as my background, just as he does—I couldn't stand alone and make my own way; no, I had to come here and find my great relatives, so that I would be someone in the world. . . . He's part of me, and all those others are part of me—the liars and fanatics and neurotics— What will I *be* in twenty years' time?"

"What you choose," he said indifferently, and indifference, or a show of it, was probably the best way of dealing with such a panic. "Do you think you're the only one in the world with some queer ancestors behind you? Fortunately there's such a thing as absolution from original sin," he said smiling, "and such a thing as free will. . . ."

The air was then so still, the cold silence so complete, that she heard from far away a train moving along the horizon, the distant low murmur of heavy iron wheels on iron tracks, far away and going farther through dusk to lighted stations where the Paris papers would be on sale and there would be telephones and the clicking of telegraph keys, and outside in the streets the noise of traffic, taxis and trams, people coming home from work or going out to dinner or to see a film. . . . She looked at the black-browed, sombre face of the man sitting beside her on the wall. He was listening to the sound of the train, too. He had been sitting relaxed, kicking one heel against the wall, breaking a match or something idly between his fingers; now he sat motionless, listening. The sound died away in the distance; Joël came out of the woodshed and crossed the yard, dusting his hands as he went; everything was shadow except the west wing, where sunlight still brightened the stones and gleamed on the slate roof, making it a landmark for the countryside, visible for miles.

"Things can seem natural here," she said, "that would be unnatural anywhere else. . . . I quarrelled with him so casually, I infuriated him without a thought. . . . I tried to kill him, as if he were nothing but a scarecrow stuffed with straw. But he's dangerous. People without hearts are dangerous. . . ." She leaned again to look at the drop from the wall. She saw herself fall, heavy skirt ballooning out, jacket flying, hair blowing upwards in the draught of descent. It seemed to her that from here she might be a sprawled figure about the size of her spread hand when she hit the water.

"It's the same world everywhere, I think," he said.

"What time do I leave?"

"Oh— After dinner, after dinner," he said angrily, getting down from the wall and starting across the shadowed yard with his long, slow strides, his hands in his pockets, his dark head bent. She followed him.

Neither Yves nor Jeanne came to dinner, and their cousin and brother was in a bitter, silent humour because, as it transpired, Yves had spent the afternoon telling his grievance to Jeanne, and her dismay had strengthened his determination to thrust Isabel out. There was no help for it, and Isabel sat with the fire warm on her back, watching waves of firelight flicker on the whitewashed wall opposite, and tried not to care; and she honestly did not care, she was honestly glad to be going, except that she was leaving the one person in the world whom it was a kind of death to leave because his life had grown into hers, as no one else's ever had done. She was more than herself, with him. She would be less than herself, alone.

[185]

The bereaving separation seemed already begun; he was a dark, gloomy stranger sitting near her, and her heart groped anxiously for his mood without being able to touch it, though her mind could almost read his mind. She was sure that his strange bondage must be in his thoughts, that he was seeing the length of it and the simple power of it as he had not done in a long time; she guessed that he must regret having told her his sister's story, merely because a secret told is no longer a secret; she thought he must resent his sister's taking sides against him; she felt he was really sorry to see her go. But that was the best she could do, and it was not really knowing him, it was not feeling his feelings as she once had done.

I think now that what she felt then was only a premonition of the little loneliness of love, of the moment that comes when at last one wants to put a tether on oneself and then finds that somehow the end of it cannot be placed in the hands that are reaching out for it. One tries with the best will in the world, but somehow the deed does not accomplish itself. And sometimes one pretends that it has been done, just doesn't look carefully to be sure, but assumes it must have been done because the will for the deed was so honest and complete, and one walks along as if tethered, but sooner or later something will happen to show that the end of the tether has been trailing free along the ground all the time.

After dinner he sat down in his usual chair in the drawing-room, in his usual posture, his legs outstretched on a hassock, his coffee-cup held at about the level of his chin, and he stared broodingly into the fire and did not speak.

She wished very much that a definite time for her departure had been set; she would have liked to know how much time was left. She sat erectly on the dark-blue velvet sofa sipping her coffee and giving swift, uneasy glances to the room, the dark panelled walls, the table where the red-velvet album lay, the blaze of the other fire, the careless clock sharply ticking on the ugly ebony lowboy, as she waited for him to say that it was time to go—and waited also for something else, without knowing what it was, waited as for an answer to a question that had been asked against her will by the hour itself, or by the silence, or by life. At last she said, as if in fearful intervention, "Shouldn't I be packing?"

"Someone is packing for you," he said crossly, but after a minute or two he turned his head to smile at her. The clock struck five in

[186]

melodious defiance of the time; a log slipped down in the fire, and a stream of golden sparks fled upwards; and the expression on his face changed. The sharp tick of the clock came marching back, through the sweet dissolving echo of its chime, and took command of the silence again.

"No," he said, putting his cup and saucer down and getting suddenly to his feet with a rare burst of vivacious energy, still staring at her, "it simply breaks my heart to look at you—the frightful clothes you wear! The clumsiness of you; it breaks my heart! I can't bear to think of you out in the world alone, Isabel, being rebuffed, being hurt—" and he began moving to and fro before the fire like a tiger teased and dangerous. When he stopped prowling, he stood wholly still. He had half forgotten her; his own emotion absorbed him; but she had never felt more aware of him, and never more sure that he moved in the same labyrinth with her. Then he looked at her again, and the coin with two faces turned, and the other face, narrow, intense, and knowing, as beautiful as towering flame and as frightening, examined her boldly. It was for a moment like nothing she had ever known before, and then it seemed to have been there always.

It may have surprised him, too; he looked surprised. Then he said, "But, naturally . . ." and was the practical-minded master of the moment again. But the sweet, dissolving echoes of her alarm spread in wider and wider rings till everything was trembling.

"Oh, don't, please don't . . ." she said.

"But why not?" he said. "Why not?" he said again, differently, recklessly, taking a cigarette and lighting it. "One may as well welcome it, under any circumstances. . . . At least, I always do. I happen to be that kind of a fool."

"But you don't know me!"

"But I do, almost. And in any case," he said, privately amused, recklessly exhilarated, "that has so little to do with it!"

"No, because what Yves said was true," she said desperately. "It was true!" She felt herself grow pale, a strange sensation.

He forgot himself and came to stand in front of her, looking down at her seriously and inquiringly, her friend again. "Tell me. What is it? What did Yves say? Nothing would really surprise me."

She wanted to tell him. Perhaps she hoped it was not as bad as it seemed; perhaps, on the other hand, just at this moment she

hoped it was unforgivable. But she could not put it into plain
words. "I was going to go away from here anyway. I saw I'd have
to go. It seemed to me that I had to." He sat down beside her on
the velvet sofa, not close, and not looking at her, holding his lighted
cigarette in a rustic way he had, between thumb and forefinger,
with the other fingers curved protectively round it, perhaps a habit
he had got into from smoking out-of-doors in bad weather. Smoke
filmed out between his fingers. "But it may not have been true, I
don't know. How can I tell? How could I tell?"

He did not think fast, but he could feel quicker than most people. "It concerned me?"

"I thought it concerned my father," she said, pressing her hands
against her face. But she ought to have known how he would take
it. If the situation that she had believed in had been true, he would
have taken it in much the same way, looking squarely at it, offering
reasonable comfort, and laughing before he was through because
there is humour in everything in the world, if one has eyes to see
it. The one thing he would not have done was be wrongly shocked.

"But it did not, you know. What are you worrying about? We
don't live sealed in our selves. There's the greatest puzzle of all,
that we're such solitary creatures, yet nothing we do or feel springs
wholly from ourselves— People turn one aspect or another of
themselves to us, and we respond to it; we're under its influence.
. . . It's the great safeguard of life, that other people feel our motives, that we feel theirs. I wasn't your father, I never felt towards
you as a father should feel; was it strange that you should be aware
of that? If you hadn't been, you'd be only half a person, insensitive,
unfeeling. Your instincts were perfectly right, don't you see? And
so were mine!" he said, beginning to laugh, taking her hand and
shaking it in emphasis before letting it go. "So were mine! You
seemed such a wild bird, afraid of a snare, always keeping out of
reach; yet you begged to stay, you hung on my words, you responded—responded, like an anxious little mirror twisting and turning to catch the full radiance of my remarkable personality—but all
the time I felt warned. I said to myself, Wait and see what she
means by this. . . . You see? . . . But it is truly unbelievable that
Yves could make such a suggestion to you, to his own daughter,
poisoning your mind against yourself, and so falsely! . . . And
that's what I've been in tug-of-war with these twenty years, that

squatting, foul-mouthed, heartless beast. . . ." He was like that; up and down, variable and changeable as moon-shadows blown by the night wind, laughing and the next moment protesting, then laughing again, but beneath it as solid as rock. When he despaired most, one still leaned on him, and when he laughed hardest, one still could look to him for comfort. "Well, never mind. I wonder if he really knows what he does in terms of other people's hurts? I doubt it. So never mind. It's only worth forgetting, like a little scratch, a little cut. . . ." But he shook his head, and she remembered Gulliver helplessly bound by threads. One little scratch was nothing; but what was twenty years with the same gadfly buzzing round one's head?

The door was opened to let Céphise in. She came in wildly, eager and gay, but she began weaving like a spent arrow as she drew near, sinking lower and lower, till she was crouched on the floor before him, and her soft black fur smelled of the cold night. He touched her topknot lightly, stirring his fingers through it. "I decided at last," he said, "that you were more innocent than you seemed, that you were rather in love without knowing it. . . ." Without meaning to, and without wanting to, Isabel shook her head. "Yes," he said more cheerfully. "You had better know now that you are dealing with someone who does trust his instincts, who's had almost forty years to learn that they can be trusted. And it did not seem strange to me at all! . . . Well." He took her hand again and touched it to his cheek. "What rough knuckles you have, don't you ever put anything on them? . . . What a strange thing it is! Well, we shall see." He got up. The battle was all to begin again, that was plain. He had found a new foothold for the tug-of-war, he was going to see what could be made of it. He lingered a moment longer, looking down at her, puzzled and a little anxious about something he felt in her. But he knew all about love and was confident that there was never anything to fear, and he could not really worry about the perilous landscape of the future that he thought only her ignorance and inexperience was making her see. He was sure that everything would be all right; he said so. "It will be all right. Don't worry," he said, and then he went off toward the hall without looking back, snapping his fingers at Céphise to make her follow.

She heard his footsteps and the click of Céphise's paws cross the hall and the passage, and then she heard the first of the doors of the empty rooms open and close, and she knew that he was going to talk once again to Yves—to her father—to her real father, who would never, never consent to give up his hopes and ambitions for himself to her. She went on sitting on the velvet sofa, confused, bewildered, afraid.

Arnaud came in at last for the coffee-cups. She supposed that he knew the truth now; his manner was different, not less kind, not less polite, but different. She could imagine the Duke tranquilly setting him right on the matter: "By the way, Arnaud, in case you have wondered about it—Miss Regan is very closely related to M. d'Ayz—not to me. But there is no need to talk of it." And Arnaud had accepted the truth with an equal tranquility. The important thing was still that the Duke was on her side, whoever her real father was.

When he had gone, she got up and went to each of the fires, beginning her farewells, and staying longest at the one where no one ever sat, which she felt she had neglected. Then she stepped just inside the dining-room and looked round at the walls, old and white and tranquil, thick to resist storms and time's slow siege, thick to resist change. She knew what Yves hungered for, because her hunger had been the same and even greater. But it was changing now. She wanted to be free, though she wanted to be safe; she would have liked to be enviably placed, but she despised shells without substance and all the flourishing ciphers of the world; she was in love; and she was not sure of anything.

She thought she heard footsteps returning through the hall, and so she slipped upstairs by way of the dark spiral staircase where drawing-room, dining-room, and pantry met, feeling her way up, walking slowly back along the corridor, past the open door of the bathroom, the open door of Jeanne's dark room, and all the closed doors. In her room Louise was doing the packing. Her forehead was furrowed with earnestness; her hands touched everything as if it might break. Isabel had done a good deal of travelling in her life, but she had never before had anyone to do her packing for her. She would rather have done it for herself, her clothes looked so shabby and makeshift in Louise's respectful hands. On the bed was a little stack of freshly laundered linen, still warm from the iron. Laid out on top of the little chest by the bed were the things that she had kept in its drawers, among them the little gold lighter with the coat of arms on its side. "Oh, that's not mine," she said, and she picked it up to take it back to its owner.

At the head of the stairs she met Barnabé's servant, who had just come through a door on the right, and afterwards she blamed herself for not having been more observant of him, but at the time it seemed somehow natural that everyone in the house should be moving about here and there. It was not like any other evening after dinner; it was special, the sort of night when windows stay lighted long after they are usually dark and all the neighbours know that something is going on. And she had the lighter on her mind, too, and all the things that it stood for, her own incredible covetousness not least. Even now she was tempted to keep it, in the hope that Yves had forgotten giving it. But she was not tempted to give way to that temptation. She did speak to the old man, and courteously; she said "Good evening," and then, making a dutiful if distracted effort to read his mind, she added, "The Duke may be in the drawing-room again, talking to Arnaud," and then she smiled and went on down the stairs. She stopped on the last step, recalling how oddly he had held his arms, one hugging the other, and how glazed his clear brown eyes had seemed, though he had smiled at her when she smiled at him; but she did not see that there was anything she should do; and so she went on through the dark cold empty chambers to Yves's isolated study.

She opened the door on an atmosphere of excited indignant discussion in which there was no element of contention; the two people in the room shared their views; their adversary had gone. Céphise was lying on the rug by the fire; Jeanne was sitting in the small arm-chair nearby; Yves was at his writing-table. His eyes turned quickly towards her and studied her as if he expected to see something new in her and was prepared to find it comical. Then he said contemptuously, "What have you come for? To have another try?" and she heard Jeanne gasp in genuine alarm.

Isabel had decided on the way to meet him coolly but politely, with proud dignity and disdainful self-restraint, but even without that greeting her ugliest passions would have risen at the sight of the man who could be blamed for everything in her life that she was ashamed of. She forgot everything but her hatred of him; she let her hatred swallow up and use the strength of every other feeling; and she felt for the last time collected and simple.

"I came to say good-bye," she said, "and to give you this. I don't want it," laying the lighter on the table.

"And now you look utterly evil."

"Perhaps my face is mirror to more than one man's," she said.

He and the room were softly lit by firelight, an unsteady light veined with flowing shadows. The far end of the room, where the doors opened on the terrace, was soft brown darkness. The glass of the doors glinted redly, reflecting the fire; other objects indicated themselves in delicate partial edgings of reflected light.

"And Mathieu would—!" he said, not to her but to Jeanne, though he continued to look at her. "Mathieu would—!" He sank back in his chair, self-consciously baffled, wilfully amused.

"He did not really mean it," said Jeanne, eagerly defending her brother. "He could not possibly have really meant it. It was an impulse. He is like that."

"Yes, he is like that. And it would not matter to him that the little bastard had tried to do away with her father," said Yves calmly, and Jeanne made an incoherent murmur of fresh distress. "But it matters to me. As I told him. Did he mention that?" Isabel saw then that they both supposed she had met the Duke as he came away from his latest battle with Yves's obduracy and believed that she had come herself to protest that defeat—or perhaps even to continue the battle. She found some small comfort in the discovery that her real father could sometimes fail completely in the reading of her heart. "What makes me sad is the thought of how great your prospects might have been—if you had been at all deserving. Not the thing that Mathieu seemed to have had in mind," he interposed hastily. "That would never do. But you've no idea what I might have done for you, along other lines. . . ."

"I wouldn't take anything from you if I were starving," said Isabel. As she spoke, the fire on the hearth flared up, and at the far end of the room she saw a stiff forefinger crooked at a slant round the edge of the stairway door, which was barely ajar.

"Well, you won't be getting anything from anyone else," said Yves in his negligent monotone. "You've gone too far."

"But, an allowance of some kind," said Jeanne, troubled. "I think Mathieu will feel—"

"I fail to see why," said Yves with an irritated glance toward her as he pushed into neatness the edges of a sheaf of papers on the table. "Under the circumstances."

"Perhaps not," said Jeanne.

"This fatal manuscript. One might think there was bad luck in it from the beginning, bad luck for us all. . . ."

"All your sins caught up with you," said Isabel. "Didn't they?" The fire flared up again, sending a warm wave of light flowing to the far corners of the room. The finger was really there. "I think, by the way," she added in English, "that the recluse is loose," and she wondered why giving the warning should make her suddenly unsteady on her feet when she had not been particularly afraid before. Yves did not understand, and she did not think she could say it again. What unnerved her was the idea that mad Barnabé was once again hunting down his kind cousin Mathieu, who was really his only friend in the world, because if someone is deaf to logic that is no more than children are, and many grown people too, but not to recognize love is to be a lost soul. It was a lost soul standing behind that door with a stiff forefinger crooked round the edge of it, listening to murmurs without meaning as he waited for the sound of the special voice.

The expression on her face attracted Yves's attention. "What did you say?" he asked, and Céphise suddenly growled softly. Isabel went on staring at the distant door. Yves started to turn and stopped half-way, looking down, his eyes abstracted. "Is he there?" he whispered. His face was green. "That's impossible. Are you sure? Go at once and— No, you had better not move. I don't know what to do."

"What is it?" said Jeanne, leaning forward to get up. "What's wrong?"

"Sit still!" he said in soft fury. She looked at him, amazed.

They were all motionless, waiting for something to happen, Isabel half expecting the lunatic to leap out suddenly with a wild yell. "Is it—" said Jeanne.

"Don't say the name," said Yves. Sweat was trickling down his large forehead; Isabel saw the glitter of it. "I don't know what to do. Is he—how far away is he? . . . What is he doing? . . ."

She did not even try to answer. Besides, she could not see anything clearly in the shadows, which might be answering a movement by the door or merely moving of themselves; they shifted and changed as the fire flickered. Then the door behind her opened briskly, and Jeanne gasped and said, "Oh, Mathieu—" and either the sound of the door or the sound of that name brought the lunatic out from his stairway. Isabel saw a pale shape moving in the shadows toward the light; it was a moment before she comprehended that he was quite naked. He was tall and rather hairy, and he looked very strong, but he moved slowly and stiffly, a strong body steered by a damaged brain, and one looked at him and loathed him as if he had made himself what he was, as if it were all his own fault.

"Mathieu?" he said in a mild voice, holding out his hand. He was like some gentle soul coming forward at a party with hand outstretched to meet the friend who had outraged him, as the other guests would see to their horror when the meeting came. Only he had no clothes on.

His cousin answered his greeting quietly and made conversation, coming forward as he spoke: the quality of his voice changed as it echoed at new angles in the room; and so did the quality of the madman's steady plod forward. Some of the purpose went out of it, though not all; momentum as well as intention carried him on past the writing-table and out of sight behind her—out of sight because she did not like to make even the slight movement of turning her head. It was disturbing to have him so near and not to be able to see what was happening. The hair at the back of her neck prickled. Then the look of unconscious longing on Yves's face took all her attention. He stared past her, his lips parted, his bright eyes narrowed, as if he watched the ball slowing towards his number on a wheel. She knew what he was profoundly hoping for; and shaping the words with extreme difficulty she said clearly, "You'll never be so lucky . . . dear Edouard. . . ."

His eyes turned slowly toward her. He caught the reference. He must have been waiting for it ever since he arranged the novel to draw her eye, but it caught him unawares for all that, and in his tenderest place, when his back was already to the wall. But because he was always a hypocrite and self-deceived, a liar to the core, living in his shallows, ignoring and ignorant of his depths, equally incapable of honest love and honest hate, it was the large implication that he resented, that he rebelled against with all his shocked little heart and soul. He picked up the weapon at hand, the paper-weight

[194]

on the table, the clear glass globe with flowers imprisoned in it, and hurled it at her. She felt the wind of its passing and turned with it to see Barnabé go down to his knees and over on his side with a heavy thud that knocked the wind out of him. She heard him grunt; then he lay quite still.

There was an instant rustle of movement. The Duke bent over Barnabé; Barnabé's servant shouldered the door shut; Jeanne twisted round, hiding her face in her arms; Yves slithered down into his chair. Isabel put one hand on the table to steady herself, and the table leaned against her in a peculiar way as if it were trying to thrust her back.

Barnabé did not move; he would never move again; and the look on Yves's white face showed that for once in his life that complete egotist could not think of himself but only of the thing that he had done, the strange enormous irrevocable thing that he had done, with his own hand, on his own impulse, at no one's behest but his own. His heartbeat must have been sounding in his ears all the more loudly against the new silence of that other heart; he must have felt the unimaginable truth of death in his own body at that moment, as she had felt it in hers.

"Take Jeanne up to her room, Isabel," said the Duke. His voice was soft with the solemnity of shock and unsteady with emotion.

Isabel went over to Jeanne, walking awkwardly, as if through deep water. She touched Jeanne's arm and said, "Come along." Jeanne did not seem to hear or to feel the touch.

Her brother came over to pull her up out of the chair and walk her to the door. "Take her up to her room," he said, thrusting Isabel out with her; and then, after a little inexplicable pause, which she understood later had only been to allow the frightened dog to follow them, he closed the door very quietly.

They stood in cold darkness; uncurtained windows looking north were bright rectangles of moonlit courtyard. Isabel took Jeanne's arm; Jeanne pulled it free. "Please don't touch me," she said politely in a thread of a voice. "I feel sick, I feel sick. . . . That was what you tried to do . . . to him." Isabel had been thinking that too, and she too felt sick. One cannot comprehend violence till one sees it done. But she was not glad to hear it from Jeanne. "I beg you, don't touch me with your murderous hands," said Jeanne softly.

Isabel came very close, at that moment, to telling her what was in her own history in the way of violence. She hung on the edge of telling for what seemed an enormous halting instant, and then she said instead, "But you see that I came by it honestly."

"Oh, for the love of God, can't you see that he was terrified for us all? That creature was dangerous—insane and dangerous—"

Isabel looked back and saw a narrow line of dim light along the bottom of the door. Her heart pounded. "Well, come along," she said. "I shan't touch you if you can walk by yourself."

"I can walk," said Jeanne, "by myself," and then she stumbled and went down on one knee. She got up again, and they went through the dark cold rooms into the passage, where the hanging lamp swayed by the staircase, and up the triangular stone steps, keeping carefully to the outside edge.

Isabel went with her as far as her room. As she turned away after closing the door, she saw Céphise pacing tardily along the corridor, head down, tail down, looking punished and uncertain. She put Céphise into Jeanne's room without saying anything and then returned downstairs. On the last step of the stairs she hesitated, not really knowing what she ought or meant to do next.

Footsteps scraped beyond the door to her left, slow footsteps, but she saw why they were slow when the Duke came through the door with Barnabé's servant beside him, still cradling his injured arm in his good one.

"Find Arnaud, Isabel," the Duke said hurriedly. "The doctor must be sent for, for this poor creature—tell him. And then go back to Jeanne, will you? Do you mind?"

"I don't think she will want me with her," said Isabel, and he paused in all his haste and anxiety to look at her and then to put his arm round her shoulders as she came down the last step.

"Don't mind," he said. "Don't mind anything. Isn't it for the best, when all is said? What was his life?" But he could not really believe that yet; no one's life, however hopeless, could seem a wise exchange for death when death was in the house; and she could not lean and take comfort from him when he wanted comfort himself. "Send Louise to her, then," he said, letting her go. "Into the drawing-room," he said to Barnabé's servant, and again to Isabel, "And I want Arnaud in Yves's room, when he has telephoned. . . ."

She ran off gratefully, glad to run his errands like a child and have no need to think. It was still early, everyone was still up. In the pantry, where the odours of dinner lingered pleasantly, Arnaud was mildly scolding Gilles for some unimportant error, and a babble of easy voices floated up the steep stairway in the corner. The placid atmosphere of a day of work near its end hung over the bright tidy room. "Arnaud," she said, and he turned, polite and inquiring, "you must send for the doctor—Monsieur Barnabé's servant has broken his arm, I think—" His expression changed; his eyes darkened with alarm; then his face masked itself in impassivity because Gilles was there. He understood all the possible connotations of that bit of news and did not mean to let them be guessed. "He is in the drawing-room. And then you are wanted in Monsieur d'Ayz's study."

"Fetch my wife," he said to Gilles, and Isabel went to the stairway and called, "Louise!" The cheerful voices below fell silent. "Louise!" The voices resumed their chat more quietly but no less cheerfully, and Louise appeared at the foot of the stairs and then came climbing up. Isabel took her half-way along the passage, passing on the way Arnaud at the telephone in the little room next to the pantry, before saying, "Go up and sit with the Countess, will you? She is a little upset this evening. . . ." She had caught caution from Arnaud, and she was glad that it was wise to make little of the evening's happenings. She did not want to make much of them.

When Louise had started up the stairs, she went into the drawing-room and found Barnabé's servant sitting on the edge of the blue velvet sofa, staring into the fire. He gave her his prompt sweet smile, the smile that meant so little because he always had to make it mean so much, but his clear brown eyes caught no light from it. She smiled back at him as consolingly as she could, but then there was nothing more that she could do; and when Arnaud's wife came in, she thought it better that she should not be there, knowing everything, when the doctor came, and so she went back to the staircase and hung around there, feeling very chilly in her thin dress, with death in the house.

While she waited, not knowing what she was waiting for, it seemed to her that she could feel an air of concerned expectancy spreading through the castle like a draught from an open door, blowing away the ordinary drowsy peace that belonged to it at that hour. Félicie could have heard nothing of what had happened, but after a time she appeared in the doorway of the pantry and then came all down the length of the passage to ask if there was anything she could do. "Nothing," said Isabel. "Go to bed. There's nothing to do, really nothing." Félicie retreated, and Isabel folded her arms for warmth and leaned against the hard stone wall and went on waiting, thinking now not only of doctors and undertakers and hearses and all the humble necessities of death that rise so suddenly and inescapably across the path of the living, but also of the police that would in this special case have to be sent for, and a slant of thought suddenly lighted an aspect of the future that made her shrink—herself as the world would come to know her after the statements had been taken and the relentless interrogations of the trial were over: the daughter of a peasant girl three times married but never married to her daughter's father, who had been tried and convicted of manslaughter. And it was not only for herself that she winced. For the first time she felt that indefinable emotion called the family feeling, and felt it about that odd trio, Henriette Miet, Yves d'Ayz, and Isabel Regan. She had not loved her mother, and she despised her father, but she felt for that one time that she belonged to them, because one of them was in trouble. But the same slant of thought showed her the blackmailer in prison, powerless to hurt the innocent for a while; and she found that she could endure anything for the sake of accomplishing that.

Arnaud came through the door on her left and passed her without a word, his pinched face rigid with strain. He returned from the entrance hall with Gilles behind him and went back the way he had come. Soon afterwards, she heard the beat of a small car's engine outside. The doctor had come; she heard Arnaud's wife admitting him to the house in her practised cicerone's way, hard, facile, and authoritative. And finally the Duke returned with Arnaud. He stared at her, baffled and uncomprehending, seeming to have to identify her anew at that moment; then he said to Arnaud, "You understand, then? It is all clear?" but only as a way of taking leave, because he then came straight to Isabel without waiting for a response and said, "What are you doing here, standing about, freezing yourself?"

The change was in him, too. His dark face was haggard, his eyes showed more than one kind of misery in their blue depths, but beneath his harassed weariness he was firm, he was decided. Some sort of final point had been reached, and everything was turning in a new direction. He would never be the same again, nor would this house, nor would anyone. The final thing had happened. "I didn't know what I should do—" she said.

"It is quite certain that you won't be leaving this house tonight," he said, turning her up the stairs and following behind her, "and I begin to feel fairly certain that you will not leave it tomorrow, nor ever, except by your own wish."

"But what will you tell the police?" she said, keeping her voice very low, and in the next instant, feeling his surprise, she corrected her ordinary experience of the world by his extraordinary standards. He was no more someone to submit himself meekly to the authority of a local constable than Yves would have been, and she wondered how she could accept that in him so easily and still abhor it in Yves. But the reason was more honourable and more sensible than any reasons of love could have been. Though he might consider himself above the law, he was not, like Yves, above himself.

"The police?" he said under his breath. "I hope it won't come to that!"

"But if the police aren't coming—" she whispered at the top of the stairs, bewildered and angry. "He *should* be punished for what he did! He *should* be! And I don't care if he is!"

"Don't you?" he said, but he understood what she meant. "Well, I do. And not merely for your sake." He looked away, and his dark proud profile was remote and unfamiliar to her in its new haggard austerity. "The truth is, I have had enough, Isabel, and now there must be an end to it. And so I must take this chance— I shall never have another as good."

"You mean to lie to the doctor?"

"If Yves makes it worth my while." He hated saying that, but he said it and meant it. He was going to bargain himself free with Barnabé's death though he died of disgust himself in the process. "I must, you see. And the worst of it is, it must be done in haste . . . but perhaps that is just as well. If there were all the time in the world, I should begin to vacillate. . . . And I have had enough."

"He meant that paper-weight for me, not for—for Barnabé. He threw it at me."

[199]

"Yes, he told me that—he offered it as a . . . a palliation. . . .
It seemed to be, in his eyes, a lesser crime. . . ."

He sounded half fearful of the strangeness that was Yves, and so
she said, "That was because it failed, you see. Because it came to
nothing."

"Yes. . . . But why did he do it, just then, at such a moment?"

"Because I taunted him."

"I didn't hear you say anything."

"I did, though."

He thought it all over, depressed and hurried though he was.
"You seem very unconcerned by it," he said at last.

"Because it didn't mean much," she said slowly. "I know. I tried,
and failed—he tried, and failed. We didn't try hard enough to suc-
ceed. It's the cheap way our anger takes us, that's all. . . ."

"Please, don't," he said, steering her toward the door of her room.
"Don't."

"I've got to learn to accept it! He is my father!"

"But when you say such things—"

"When I say such things?" she said, suffering over what she had
said.

"No," he said apologetically, "I am too busy to change your mind
for you just now. . . . Let it be enough that everything will soon
be all right."

"But how can you trust him?" she said, pulling free of his hand
on her arm to face him. "You only think you can because you're
tired! Nothing has changed! He will promise, and then he will break
his promise as soon as things are arranged, as soon as you have told
your lies and made it safe for him, and then it will all begin again!"

He shook his head. "No. This has broken him, Isabel. This has
made its impression on him. He is quite altered. And in any case,
he will keep his promise. If he gives his word— I must go," he said,
suddenly distrait and aloof—how he hated what he was doing!
"Have you matches? Here." He gave her a box from his pocket,
warm to the touch, and went away.

Everything was changing, and she was afraid. She was changing
too, of course; she was growing up; she was ceasing to be a child in
search of a home and learning to find a home in herself. It was all
for the good, but it hurt, and it seemed to accomplish nothing. It
is never very pleasant to reach a goal and find that it counts for

nothing, that it is no more than a dirty milestone half buried in weeds at the side of the road, unimportant until it has been left behind, and then important only as a measure of progress. She had come to the castle swathed like a mummy in the tight wrappings of a dream; and now the dream had come undone, and she had fallen apart in a chaos of truths.

The fire was almost out. When she had lighted the candle, she put on her coat for warmth and sat down in the wing-chair, huddling herself into its depths in a sudden terror of death and change and loss. She tried to think of the bargain that was being made with Yves in order to examine its risks and test it for flaws, but her thoughts soon slipped away from that, and away from the memory of shadows and a fall, away from the mixed vision of herringbone cobbles and a quaint child lifting a brightly striped mallet into the innocent air, away from the hard silver chill of a pair of scissors in her own hand and her ignorant scuffle with Yves at the drawing-room door, away from her wakening from a dream of truth into a nightmare of false reality, away from all those disasters into a new consoling dream: a dream of going away to become somehow suave, experienced, independent, admired, highly placed, and then returning—returning witty and worldly, equal to anything, elegant in black with pearls and a fur piece and a smart hat. . . .

She went over the route of it again and again, each time more vaguely, hurrying on to the moment of returning sure of herself, equal to anything, but knowing what she wanted and certain of getting it—and wanting not an impossible marriage, hovered over by Yves, resented by Jeanne, in this aged hateful castle of the past, but something else, some sort of love affair, outside the world's ways, secret and never-ending, always their own affair and no one else's. She imagined it, she shaped it elaborately and defined its details, she listened to endless conversations of the future, his voice and hers saying all the things that she truly wanted to say to him and wanted to hear from him, and she was nearly happy.

And then outside she heard the cranking of a small car's engine and the beat of its loose pistons as it caught; and the future Isabel faded away and the present Isabel in a cheap blue dress and a shabby coat became what she had to deal with in the hours and days to come.

The doctor was going. She went to the window and was in time to see the red tail-light disappearing round the corner that led to the ramp. Moonlight was still bright, but the moon was lower in the western sky, and a rising bank of clotted cloud menaced it, and the shadow of the central wing had come closer across the silvery stones of the courtyard. While she watched, the golden rectangles of light falling from the drawing-room windows vanished; as they vanished, there was a tapping on her door and the Duke opened it and looked in.

He had expected her to be waiting up for one last word—but if he had found her in bed and oblivious, he would have been only pleased that she could sleep. She knew that; she knew that he was the easiest man in the world; but that did not help. "Well," he said, tall and dark and tired in the doorway, and she went uncertainly over to him. "It's done."

"There was no trouble?"

"None." He leaned against the jamb and smoothed his face slowly and wearily with the palm of one long narrow hand. "We simply took poor Barnabé back to his room— Arnaud and I dressed him a little and carried him as far as the stairs, and then Gilles was fetched to help me get him the rest of the way. The doctor saw him there and accepted the idea of an accidental fall on the stairs without question—they are such wicked stairs, you know. . . ."

"The—the bargain was already made?"

"No, not exactly, though I had laid out the terms of it—that was the first thing I did, before you had been gone one minute from that room! I spoke without any conscious thought at all, I believe, and yet as much to the purpose as if I had planned it for years. . . . Strange. . . ." But she did not find it strange. His long frustrations, gathered up into a single force by the shock of that sudden death, had made his plans for him out of the obvious material at hand, and acting on them had been his best and only way of escape from that intolerable shock. "But then I remembered that poor fellow's injured arm and had to see to that. And then we moved Barnabé's body—but that committed me to nothing, you see, with four good witnesses to tell what had really happened, and it had to be moved in any case, I could not have let him be seen like that by strangers. . . . And four good witnesses. . . ." But this time he said it dubiously. "Jeanne, I mean," he explained when she looked questioningly at him. "It just occurs to me that she might not perhaps have been very good. She would not have wanted him punished— Yves. No, I think she would have sworn to absolute untruths, believing them to be true, in order to save him. . . ." He contemplated that averted danger, and then he said, "Oh, you see that it had to be done, don't you? You see what it might have turned into, if there had had to be any sort of official inquiry. Every detail of our life here exposed—and then public disagreements among us— I could not have let it come to that."

"No," she said, "you could not. . . . But why couldn't *he* see that too—see that you would have to get him out of it?"

"He was in no state to see anything. He was all but in pieces. And that's to his credit, Isabel."

"I suppose so," she said dully, thinking of the things that Yves had done to the man beside her without turning a hair.

"Well, Arnaud and I carried poor Barnabé as far as the stairway, and—but I've told you that already. And then I talked to Yves again. He had gone into his bedroom, I talked to him there. . . . I put the case to him, I hammered it home. . . ."

"And he promised?"

"He promised. He gave his word the moment after Arnaud announced the doctor in the next room. What else could he do? He saw that I was at the end of my rope. . . . Oh, doubly so—this dreadful affair, on top of everything else—to say nothing of his behaviour when I went to him just after dinner. You see, though I put my ideas for a possible future for you in the most tentative way—you will not be hurt by that, you have such intelligence," he interrupted himself to say with an unexpected intonation of respect in his voice, and she looked away, hardly knowing what she felt. "Well, he was so astonished, so incredulous. . . . And Jeanne too —she was there—equally incredulous, equally astonished. . . . I began to think myself a very simple sort of person." But he laughed. He was not simple at all. And the anger of that moment was still in him, though dying, now that everything was changed. "I would not be so tentative now. What can be important to any man except happiness, Isabel? Death will come to us all at last, and what will we have had, if we have not had happiness? I did not know, till they answered me, how much I needed it, or how far this past month had carried me."

"And he promised," she said, fleeing from that point to which he had been carried, but he did not notice that.

"He promised. He saw that I would endure no more from him. Yes, just then I *would* have brought in the police, and happily, if he had refused!" he said, shaking his head at the memory of himself in such a reckless passion. "It's not so bad, Isabel. It has really changed him. I hardly knew him, in those minutes afterward—not merely frightened—of course he was frightened, but beyond that he was genuinely, profoundly shocked—shocked at himself. . . . How odd it is for me to have someone to talk to about it, someone to confide in. . . . I am glad of you."

"And he will keep his promise?" she said.

"He gave his word."

She concentrated on that, turning it over in her mind as well as she could, and it seemed to her that everything had indeed reached a new balance and would be safe there. She could imagine Yves reviving from shock, returning to himself, and renewing his old ways, but she could also imagine him feeling himself bound by a clear unequivocal promise, in exchange for value received.

It is easy to be wise after the event, but they were in the middle of it all, not high above the night and seeing it whole but enmeshed in all its immediate intricacies and ambiguities, forced to weigh imponderables as best they could. In that moment she was only thinking of him, only wanting to see him free of his other incubus; and besides, she could not torment him with her doubts, doubts that she was in truth doubtful about, at that late hour, when he leaned against the jamb in a slump of exhaustion, keeping his steady composure but hardly capable of more than that, his fine face drawn with weariness and strain. And so she turned it over in her mind and really decided that the case was sound. "In a way," she said, "you were safe all along—because once he had told, he could have got no more from you. And so he couldn't have told. He could only threaten to tell." She reassured herself more than him with that reasoning because he was too tired to follow her through the logic of it. But he needed reassurance less than she did, because he always chose to believe the best of people.

"And he will have an allowance still, of course. I have tried to be fair." He yawned suddenly. He was at peace at last; he was content. He had got through the worst of it and could leave it behind.

"And so you can go to bed now and forget it all," he said. "Are you all right? Shall I ask Félicie to sit up with you? Shall I ask Jeanne for one of her tablets?"

"No, I'm all right."

"You look very white, however."

All his attention was coming on her again, and she could no longer pretend that it was in any way fatherly. He was even trying to make her meet his eyes, absently smiling a little, half wondering, half sympathetic, at the difficulty he was having in doing so. But he knew her feelings so well in his heart that it did not enter his head to worry about what she might be making of them.

"Oh!" he said abruptly, straightening up. "If you won't have a tablet, have this—it should distract you a little. I seem to have an extraordinary facility for letting these things slip my mind. But it came only today." He brought a letter out of his pocket; she took it and looked at it. He waited. He had brought up the subject of Henry—Henry and Henry's proposal and Henry's mistake—and of course he expected some comment from her; but it did not occur to her to make one. After a moment he touched the top of her head lightly and went on down the hall.

He stopped to knock on Jeanne's door, and Jeanne came out into the hall to speak to him, closing the door behind her. Isabel could hear only the murmur of their voices, but she guessed that he was telling the version of events that had been accepted by the doctor and—he was shaking his head very decidedly to a little gesture that his sister made toward the stairs—advising Jeanne not to go down to Yves just then. He closed her firmly into her room before he went on to the turn in the corridor, round which he disappeared to the comforts of his own room, his own bed.

Isabel shut her door and tore open her letter as if its words promised to be her life-line, and all the while every pulse in her body was shaking her with a violence that seemed as separate from her real self as it was from the letter that she was reading.

Henry had written on the train; the writing was jiggly yet clearer than usual, as if he had tried specially hard against odds to make it legible; and it had been posted in the station at Paris. "I'm in a compartment with five Frenchmen," it began, "all smoking cigarettes—French cigarettes—and talking nine to the dozen and generally showing off, very tiresome. One of them is wearing jodhpurs!!!"

But he must have written that unthinkingly, rushing at a beginning in order to make a beginning, because the rest was quite different, so respectful and ignorant that it endeared him to her.

He apologized for having misunderstood her, he explained that he understood much better now her position in the household and the gratitude she was bound to feel towards her kind cousin, he no longer offered her a refuge, but he still offered love and marriage. He seemed to have forgotten her commonplace past in his office and forgotten as well her fluttering alarms and fears of the day before as he rode away in a compartment full of chattering Frenchmen and remembered her in the castle, dark-browed and stately in ancient rooms, with firelight on her plum-coloured hair. . . . She could see that picture for herself—because she was not that girl. Nor was she the Isabel he had known in London, irresolute, hardworking, daydreaming, striving uncertainly for refinement as her only preparation for the dream's coming true. She wondered what he thought he was in love with.

Once again there was a postscript: "I have business in Paris for a few days— I shall be at the Bristol. Write to me there—write and say 'Yes.' Or better yet—much, much better—come to me there, and we'll go home together. Will you?"

She bundled the letter back into its envelope and began hurrying about the room preparing for bed, opening her suitcases to find her nightgown and slippers, her dressing-gown and toothbrush, turning down the bed, drawing the red-flecked curtains, keeping herself in movement to keep out of reach of thought. When she came back from the lavatory, Jeanne's door stood open, and she saw Louise sitting alone in the room, primly upright on a straight chair in the corner, her hands in her lap, patiently grimacing through a yawn.

It was easy to guess that Jeanne had probably gone down to soothe and console Yves after all, but Isabel saw no harm in that. Whatever she might still have been dreading for the far future, when his deed and the dangers of it had grown small in the past, she was sure that he had been scotched for the present. She got into bed, but she did not put out her candle at once, and she was still awake, propped rather high on her pillows, when Jeanne's footsteps returned up the stairs, very audible in the midnight silence of the house, and very slow.

They creaked to a halt outside Isabel's door; when, after a full minute of silence, they had not moved on, Isabel got out of bed and went to the door to open it.

"You are still awake, then," said Jeanne politely. "I saw a light along the threshold. . . ." Her hair was still dressed, and she was wearing a handsome dressing-gown of black wool whose high collar was embroidered with small blue flowers, but she looked bent and gaunt and old. Her deep humourless eyes were cold with loneliness. "He cares nothing for me," she said. It was an odd communication, but it seemed to Isabel, fresh from her private despairs, the right way for human beings to greet each other—with important truths, with thoughts that really needed saying. "I went down to comfort him a little—to tell him that it did not count, what he had done—to comfort him. . . . He cares nothing for me. Nothing."

"He cares nothing for anyone," said Isabel, "except himself." She was sorry when she saw Jeanne waver before the force of that, but she had nothing better to offer to the truth than another truth as true.

"Oh, what a good daughter you are," said Jeanne softly, raising her clasped hands to hide her mouth. "What a blessing—what a happy discovery for him! I should not say this, forgive me, but I wish you were dead. I wish you had never been born. With all my heart I wish it," and Isabel stepped back from the cold pure well of truth to the distances of saying the right polite things whether she believed them or not.

"It's been a dreadful shock for everyone—it will take time to get over it. I mean, it's made everyone not quite himself. . . . I suppose he was only upset and didn't really mean to be unkind—"

"I wish you had never been born," said Jeanne, closing her eyes.

Isabel turned away. People had sometimes spoken brutally to her before, but never with that kind of unhappy reluctance, which gave each word the full terrible weight of its meaning. "Yes," she said, and she closed the door and went over to her bed and crawled into it, laying herself down as carefully as if any brusque movement were certain to break her.

And Jeanne went on to her room, dismissed Louise with a smile, said good night in a calm voice, and lay down on her own bed to lie awake all night exploring the dimensions of her new intolerable burden. Early in the morning, she got up, took out her sleeping tablets, and swallowed them all.

Because, of course, Yves had spoken; cornered and conquered for the first time in his life, facing the loss of all his lovely tyranny, in fear and frustration and simple detestation he had spoken—and probably without completely understanding what he did. When his secret became worthless to him, it lost its force, too, as far as he was concerned. How could he conceive that it still had real weight and importance when it could no longer buy him anything that he wanted?

And so, when she came to him, offering her foolish tenderness to make up for everything that he had lost, at a moment when he was only beginning to look forward and see how great the loss was going to be, he had flung his worn-out useless secret at her, wanting to wound her but never dreaming, perhaps, that it might kill her.

It was her brother who looked in on her when he got up and found her in that white cold heavy sleep; it was his shout down the small stairway to Arnaud that woke Isabel from her nightmares; it was he who decided not to waste time summoning the doctor but bundled Jeanne up in her bedclothes and carried her down to the car—Yves's great beautiful car, not his own—to drive her not to the doctor's house but to a private clinic ten miles away to the north, where there would be every kind of medical equipment at hand. He was never helpless in an emergency; he had instincts and common sense, and he was not shy about using them.

Isabel, sleep-dazed, stood back in her doorway to be out of the way and watched in an increasing rage of revolt that he should have had to suffer this adventitious trouble when he had already endured so much. She thought she understood the cause, and she blamed Jeanne, blamed her for her stupidity in letting herself adore Yves and so making herself so fatally vulnerable to disillusionment. She was able to pity her a little only because of Jeanne's cruelty on the night before, I suppose on the principle of pitying an enemy brought low; mostly she blamed her. All the while she was getting dressed, after the car had roared away down the ramp, she blamed her, never suspecting, until she went downstairs and came face to face with Yves in the drawing-room, how good a reason Jeanne might have had for not wanting to live any more. The first sight of him reminded her of his ancient power; once reminded, she found the truth in her memory of Jeanne's desolate eyes at midnight and guessed everything.

[208]

Yves looked sick, wretched, and defiant; the small sharp lines of a rebellious and terrified remorse fretted his handsome face. The cipher was open to her most casual inspection, and she could hardly bear to look. A full comprehension of how uselessly Jeanne had been broken came to her; the wanton waste of the deed appalled her as much as anything else. She stared for perhaps a large part of a minute at the father that she had waited so long and come so far to find, a weak trivial man without honour or pride or truth in him. There was nothing to be said and nothing to be done. She moved away to the grey warmth of the banked-up fire; the morning was cloudy, and the room was cold.

Arnaud, white as wax, his old face tremulous with distress, came in with coffee for Yves; seeing her, he went to get another cup. He was long in returning; and when he came, he said that the Duke had just telephoned, that the Countess had been still alive when they reached the clinic and that there was some hope of a recovery. Yves said, "Thank God! Thank God!" and Arnaud nodded his head in agreement. Isabel went back to the hearth with her coffee and stood there studying the room as if to assure herself that some things, at least, were out of reach of change—the rich carving of the dark panelled walls, the chimney-pieces that had snared white delicacy in the permanence of stone, the ebony lowboy winking in the grey morning light like a whole great set of dominoes, the sharply ticking clock. But there was no comfort in the room that morning. It seemed on the edge of dissolving into grey ruin with everything else that had been steady and safe and long established in the castle. Nobody had put it in order, and nobody would: Gilles was keeping watch outside the open door of a dead man, Félicie had gone in the car with Jeanne, and Louise was beyond her duties in the morass of blaming herself for having allowed herself to be dismissed with a smile before the Countess slept.

Oddly enough, Isabel did not slip into that morass herself, perhaps because she was in a way so completely to blame. When one has to say, "Without me none of this would have happened," not "without this particular act of mine," or "these particular acts," but "without *me*," "without my existence in the world," one begins to see that something a bit bigger than oneself is at work in the matter. Jeanne could have said exactly the same thing— "Without me, without my existence in the world, none of this would have happened." Yves could have said it. It could have been said of Barnabé.

But it could not have been said of Mathieu, not quite. For him, the morass waited.

He had misjudged the case, there was no denying that. He had pushed Yves past the point of cowed obedience into the dangerous recklessness of despair; he had turned on him too suddenly and too completely; he had cornered him; he had taken too much from him; and finally, he had let himself believe that Yves would keep his word. He would see all that; and what was more, he would know why he had made those mistakes. He was not one to be dishonest with himself ever, and he would recognize the personal desires that had momentarily overbalanced his judgement. She did not see that he would ever be able to forgive himself.

The egotistical clock struck the half hour of its mysterious choice, and she finished her coffee. The cushions on the blue sofa where Barnabé's servant had sat were still crushed; chairs were out of their usual places; even the coffee was bad; and the hot milk had a skin on it that hung over the lip of the china pitcher. And Yves seemed to be preparing to break his silence. She filled her cup again and took it into the great bare icy hall, her footsteps loud on the stone-coloured tiles, and from the hall she wandered outside, where the air came damp and unexpectedly mild against her face and birds were chirping. But a small dark van, disproportionately long, was parked in the far corner of the courtyard, and a bicycle leaned against the wall nearby.

Giving them a furtive glance, she crossed the pavement and entered the central quadrangle, and all the pillars and fanciful balustrades, coldly white, opened and arranged themselves round her in a slow formal silent dance. She put her cup and saucer down on the wooden cover of the well and touched the pocked stone flank of the nearest nymph.

Whether Jeanne lived or died did not matter; he would come back needing comfort, and she would not know how to give it. He rose before her in all his most formidable aspects—supremely authoritative, unthinkingly self-assertive, painfully fastidious, terrifyingly discriminating, and perfectly incapable of concealing his real opinion of other people's behaviour for a single instant—and nothing now stood between them to shield her, neither the false fatherhood with which she had invested him, nor her true father's power to intercede and prevent. All the barriers were down.

In a corner of herself, a dark still pocket of personal life isolated from everything that had happened, she felt desire and dread. They were one feeling in her, two opposites mingled in a mixture that was always on the edge of imbalance. There was a saying that Betty's brother had once daringly quoted to her, meaning nothing serious by it, merely striking out on a bold line of conversation from which he had quickly made a retreat, blushing furiously: Love is not just one thing, it is twenty; but it is not nineteen. She did not think of that now, but it was in her mind, part of the chaos of herself that prevented her thinking steadily of anything.

Only two days before, she had woken believing that what she felt for him was as wrong as wrong could be and had to be suppressed at all costs, and that resolution had had one long day to sink into the farthest depths of her heart and harm things there. And she had never had a very good opinion of herself in the first place. She could catch glimpses of what he saw in her—an uncritical and persistent desire to please him, a prejudiced devotion not at all stupid at base, the freshness of inexperience, the simplicity of innocence; but she saw other qualities as well, her evil fits of temper, her unforgiving hatred of Yves, and the hunger for honesty and independence that made her subservience seem the worst sort of hypocrisy. He would not love those things in her, she felt, if he knew they were there. Besides that, there was the fact of her birth, which probably was more important to her than to anyone else in the world—but that is the way it is for the illegitimate. Other people may make nothing of it, but for the illegitimate it is a kind of fence or wall or magic circle that sets them always apart. For them, the least that can ever be said is that it makes a difference. And besides, she kept hearing now the clear echo of phrases that she had hardly heard when they were spoken: "The clumsiness of you . . . the frightful clothes you wear. . . ." They ought to have reassured her; they ought to have made her perceive how well, perhaps, he did see her; instead, they humbled her to the ground.

Henry's hand seemed stretched out to rescue her from the bitterest of failures. She was not afraid of disappointing Henry. He would like to look at her however she dressed; he never noticed women's clothes. And she was fond of him, and she admired him too, and the thought of him did not make her dizzy with desire and dread. She had not seen him doubly caged and then suddenly set free like a terrifying tiger.

She looked round the silent beautiful court, trying to lose herself in its timeless serenity, but the arch was a tear in the tapestry to show her the future on the threshold—a paving of flat grey stones neatly fitted together, across which the long grey car would come and slow to a stop, soon, in a few hours, or a few minutes. And its door would open, and she would be caught.

The air hung silent and still; birds chirped, but there was no other sound. No car came; the silence continued. She wanted to know whether Jeanne would live or die, but she could not stay for that. "I'm going!" she said aloud, and she walked away towards the arch, forgetting her cup and saucer on the well.

She was almost running when she entered the hall; and Arnaud, who was just crossing it as she came in, glanced beyond her as if he thought she had had later news than his from some source outside; when she told him that she was leaving for Paris and wanted to be driven to the station in Tours, he was simply bewildered. "No," she said, to soothe him, not to excuse herself, "I was supposed to go last night, you know, and couldn't, when— I must go now. It was all arranged."

The extreme urgency of her manner and the look of panic unloosed in her face must have impressed him; he went off to find Joël and send for the car; but she knew that she had shocked him. That did not trouble her, however. Only one person's opinion mattered to her; if she could not bring herself to be ruled by that, she certainly could not care what anyone else might think—Arnaud, or Joël, whom he sent belatedly upstairs to bring down her suitcases, or Yves, whom she met in the hall when she came down in her hat and thick blue coat and whom she passed without a word.

The old black touring-car waited outside, shaking with the thrum of its engine; Joël was holding the door open. She climbed in and sat down on the hard seat in the enormous leathery tonneau, and he closed the door and got in himself behind the wheel. Arnaud stood in the portico, confused and distressed; Yves was visible in the shadows of the doorway behind him. She stared solemnly at them both, with nothing to communicate to either, until the car moved toward the cobbled ramp and sent them out of sight.

And so she left the castle as she had entered it, wearing her same blue suit and dark-blue coat, sitting alone on the back seat of a strange car, weak with relief; and in other ways, too, her flight resembled her quest. Both, in spite of her little displays of purpose in them, were equally involuntary, their impetus arising from the pressures of the world about her, their direction taking its course far more from what lay behind than from what was ahead. She ran away, in short, as childishly as she had come.

But there was one difference. She had come thinking that she was wholly right to come, that every standard of morality and humanity justified her coming; she went away knowing that she was wholly wrong to go. She had come to conquer a neglectful father in order to win what she considered to be any child's rightful heritage—a sense of pride, a sense of security—but she went away to do battle with herself.

The ride was windy, but the wind was soft and damp, and it had all the smells of the country in it, the smells of ploughed fields and manure and leaf-mould; she felt the nearness of spring, and she felt freed. For a time her chief worry was that she had in her haste forgotten something—her passport, or her purse, or Henry's letter. She went through her handbag to make sure that they were all there; and then, when she had looked out for a while at the blunted contours of Touraine under a grey February sky, she had to rummage through her handbag again to make twice sure. In the course of the second check, she came upon the glossy postcard for the last time. The pale walls and towers of the picture looked more than ever magical and unreal, a dream and never a reality, with her memory of the truth set beside it. She looked at it, and then she tore the card up into small stiff pieces and let them go into the wind.

Tours was busy and bustling with morning traffic; trams made a great clatter in the streets. The continuous inconsequential noise of the town sounded strange to her after the weeks of silence; she felt like someone rejoining the world after an absence in the farthest of fairylands. When she saw the station square, its image came down slightly askew on her memory of it; for an instant there were two station squares, then only one.

Joël went inside to inquire about trains and came back with her ticket in his hand, bought, as he said, on instructions from Arnaud, who had evidently helped himself through the flurry of her going by falling back on the orders he had received the night before. She wanted to pay for it herself, but she did not have the right change to accomplish the transaction deftly; and when she saw how she was embarrassing Joël, she gave it up.

She had not expected to have to wait long for a train to Paris, and in fact she did not have to wait at all. As soon as the little awkwardness about the ticket was past, he took out her suitcases, and she followed him into the gloomy station with its cold cement and its smells of coal-dust and oil and metal and smoke and its murmur of metallic noises and footsteps and people talking. He found an empty compartment on the Paris train and installed her in it; she thanked him, said good-bye, and sat back to wait for the train to start. The little scream of the warning whistle came at last, she felt the tension as the engine took hold, the platform began to slide past, the train emerged into grey daylight, and the ghost self that she had left behind in choosing to go—because she might equally have chosen to stay—began to live the hours of that journey far from the train, in the courtyards and stately rooms of the Château de Ferronçalles, following the probabilities of events there.

The heavy iron wheels clicked regularly along the joints of the iron rails, chanting their ominous phrases; a few drops of chilly rain streaked the windows; and she imagined the long grey car coming into the courtyard, Arnaud hurrying to meet it and ask the news, the miserable scene with Yves, and finally, when everything had been settled in that quarter, the inquiry for her.

When she got to that point in the day's distant unwinding, she was glad that she had gone—glad because she was so afraid of him, and glad because she could see herself as only one more responsibility for him, an emotional dependent tangled in a private cobweb for whose weaving he was in no way at fault but from which he would have felt obliged to help her get free if she had stayed. She was glad of the miles growing between them, the safe distances expanding.

But at the same time, helplessly and hopelessly, she was sinking into the last of her personal despairs of herself. She hated the cowardice and treachery of her going, she despised her weakness, she began to believe that her true self had emerged in that moment of final panic and that she really deserved no one's love—and possessed no one's. She saw him as being glad, too, as feeling in spite of everything a soft sensation of relief. Surrounded by his new freedom, surrounded as well by his inescapable regrets, none of which he would for an instant blame on her but all of which would inevitably be associated with her for him, he would find his heart unconsciously lightening because she had gone. And then, of course, he would dutifully set about bringing her back, because he was that sort of man—but she was never again going to be the sort of girl who wanted anything that she had not earned, whether it was a place in the world, or a home of her own, or something so trivial as cigarettes lying loose in an open box, or something so necessary and precious and indispensable as love.

At Blois she was joined by three women in black, and she lost herself in their elliptic conversation for a while. They left the train at Les Aubrais, but there she bought some sausage rolls and a packet of barley sugar at the station buffet and lunched on that as the train moved on, which was a distraction. On the platform at Etampes, there was a man curiously dressed in riding-breeches and laced boots and a Tyrolese hat, who turned up a moment later at the door of her compartment, sliding the door open, putting his yellow leather suitcase up on the rack, settling himself on the opposite seat, and before long making an observation about the weather. She answered him politely, and he turned out to be a very decent sort in spite of his clothes. He told her the story of his life with all the cool logic and impersonal detail of an old-fashioned autobiographer and parted from her as the train was slowing to a stop in the station at Paris with a deliberate casualness that she recognized through her reviving agitation as the true essence of courtesy.

But she hardly had time to feel grateful for that. The train had stopped, and she could no longer believe that her end-of-the-rainbow waited for her beyond the gloom and echoes of any railway station in the world. She knew that she had arrived only at the resumption of responsibility.

It was raining in Paris. She got a porter at once, but they had to wait outside for a taxi until one came delivering another traveller to the station. She gave the driver the name of the hotel where she had stayed before with Daphne, and then once again she rode through the vast ornate spaciousness of Paris, now subdued and glistening in rain but as thronged with people and noise and movement as before, its endless life going on as it had been going on while she was away.

The hall-porter at the hotel was the same hard sharp weary man as before; she remembered him, and he seemed to recognize her— that sort of look came into his hard pleasant eyes as she passed his counter. She asked the clerk for a bedroom and sitting-room because Daphne had asked for a sitting-room before and she thought it was the proper thing for ladies travelling alone.

She was shown to a suite on the same floor as before but looking out on a street instead of the glazed roof of the court. The street was narrow, deserted at the moment, wet with rain, and loomed over by the joined massive façades of narrow buildings of differing designs. Some of the ground floors contained shops. The one at the corner said *Pâtisserie-Confiserie* in gold letters on the plate glass window; the one next to it said, below the name of the proprietor, *Produits de Beauté*. She had not yet taken off her coat or hat, and so she went out into the red corridor at once, before she could argue herself into delay, and down the red-carpeted steps and outside into the thin persistent rain. She turned the wrong way and had to walk all round the square before she came to the *Produits de Beauté*. She asked the clerk, who was a handsome woman with glorious red-gold hair, for something to use on rough hands, and the clerk recommended something in a pink glass jar that cost a fantastic sum. But Isabel bought it and went back to the hotel, feeling very foolish.

Then she took off her coat and hat, sat down on the sofa, and discovered a hole in the heel of her stocking just above the edge of her shoe. She sat up straighter and surveyed the salmon-coloured walls, the pink-and-mauve carpet, the ugly uncomfortable furniture of her extravagant sitting-room. There was a fireplace, but it was closed off by a metal shutter. The little balcony outside the tall rain-streaked windows was spattered and splashed with bird-droppings pale against sooty stone. And then she tried to think what she was going to do in the coming hours—and the coming years.

It was for comfort that she took out Henry's letter at last, but she found no comfort there. With the murmur of a great city outside the windows, he had become Mr. Dolphin again, very recently her employer, a man of lofty power and authority at her place of work for all his casual ways, and it appalled her to read in his handwriting "Dearest Isabel, I do love you—" She hurried the letter into its envelope again and no longer considered putting on her hat and coat and going down to ask the hall-porter exactly where the Bristol was and how to get there and then setting out in the rain, or of telephoning, asking for Mr. Henry Dolphin, saying, "Hullo, Henry, here I am." She got out her fountain pen instead, sat down at the writing-table, and hunted through the drawers until she found a single sheet of blue paper that some other visitor had asked for and had not used.

But as soon as the nib approached the paper, Henry simply vanished from the world. It was not to Henry that she meant to write, but to the man who entirely occupied her thoughts and life, the best man in the world, whom she loved with all her heart, whom she would have died for, and who terrified her, and whose desires and expectations she was now sure she would never have been able to satisfy in any way.

If he remembered the name of the hotel that Daphne had described to him so thoroughly in that first night's desperate manufacture of conversation, and she did not think he could have forgotten it, he would guess where she had gone, and he would send a wire, or he would telephone, she was sure of that. But if he did not telephone, she would have to write, explaining, before she went on her way.

She wanted him to telephone. She wanted to hear the sound of his voice once more, with all the safety of distance between them; and she felt that she would know from the words he chose and the way he spoke them what he really wanted of her. And then she could promise to accept from him enough to make him comfortable about her and convince him later in letters that she did not need it—because she was more than ever certain that he would not want her back. If his new opportunities had not changed his view of her, her treacherous flight would have done so.

But he did not send a wire, and he did not telephone; he was really bestirring himself that day. When he got home at about half-past ten and found her gone, he turned the car in the courtyard while Arnaud was fetching him a coat, and then he set off for Paris, an immense step for him who had not been in Paris for at least ten years and was unfamiliar with the car and unacquainted with the roads. While she was listening to the story of the yellow suitcase stranger, he was driving along the wet highway, thinking out his problems and hers too as he drove; when she was buying her costly little pink jar, he was meeting the thicker traffic of the outskirts of Paris; at the moment that she found the sheet of unused paper, he was downstairs asking the number of her room.

Two minutes later he knocked on the door and opened it, all pretty much in one gesture, and she scraped back her chair in a wild flurry and got to her feet.

He was wearing Yves's brown leather coat, which gave him a very different air, and the enormous change that being in Paris was for him showed somehow as a kind of refreshment of the spirit that had nothing to do with the weariness of his body. For the smallest clear fraction of a second she saw him as the passers-by in the street would have seen him, not as the shabby moody eccentric Duc de Ferronçalles, inseparable from the magnificent castle that had been his mould and had become for her his mirror, but as a dark stranger, uncommonly attractive, unknown and worth knowing. Then he smiled at her, a little wryly, and she knew that everything was going to be all right, everything, if only she had the courage to step through the last tatters of the false reality and leave them behind.

He was ready to help her in any way that he could; her going had wakened him to a good many things. "Is that letter for me?" he began, as easily as if he had dropped in from next door, as lightly as if he had nothing on his mind but the puzzle of her flight and found that puzzle only amusing. He came to look at the sheet of blue paper. "It does not tell me much," he remarked, and he laughed, but as he moved away across the room, she saw that he was not feeling gay at all. His eyes were sombre, he looked every year of his age. He sat down rather heavily on the hard sofa and glanced about the room. His face showed plainly what he thought of it, but he made no comment. "And so you ran away," he said, but without any special emphasis of rebuke or disappointment in his voice, merely offering it as a statement, to get everything quite clear before going on to other things. "You did not even wait to learn whether poor Jeanne would live. . . . You don't even ask news of her now. . . ." Isabel looked down at the ugly carpet. "Well, she will live. But perhaps you think that is nothing to thank God for. I don't really know myself whether it is," he said slowly, taking out his worn cigarette case. She noticed that one of the leather sleeves of the coat was dark with rain. She could picture him driving with his elbow on the door of the car, enjoying in spite of everything the freshness of the rainy wind blowing across his face. "It is different, a little different, with Barnabé at rest at last, no longer alive and suffering. . . ." He leaned to toss the burnt match into the ashtray. "It will perhaps be a little easier to bear, a little less . . . sharp a burden. . . . And I can tell a few lies, talk of inherited tendencies that share the blame— I thought of that as I was driving up. In any event, one must face it," he said, looking squarely at her for the second time. Then he looked quickly down at his cigarette. "And so you were right, and I was wrong. I thought I could trust him to keep his word, once he had given it. And he did give it."

"I think," she said with difficulty, "I think he forgot how heavy a blow it would be, when it stopped being useful to him. I mean, once it stopped bringing him everything he wanted, it didn't seem very awful to him any more. And so—"

"You understand him."

"I ought to."

"No, no—you understand me, too—and you understand Jeanne. You are simply not stupid about people."

"Don't," she said. "Oh, don't. . . ." She meant that she was in such a state that every word of praise would only sound like the falsest of flattery. He instantly broke off and went back to start again, and she saw that she was going to be very carefully handled. She was glad of that, and simultaneously she hated it, all in one anguished moment of humiliation.

"When I got home, Arnaud met me with the news that you had gone," he said, and she looked involuntarily at him, astonished that Arnaud had thought her going that important. "But I had gone off without a coat the first time, and he would not let me set off for Paris like that, and so he brought the first thing he could lay his hands on. . . ." He looked down at the coat and laughed again. "And so I arrive looking very smart, quite by chance!" But he got up and took off the coat then and laid it on another chair. "However, it is a good coat. And a splendid car, that car of Yves's. I came like the wind. . . ." He sat down on the sofa, once again looking strange to her with that room around him, but in the next moment he seemed more her own than he had ever been before, because there was no one within a hundred miles and more who

loved him as well as she did, and no one in all the world in whom
he had confided more completely. And he was doing his best for
her in every way, but the problem was her own, and she had to get
through it as best she could by herself. She had to stop being a
child, waiting for other people to set the world right for her.

He looked very tired; and she decided, working it out like a problem in arithmetic, that he might be hungry too and that in any case
he would be glad of a cup of tea. Feeling very shy and very awkward
but thoroughly determined, too, she went over to the plaque of
bells on the writing-table, rang for the waiter, and ordered tea and
sandwiches, praying within herself that they would be edible and
thankful that she had watched Daphne experiment with the bells
before. When she went back to her chair, her legs felt twice as long
as usual.

He made no sign of having noticed anything at all. "No," he said,
"I am glad that you understand him. You make it easier for me. I
have been thinking that I should never be able to forgive him now."

"Why should he be forgiven?" she said, but no longer pugna-
ciously.

"Because it's so difficult to hate?" he suggested, and in the same
tone of casual inquiry, "Why did you go?"

Beyond the glass of the windows the rain thickened, sighing
through the cold darkening air. "I was afraid," she said. "Everything
had gone wrong."

"Yes," he said thoughtfully. "If I hadn't misjudged Yves, Jeanne
might have had a few more good years. But it's no use making
things worse than they are. Do you see? It's all bad enough as it is,
but there are a few good things in the mixture, after all. . . . Do
you think it's no consolation to me, having come upon you? Or do
you think that I should not allow myself to find that consoling?"

She knew that she should have expected him to take that sensible
line. It was exactly like him, because it was sensible and realistic
and patient and mature. The truth is, I suppose, that he had
learned to be as tolerant of himself as he was of everyone else—and
that was the difference between them: she did not know how to be
tolerant of herself. But she had begun to try. She got up from her
chair and went over to the window and came back to take hold of
the back of the chair as she said, "I only want—I only want to be

meeting you for the first time, without being—being mistaken about anything. . . ."

"That is like wishing I were a bus conductor!"

"I meant that! I would not care what you were!"

"I believe it," he said, smiling faintly, probably not so much at what she said as at that sign of her old fierce devotion daring to show itself again. "What puzzles me is that you don't seem to see that I might feel exactly the same about you."

She looked at him; she met his eyes over that; and she found it hard to breathe steadily. The rain swept against the windows, turning their long rectangles into a richness of mottled twilight blue. Then the tea came, and she could breathe again.

He sat quite still and let her serve him, remarking about the sandwiches, "Good enough!" and then saying, "But there might be a bit more light, don't you think? so that I won't make the mistake of attempting to eat one of these little plates. . . ." She turned on the lights, the room blinked into a shaded bright cosiness, and he said, "Excellent," and she then had the pleasure of watching him eat and seem to enjoy a meal that she had provided for him. She did not draw the curtains; he seemed to like seeing the sky darken over Paris and the lights coming on in unknown rooms on the other side of the street. He finished his tea and sat back. "And all the same," he said abruptly, "I wish—God knows how much I wish that I could erase these past four days for you. . . . Expunge them. . . . Rub them out. . . ."

"When I was frightened," she said slowly, "and you comforted me. . . . When I despised everything that I was, and you would not agree that I should. . . . When I was ashamed, and you made it right. . . . I don't ever want to forget any of it."

"But did I make it right?"

"Yes," she said untruthfully, and she crossed the little space of pink-and-mauve carpet, sat down beside him on the sofa, and took his hand. He let her hold it, making not a move himself. He was prepared to be infinitely cautious, infinitely patient with his wild bird. But she was nothing so fine as a wild bird and never had been. She was in love, and a little afraid of love, in love with him, and more than a little afraid of him, but growing less and less afraid of everything as the minutes went by. She bent her head and just

[221]

touched her lips to the back of his hand. "I must write to Henry, I must answer his letter," she said.

"By all means, write to Henry."

"I love you so much."

"I know," he said, smiling the same faint smile as before.

And then—but the rest does not belong to that Isabel's story. The rest is mine.